Text Classics

DAVID BALLANTYNE, one of New Zealand's greatest writers, was born in Auckland in 1924. As a child he lived for a time in Hicks Bay, a remote seaport on the east coast of the North Island and the setting for *Sydney Bridge Upside Down*.

Ballantyne left school at fifteen after his father died, and soon started to work as a journalist in Auckland. He was something of a prodigy. His first novel, *The Cunninghams*, was published to critical acclaim, in both the US and New Zealand, when he was twenty-three. He married his wife Vivienne in 1950, and they had one son.

By 1954 Ballantyne and his family had decamped to London, where he worked in journalism. He wrote stories, television plays and a novel, *The Last Pioneer*, published in 1963.

Ballantyne and his family returned to New Zealand in 1966. His masterpiece *Sydney Bridge Upside Down* was published in 1968. He was beginning to struggle with alcoholism but continued to write, and was to produce seven books in all.

David Ballantyne died in 1986.

KATE DE GOLDI was born in Christchurch. She is a regular radio and television book reviewer in New Zealand. Her books for young adults are published internationally to great acclaim.

ALSO BY DAVID BALLANTYNE

The Cunninghams
The Last Pioneer
A Friend of the Family
And the Glory
The Talkback Man
The Penfriend

Sydney Bridge Upside Down
David Ballantyne

Text Publishing Melbourne Australia

The Text Publishing Company acknowledges the Traditional Owners of the country on which we work, the Wurundjeri people of the Kulin Nation, and pays respect to their Elders past and present.

Proudly supported by Copyright Agency's Cultural Fund.

textclassics.com.au
textpublishing.com.au

Copyright Agency
Cultural Fund

The Text Publishing Company
Wurundjeri Country, Level 6, Royal Bank Chambers, 287 Collins Street, Melbourne, Victoria 3000 Australia

First published in New Zealand by Robert Hale Limited 1968
First published by The Text Publishing Company 2010
This edition published 2012
Reprinted 2021

Cover design by WH Chong
Page design by WH Chong & Susan Miller
Typeset by Midland Typesetters

Printed in Australia by Griffin Press, an Accredited ISO AS/NZS 14001:2004 Environmental Management System printer

Primary print ISBN: 9781921922374
Ebook ISBN: 9781921961007

CONTENTS

INTRODUCTION
Sydney Bridge Redux

New Zealand literature began in 1882 with the introduction of refrigerated shipping. This was the inimitable opening line of the New Zealand Lit course offered at Canterbury University in 1981. It was delivered by Dr Patrick Evans whose undergrad fame preceded him: his jokes were so good people actually wrote them down in lectures. Evans' thesis, as it unfolded, was mesmerising—and deeply unsettling. Born in discussion with Dr Peter Simpson, developed through his lectures and burnished in several provocative essays published in the late 1970s and early 1980s, it went something like this:

Refrigerated shipping—the vehicle for the frozen meat trade—entrenched the basis of the nascent New Zealand economy: the farming and slaughter of animals. The consequent despoliation and industrialisation of the landscape, and the transformation of the New Zealand colonist into 'a systematic and calculating' butcher, described the progress of the 'New Zealand dream' from an imagined South Pacific Eden (a 'better Britain') to a fallen society with, literally, blood on its collective hands. New Zealand became, not the pastoral paradise envisioned by British utopians, but a society in which an industrialised violence was merely the sanctioned version of other widespread malignancies. In short, we passed from innocence to a decidedly ugly experience.

New Zealand literature, Evans argued, oscillated between work that danced around the 'truth' of this national mythology, and work that confronted it in various compelling ways. Using short fiction and novels from the mid nineteenth century through to the late 1960s he laid out the evidence for a 'slaughterhouse fiction': the farmer in *The Heart of the Bush* confessing to his wife that not only is he a sheep slaughterer but also the killer of their loved childhood dog; Pat, the servant, in Mansfield's 'Prelude', beheading a duck for dinner in front of the Burnell children (*Even Isabel leapt about crying: 'The blood! The blood!'*); the very title of Jean Devanny's *The Butcher Shop*; the 'severed heads, human incineration, necrophilia, drowning, car crashes' of Ronald Hugh Morrieson's fictional world, and much, much more.

It was chilling stuff, and somehow, in 1981, the culture around us seemed to be disposing itself in ways that underscored everything Evans was pointing up. The Springbok Tour (always spoken of in upper case) was underway and the violent clashes between protestors, police and Tour supporters revealed the fault-lines just below New Zealand's apparently harmonious surface. Significantly, those lines ran between town and country. The laagers of farm vehicles providing barriers against protestors at provincial games were one of the more potent symbols of a country at war with itself.

I was twenty-one that year, newly politicised, idealistic, eager to anatomise our cultural tics and hypocrisies, to debate the national stories we comforted ourselves with (land of plenty, racial harmony, egalitarianism, social radicalism, shared visions, etc). Patrick Evans' alternative cultural narrative seemed like nothing so much as an eerie annotation to the ugly community upheavals we were all witnessing.

And reared as I had been on British and American literature (children's and adult), this immersion in New Zealand fiction, and the invitation to assess it on Evans' terms, was nothing short of a cultural awakening. Book after book that year galvanised and disconcerted me. Our damaged relationship with the landscape, our repressive puritanism, the casual violence of family relationships, the inarticulate gropings of romance Kiwi-style, the sweat and tedium of work, and, so often, a watching child—a child doubly burdened by preternatural insight *and* fatal misunderstanding of the behaviour and events unfolding around him. These themes and the fictional worlds that buttressed them blew open my reading habits and preconceptions; they certainly marked a crucial step in my own progress to becoming a writer.

But the book that contained all the foregoing, and some other, haunting quality, the book that really knocked me sideways was *Sydney Bridge Upside Down*.

There are many ways to describe *Sydney Bridge* (in our house Sydney Bridge is always the book, not the splendid piece of engineering): a coming-of-age story, a gothic anti-romance, a ruined-pastoral thriller, a family tragedy. It has been variously assessed as proletarian fiction, young adult fiction, post-provincial fiction. It is all those things, of course, *and* the pre-eminent example of slaughter-house fiction: an abandoned meat-works is both the central symbol of the novel and the site of the story's most troubling events.

For myself, the most piquant description of the book was Patrick Evans': *Sydney Bridge Upside Down*, he said, when introducing it to us, is *the* great, and *unread*, New Zealand novel. Merely picking up the book to read it, then, was instant admission to a select literary community. Actually reading it was a beautiful and sinister and unforgettable experience.

Ironically, my first reading was in a sheep-shearers' hut on a high country Canterbury sheep station. It was waning autumn and the day after a wedding. I lay in a hard, cold bed most of that day, incapable of leaving the story, which —in the way of these things—was hung about with the emotional and sensory circumstance of the reading. So, though the story is set 'up the coast that summer' (almost certainly Hick's Bay, on the east coast of the North Island) and in the mid-1960s, it was also somehow now shot through with the melancholy colours and light of late April, and the mountain air, and the queasiness of the morning-after.

Nearly thirty years later, the novel's opening is still one of the most entrancing I've ever read:

> There was an old man who lived on the edge
> of the world and he had a horse called Sydney
> Bridge Upside Down. He was a scar-faced old
> man and his horse was a slow-moving bag of
> bones, and I start with this man and his horse

because they were there for all the terrible happenings up the coast that summer, always somewhere around.

The DNA for the novel is so artfully laid down in that passage: the mythic setting ('up the coast'); the faintly threatening old man and his horse, suggestive of Quixotic notions and old conflicts; intimations of watchfulness, of secrets, of decline. And the sing-song voice of the story-teller, evoking a fairy-tale ambience, alerting us to an 'other' world and the possibility that nothing is quite as it seems.

It *seems*, on the surface, that Harry, his brother Cal, and his Dad are simply waiting out the summer in their tiny hometown, Calliope Bay (referencing the muse of epic poetry is entirely deliberate, of course) while Harry's Mum is away in the city. Harry's holiday is marked by forbidden adventures at 'the works' with his mate, Dibs, and the trailing Cal, picnics with the Kelly family, spiky exchanges with his snoopy neighbour Susan Prosser and, most excitingly, naked morning frolics with his sexy cousin Caroline who has come to stay. Caroline is, for the summer, de facto mother and sister, but something much less comfortable, too: the object of men's frank admiration and a thoroughly sophisticated sexual tease.

So, beneath the surface of this summer-holiday story, behind the faux-innocent narrative voice, is a simmering and most disturbing sexuality—the sense of danger around sex permeates the novel. Harry's innocent romps with Caroline give way to agitation about his cousin's safety and an increasingly frantic desire to protect her. Meanwhile,

Susan Prosser is watching narrow-eyed over the fence. Mrs Kelly, Cassandra-like and enigmatic, intones meaningfully as she hands out the picnic food. And Mr Wiggins, the laddish butcher, is disconcertingly ever-present. Only Harry understands the multiple pending threats.

Apparently.

I have read *Sydney Bridge* a number of times since that first fervid immersion, and each time it has been equally powerful, but subtly different—because of course I am different, and because a great book always accommodates revisiting and new insights. Most recently, it seemed more sinister and somehow much sadder than I can ever remember, but I marvelled all over again at Ballantyne's restraint and control, at the quietly brilliant way he wrong-foots the reader. This is a novel of suppressions and elisions. You must pay attention to what is not on the page. It is after all, and amongst much else, a thriller, and much of the story's impact comes from the reader's growing anxiety around exactly what is happening and who is responsible for the 'terrible things'.

The last chapter remains as mysterious and seductive as ever. I have spent hours anatomising that epilogue. And every time I have anticipated and dreaded the final two sentences, knowing they will break my heart.

Perhaps the real mystery is why *Sydney Bridge Upside Down* is still—more than forty years since its publication—not read. In a sort of faithful, and hopeful, ongoing test of Evans' long-ago claim, I check it out quite regularly, ask people—book groups, librarians, teachers, other writers—if they've ever read it, if they've even heard of it: nope.

One reason, of course, is that it's been out of print for thirty years. But why has it stayed out of print? Patrick Evans had a characteristically provocative theory about David Ballantyne's critical neglect and lost readership. Ballantyne, he argued, had never attained a recognisable public persona, any public persona for that matter—and since this had become an almost essential condition of literary success, it was his, and the book's, burden. He contrasted memorably Ballantyne's lack of serious attention with the reverence accorded Janet Frame and her work, insisting that Ballantyne, too, was a writer of 'considerable skill and coherence of vision'. But Ballantyne presented a picture of his country that was, forty years ago at least, unpalatable to his potential readership: a dark, unredemptive vision challenging some of our most clung-to mythologies.

I'm thrilled that a publisher has now recognised the power and beauty of *Sydney Bridge* and that it will be out there again, finding its readers, pulling in a new generation, giving them the opportunity to experience what all great fiction offers, and what this book has always delivered in spades: transport, discomfort, and, ultimately, transformation.

Kate De Goldi, 2010

For Jean, Des, Den —
and remembering Bill

I

THERE WAS an old man who lived on the edge of the world, and he had a horse called Sydney Bridge Upside Down. He was a scar-faced old man and his horse was a slow-moving bag of bones, and I start with this man and his horse because they were there for all the terrible happenings up the coast that summer, always somewhere around.

I start with Sam Phelps and Sydney Bridge Upside Down, but now I go to a cliff-top on a January day, a sunny afternoon, mid-afternoon. I was there with Dibs Kelly.

Dibs said I was too scared to climb the dead tree. I put a hammerlock on him and shoved him to the drop from the cliff-top to the rocks beside the wharf.

'You know why I won't climb that tree,' I told him. I put on some pressure. 'Eh? Eh?'

'That hurts a bit,' he said.

'Give in then,' I said. 'No, answer the question first.'

'I told you,' he said. 'I don't know where Mr Dalloway's

gone for his holidays—hey, that hurt!'

'I mean the tree now,' I said. 'What did you say about me and the tree?'

'Nothing,' he said.

I told him what I could see. By pushing his head into the grass, I said, I could look over him and see the rocks, waves hitting the wharf piles, a dinghy swaying at the bottom of the funny steps near the end of the wharf. It was a long way down, I said, shifting my elbow from his neck. He pretended to cry. He made choking sounds into the grass. He coughed.

'I'll tell you then,' I said, loosening the hammerlock. 'You know, all right, but I'll tell you, boy.'

I explained why I wasn't climbing a tree that would fall over the cliff with a good push, let alone with me trying to get up it, so who wouldn't be scared to climb it? I'd be looking for a quick trip to the rocks if I climbed it.

'Anyway,' I said, 'who did you hear crying like that?'

'A girl,' he said.

'Which one?'

'I don't remember.'

'Susan Prosser?'

'I don't remember, Harry.'

'I've never heard anybody else crying like that,' I said.

'It happens all the time,' he said. 'You just don't hear them. Haven't you heard your mother crying?'

'Not like that,' I said.

'You listen,' he said. 'When she comes back, you listen.'

'People cry differently,' I said. 'When my brother cries, he yells, he enjoys it. When I cry, it's because I'm gulpy and

2

the damned tears start without me wanting them to. But I don't cry much.'

'My mother says she likes a good cry,' Dibs Kelly said.

'What about?'

'Oh, anything.'

'I've never heard—' I was going to say I'd never heard my mother crying the way Dibs had been crying, nor did I think she would agree with Mrs Kelly about liking a good cry. My mother was different from Mrs Kelly. My mother did her crying in secret.

I didn't say this, though, because Dibs humped me suddenly and I had to let go of him. He'd hurt me, I staggered. He followed up fast and knocked me down.

I got my knees working, he couldn't keep me pinned.

'I'll dong you, boy!' he shouted.

As he came in, I caught him, my feet in his stomach. He went flying, smacked the dead tree pretty hard. The tree did not fall over the cliff. Dibs Kelly did.

I go back now to the beginning of that day, my brother and myself in pyjamas for breakfast with our father, sausages and fried potatoes, plenty of toast and raspberry jam, cocoa for us and tea for him.

'Just because your mother's away,' he said, 'it doesn't mean you can run wild. Just because it's the holidays it doesn't mean fun and games all day every day. An hour a day won't hurt you. You could do a lot of weeding in an hour. Other things as well. What about those passion-fruit, Harry? The vine's all over the shed now. Lot of passion-fruit on that roof. But you do the climbing. Cal can catch them.'

3

'I can climb,' Cal said. 'Aren't I a good climber, Harry?'

'You're not so bad for your age,' I told him.

'I can climb to the top of the chute,' he said.

'Shut up!' I told him.

'Keep away from the works!' Dad shouted.

'Cal means long ago,' I said. 'He hasn't been in the works for years and years.'

'Three men died there,' Dad told Cal. 'They knew of the dangers, but it didn't stop them having accidents. If it could happen to them, men knowing what might happen if they weren't careful, it could happen to you. So keep away. Or you know what I'll do to you.'

I knew what he would do to Cal. He would chase him with his whip.

My father's whip was long and black. He'd won it at poker many years before from a drunken stockman. He kept it on a nail above the copper in the wash-house, and he could certainly get to it quickly when he was in the mood to use it, his missing leg didn't slow him, not then or when he was chasing me, whizzing along behind me with his crutch flashing and his whip cracking, and me thinking it was fair to let him catch me twice, since I had two good legs and could have got clean away if I tried, but no more than two flicks because it was very cutty and there was blood on my legs whenever he caught me. I would let him get his two flicks in and then I'd be off, up into the hills or across the swamp to the river-bank where I had plenty of hiding-places, usually the swamp because the single-plank bridge was too awkward for his crutch. He had to stay

4

behind and watch me go, cracking the whip and shouting, making me feel sorry for him.

I liked Dad. Cal liked him too. We had good fun when our mother was away. We didn't mind if she took her time about coming back.

'Want me to go to the store, Dad?' I asked as soon as he'd made Cal promise to keep away from the works. 'I can go to the store after I've done the weeding. No trouble.'

'Not today thanks, Harry,' he said. 'That reminds me, though. I must put in an order for the paint, must do it on the way to work.'

'Expect you'll let Cal and me help to paint the house?' I said. 'Get it done quicker if you do.'

'We'll have plenty of time,' he said. 'But you boys can help, all right. I'll do the high bits, you two can do some of the low bits.'

'Expect we'll have it done by the time she gets home?' I said, in case he had a hint, or a warning, of when she'd be back.

'That's the general idea,' he said. He looked into his cup, seemed to frown. 'But she won't be back for a while yet. Not according to her letter. She'd be coming with your cousin if she was in a hurry to get back. She wouldn't let Caroline make the trip alone.'

Cal and I scowled at each other. We had forgotten about our cousin. Dad laughed. 'She's an interesting girl. Your mother says so.'

'She's old,' I said. 'You said she was too old to play with.'

'Well, rather too old for childish games,' he said. 'But I

5

dare say she'll be grateful if you boys show her some of the sights of the district. You can be her guides.'

'As long as she's not coming here to boss us,' I said.

'She's coming for a holiday,' he said. 'City girls often come to places like Calliope Bay for holidays.'

'The same as country teachers like Mr Dalloway have holidays in the city, eh?' I said.

It was Dad's turn to scowl. 'Who said Dalloway's gone to the city?'

'I forget,' I said. 'No, that's right! I made it up.'

'Take care, Harry,' he said. 'Nobody likes liars.'

'I think he *might* have said he was going to the city,' I said. 'One day at school.' I reflected while my father watched me. 'But I'm not sure. Sorry, Dad.'

'It's all right,' he said. 'Anyway, you're not to mis- behave when Caroline's here. I want you boys to make her welcome. Show her that country people are hospitable.'

'Yes, Dad,' I said. 'Trust us.'

'I wonder,' he said. But he was smiling as he hopped to his crutch, against the wall near the stove. 'Don't leave the dishes too long,' he said, hopping to the door. 'They bring the flies.'

'I'll do them right after I get dressed,' I said.

He studied our pyjamas. 'About time they went into the wash,' he said. 'Remind me about them next Monday.'

'I'll get some driftwood for the copper, Dad,' I said. 'After the weeding.'

'No hurry,' he said. 'Later in the week will do.'

Cal and I went to the back steps to watch him get on to his bike. It was always interesting to see him take off.

6

He had to work fast with his leg, pushing himself away from the tank-stand, jabbing down quickly on the pedal, stopping the wobble just in time, then speeding up the side-path.

Back in the kitchen, I threw the pot of raspberry jam at Cal. 'Catch!' I yelled.

He missed. The pot exploded on the wall. Jam splashed everywhere.

'Dad!' yelled Cal, running up the passage to the front door. 'Hey, Dad!'

'You're too late,' I said. 'He'll be nearly at the river by now.'

It never took Dad long to reach the river, I thought as I cleaned up the glass and jam. He covered that half-mile stretch of road as quickly as any person with two good legs. The only time he slowed was when he got into the roadside metal. Then he had to use the crutch to keep his balance, poking the metal with it until he was clear. Once I had seen him doing that after a skid, and I thought it was great how he stopped himself from toppling into the ditch. He was a great rider.

Cal came back. He said: 'That jampot nearly cut me.'

'It slipped,' I told him. 'And if you don't wash the dishes, another one might slip.'

I was only kidding. He was too short to wash up. I did that. He did the wiping.

After we had done the dishes, we took off our pyjamas and had a run with nothing on. We ran up and down the passage and in and out of the rooms, and some of the time he chased me and some of the time I chased him. When

I caught him I gave him two smacks on the behind and, to be fair, I let him catch me a couple of times. Mostly we stayed inside when we had this sort of fun, but some days I'd chase him outside and then scare him by shutting the door, and he'd bang on the door and keep looking around in case somebody came down the side-path or Mrs Prosser next door happened to look out of her bathroom window; she could see our back porch from her bathroom. One day, during one of these games, I went to the dunny which was beside the wash-house, and I suddenly thought I would be trapped if anybody called, I'd have to stay in there until the caller left, and what if the caller realised I was in there and decided to wait until I was finished? I got so excited I couldn't do anything for a while, not until I'd made myself think of the river on a cold day. When I did leave the dunny, the coast was clear. Lucky for me, I thought.

'Righto, boy, now we'll do some weeding,' I said after Cal had got in his second lot of smacks. 'Ten minutes in the garden. Before the sun's too hot.'

'Why don't we pick passion-fruit?' asked Cal. 'Dad said I could help.'

'*I* give the orders,' I said.

But we did pick passion-fruit, because that seemed like more fun to me too. I stood on the shed roof and tossed the passion-fruit to Cal, and he caught most of them, the only ones he missed were the ones I aimed at his head, he ducked those.

Up on the shed roof, I could see along the backyards, all five of them. Of course there were once a lot more backyards, they used to go nearly half-way to the river.

Nowadays, with the works closed, there were only five houses left in Calliope Bay, the others had been pulled down. Every backyard was very much like the next—vegetable garden, shed, passion-fruit vine—except for the Kelly backyard. The Kelly backyard was full of rusty truck and car parts. This was because Mr Kelly, a short gingery man, was a carrier. He owned a Reo lorry and kept it in his backyard, which was where he had let other trucks and cars go to rust. Another reason for the mess was that Dibs Kelly's big brother, Buster, fixed motor-bikes there. Buster Kelly owned an Indian, and everybody said it was a tremendous roaring thing. Buster sure made that Indian go.

'No, it wasn't the only reason I called,' I told Mrs Kelly later in the morning. 'Of course, if Buster does turn up and offer me a ride, I won't say no. I rather like speeding along on the back of his Indian. How about you, Mrs Kelly?'

'On that roaring thing?' said Mrs Kelly, who was plucking a fowl. 'Not for me, thanks!'

'It's quite safe,' I told her. 'Personally, I trust Buster.'

Mrs Kelly, who was large and purple-cheeked, gave me one of her knowing looks. She said: 'It's not *me* you must convince, young man. Wasn't it your mother who said you were not to ride on Buster's bike? Or was it somebody else's mother?'

'My mother did say that,' I said. 'But it was ages ago. I don't suppose she'd mind now.'

'Buster wouldn't want to go against her wishes,' Mrs Kelly said. 'We can't be sure what they are until she gets back. And she's only been gone a week, so she won't be thinking of coming back yet.'

'She won't mind,' I said. 'Especially when she sees how we've fixed things while she's away. We're not just having fun, Mrs Kelly.'

Mrs Kelly finished plucking the fowl, dangled it. 'Do you miss your mother, Harry?'

'Not much,' I said. I watched her wipe the bench. 'We're having a visitor, you know,' I said. 'Our cousin Caroline. She's coming from the city.'

'So I heard,' said Mrs Kelly. 'How long will she stay?'

'I don't know,' I said. 'Hope she doesn't stay too long. By the way, Mrs Kelly, when will Buster be back?'

'Not till the week-end,' she said. 'You're out of luck today.'

'That's all right,' I said. 'I've got plenty to do.'

'Harry?' Cal said from the doorway.

'I have to look after *him*,' I told Mrs Kelly. 'He misses his Mummy.'

'I don't!' Cal shouted.

'He pretends he doesn't,' I told Mrs Kelly.

'When people first came to Calliope Bay,' she said, 'what troubled them most was loneliness. I don't mean the people in the very old days, the first one or two who farmed in the district before there was any sort of settlement. I mean those who came to build the works, then those who came because there were jobs for them at the works, then those who moved in when others moved out, then of course those who came to help pull down the works. All these people were very lonely for a time. They seemed so far, far away from everything. No part of the country, of the world even, seems so faraway as this. And when people are faraway and lonely they often behave curiously, this is well-known. The teacher, many years ago, who tied a child to a tree in the school grounds would not have done so in any other place. Or, nowadays, the way Mrs Prosser hides is because she lives in such a faraway place. She is lonely, so she holds back. Even the rest of us, popping into one another's homes and chatting, can see and hear only so much. I know I hold back when I go visiting, I know the others do too. Now, I asked your mother if she was looking forward to her holiday in the city. She said she was. "Are you sure, Janet?" I asked. Then she said she didn't like leaving you boys, she said she would be thinking all the time she was away that she should have taken you with her, she would not be able to truly enjoy her holiday for thinking of you. On and on in this fashion. Was it the truth? Or, once she had made the two dozen bottles of ginger beer, did she give another thought to those who would drink it when she was gone? This is not for me to say. I can only suggest that escaping from loneliness is not always a matter of going from one place to another. How many bottles are left, Harry?'

'Eighteen,' I said.

'Seventeen and a half,' Cal said from the doorway.

'I counted them last night,' I said.

'I opened one a while ago,' he said.

'You'll catch it,' I said. 'You heard Dad say we were drinking it too fast. Have you been out to the wash-house lately? Seen what's hanging above the copper?'

'I was thirsty,' Cal said. 'What's the use of ginger beer if I'm not allowed to drink it on hot days?'

'It's your funeral, boy,' I said.

'Would anybody here fancy a piecey?' asked Mrs Kelly.

'If it's not too much trouble,' I said. I followed her to the pantry, hoped she would put some of her great plum jam on the pieces of bread. 'I was interested in what you were saying about loneliness,' I told her. 'It reminded me of something Mr Dalloway said last term. He said we live on the edge of the world. Us here in Calliope Bay. Like, it's a wonder we don't fall off, we live so close to the edge. Do you agree with that?'

'Up to a point,' she said, putting plum jam on the pieces. 'What prompted him to say that? What time of the day was it when he said that?'

'The afternoon,' I said. 'During geography.'

'He said it as a joke, did he?' she asked, handing me a piece then walking to the door to give Cal his piece.

'He seemed serious,' I said. I bit into the bread.

'Mr Dalloway, I notice, hurries away from the edge the moment the holidays come,' she said. 'Takes no risks, it seems.'

'I think he's gone to the city,' I said. 'I like this plum jam, Mrs Kelly.'

'So do I,' Cal said.

'I prefer plum to raspberry,' I said. 'Or maybe it depends on how it's made. My mother's raspberry jam is runny.'

'That occasionally happens, no matter who the cook is,' said Mrs Kelly. 'Care for another piecey, boys?'

'No more, thanks,' I said. 'I'll be giving this kid his lunch soon. By the way, would you like some passion-fruit? We picked a lot this morning. Plenty to spare.'

She shook her head. 'We have so many of our own. I must tell Dibs to pick them before the shed collapses.'

'Do you reckon he'll be long?' I asked. 'We thought we'd have a game before we do the weeding.'

'He usually dawdles when he goes to the store,' she said. 'I'll tell him you boys were asking about him.'

'Tell him we'll be near the works,' I said. '*Near* the works, not *in* the works. We got something we want to show him.'

'Very well, boys,' said Mrs Kelly. 'Now I must change my dress before Mr Wiggins arrives.'

I go on to my time at the works in the late afternoon of that day. This, of course, was after Dibs Kelly had fallen over the cliff. And that part on the cliff-top was, of course, after I had shown him what Cal and I had found in a killing-room at the works. I was up on the top floor of the works, looking through one of the holes where chutes had once started from. I was trying to see Cal.

'Cal!' I called, and 'Cal-Cal-Cal' went the echo through the works. 'Are you ready?'

I saw him then, down through the holes on the other floors, waiting down there near the end of the one chute the men had not destroyed.

He waved.

'Keep clear!' I called.

I sent down eight of the bricks I had taken from the only wall left up there. I didn't know why the men had let that wall stay, after pulling down the other three walls and the roof, but I was glad they had because the bricks in it were useful for things like creek dams and cave fireplaces.

13

Earlier that summer we had found a new cave in the hill up from the wharf, and we were using a good few bricks in it.

Sometimes I followed the bricks down the chute. Not this time, though. It was best to wear sandshoes to help with the braking, and I wasn't wearing sandshoes this time. Actually, I was only up there just now because I met Cal on my way back from the cliff-top and he looked sad about missing the fun Dibs and I had been having, so I agreed when he said it would be a good idea to get some more bricks for the cave, I said we could leave the bricks beside the furnace-house and take them to the cave tomorrow.

The risky part in getting down was between the top floor and the one below. The stairs between these floors had gone, you had to use footholds in the wall. This was easy enough, but it was exciting to pretend it was very dangerous, and I used to walk around the top floor several times, sort of preparing myself for the trip, breathing in deeply, frowning.

Doing this now, I happened to see the butcher's white van parked in the river. When the river was low there were two main streams at the crossing, a strip of shingle separating the streams. Cars and trucks simply sped through the streams and across the shingle when the river was like this, but it obviously hadn't worked out right for Mr Wiggins today, because his van had stopped in the near-side stream, and there were signs he was in trouble.

One of the signs was that Mr Wiggins was squatting on a mud-guard, looking at the engine. The water was half-way up the van's wheels; he couldn't have stopped there on purpose.

'Hey, Harry!' cried Cal, popping up through the chute hole. 'I climbed it again!'

'Mr Wiggins is in trouble,' I said.

Cal came across to look.

'It's the shallow part where he is,' I said. 'The other part's where trucks usually get stuck, eh? Remember when Mr Kelly got stuck and the water was in the cab by the time they hauled the Reo out? It's lucky for Mr Wiggins he didn't get stuck in that part—'

'Somebody's with him,' Cal said.

'That's Mrs Kelly,' I said. I could see her on the running-board; she was staring at the river.

'Mr Wiggins is taking off his boots,' Cal said. 'Must be going to swim for it.'

'He can walk to the shingle from there,' I said.

We watched him jump into the water, then back towards Mrs Kelly.

'She's too heavy for him to carry,' Cal said. 'He'll sink, she'll fall in.'

But Mr Wiggins, for all his staggering, got to the shingle with Mrs Kelly on his back. He must be very strong, I thought. Then I remembered that he had been here at the works in the old days, one of the powerful fellows who killed animals with sledgehammers.

'Now he's going to push the van,' I said.

'What happened to Dibs?' asked Cal.

'See?' I said. 'That's why he unloaded Mrs Kelly. He knew he couldn't push it with her aboard.'

'Where's Dibs?' asked Cal.

'Search me,' I said. 'Doesn't look as if Mr Wiggins can move the van.'

'Wonder where Dibs got to,' Cal said. He was looking the other way, out across the paddocks and dunes and beach to the wharf and the sea.

'Mr Wiggins needs help,' I said. 'He can't move the van on his own. Let's go down and help him.'

'I can see Mr Phelps and his horse,' Cal said. 'I can see them near the woolshed. I bet Sydney Bridge Upside Down could tow Mr Wiggins out.'

'Sam Phelps wouldn't let his horse do that,' I said.

'I'm going down,' Cal said.

'I'll go first and catch you if you fall,' I said.

I went quickly. I knew the footholds so well I just skimmed down the wall to the next floor. The only time this trip was risky was when there was a high wind; the wall wobbled a bit then and I understood what my father meant when he said a good gale would flatten the ruins one of these days.

'Get going!' I called to Cal.

He came down very shakily for a kid who was like a squirrel when using the chute. Of course he was short, it was harder for him to find the footholds. I always held up my arms, ready to catch him. I blinked as cement chips fell.

He made it, and we ran down the stairs.

'What about the bricks?' asked Cal when we were in the yard. 'We going to stack them?'

'They'll be safe,' I said. 'We're in a hurry. Mr Wiggins needs our help.'

When we reached the road, he said, 'Dibs might sneak our bricks.'

'He'd better not,' I said.

'It's funny Dibs isn't here,' he said.

'Must be playing somewhere,' I said, running faster.

'Wait for me!' Cal called.

I stopped. 'Don't you care about Mr Wiggins? How would *you* like to be stuck in the river?'

'I don't care,' he said. 'I'm going to find Dibs.' He turned and ran towards the railway line.

'Cal!' I called. 'I'll fix you, boy! Come here!'

But he kept running, that mad kid, so I went on alone. I didn't go very fast because I really wasn't so eager to help Mr Wiggins. Also, I was busy thinking how I would pay Cal back. I got damned angry about him, turning traitor after all the fun I found for him.

He didn't miss anything at the river. Mr Wiggins' van had gone. So had Mr Wiggins and Mrs Kelly. It was as if I had only imagined seeing them.

2

THERE WAS a bit of a mystery about old Sam Phelps, and I don't mean because of how he stuck to Sydney Bridge Upside Down instead of buying a younger and quicker horse to haul the freight wagon along the railway line from the wharf to just outside the works. That was mysterious enough, though not so hard to understand when you remembered how few ships called at Calliope Bay nowadays, how few trips Sam Phelps had to make along the line. No, what I mean about a bit of a mystery was how people said he had once lived in a good house with his pretty daughter. The pretty daughter, they said, had run away, then Sam Phelps had moved from the good house, then the house had been pulled down. After that, they said, he had gone to the pack. Nobody seemed to know where his daughter had gone to, and if *he* knew, they said, he certainly wasn't telling. Actually, as I said to Dibs Kelly in the cave one afternoon during those summer holidays, you would have a tough job getting Sam Phelps to tell you anything. It would be useless asking him when exactly the *Emma Cranwell* was due to berth. Like as not he would turn from you without speaking and begin stroking Sydney Bridge Upside Down's hollow, maybe hoping in this way to fill it in, though I reckoned it was more likely he was helping to make it deeper.

'So you can drop that idea, boy,' I told Dibs, taking another of his cigarettes. 'We'll wait here for Cal. He'll tell us when the ship's in sight.'

'Hope he hurries,' Dibs said. 'It's getting a heck of a smoky in here.'

'Are you dizzy yet?' I asked.

'No,' he said. 'I've only had two.'

'This is my third,' I said, waving the cigarette. 'Better than my mother's cigarettes, but not as strong as your last lot. You using the same leaves?'

'They're off the same bush,' he said. 'The others might have dried out better. These are strong enough for me. I'll be dizzy if I have another one.'

'Have another one then,' I said. 'You need to be dizzy to see fantastic things.'

'I've been dizzy before, but I've never seen anything fantastic,' Dibs said. 'I get dizzy, then I feel sick.'

'Hey!' I shouted. 'Just then you seemed to have a big moustache and a helmet. It's beginning!'

'Now what do you see?' he asked.

I coughed. I began to choke.

'What do you see?' asked Dibs. 'What do you see?'

I got my breath back, staggered across the cave and bopped him. 'Couldn't you see I was choking? You're dippy sometimes, boy. Now I've changed my mind about letting you use the pistol.'

He wriggled past me to the cave mouth. 'I'll tell Buster you've got it,' he said, ready to run.

I didn't move. 'So what?' I said. 'It was in the killing-room and I found it, so it's mine. What's it got to do with Buster?'

'Kids aren't supposed to have pistols,' he said. 'You ask Buster.'

I didn't mind his threats, I was a bop up on him. 'I'll tell him myself if he gives me a ride on the Indian,' I said. 'I'll let him use the pistol. Maybe he can get some ammo.'

'A good idea,' he said. 'We could shoot pigs, eh?'

'Yes, and sizzle them in here,' I said. 'Buster might have some ammo hidden in his room. You have a look tonight, Dibs. We can have fun with that pistol.'

'It's an old-fashioned pistol,' he said. 'I don't know what ammo would fit that sort of pistol.'

Cal showed up behind Dibs and asked: 'Why can't I have a smoke?'

'Because you'd tell Dad,' I said. 'What about the ship? Have you seen her yet?'

'No,' he said. 'Why don't you or Dibs have a turn? Why do I have to keep looking?'

'Because that's your job today,' I said. 'We got other jobs. What about Sam Phelps? Is he on the wharf?'

'Yes,' said Cal.

'And the horse and wagon?' I asked.

'Yes,' he said.

'See!' I said. 'He knows the ship won't be long.'

'Takes an hour for her to get in after she's passed the heads,' Cal said. 'I'd have plenty of time for a smoke. Be a sport, Harry. I won't tell Dad.'

'It's not only the ship,' I said. 'You're supposed to watch out for the Kelly kids.' (Dibs had two younger brothers and two younger sisters, but I won't mention them often, you can take it for granted they were always around. I ignored them mostly then and that's what I'll do now.)

'I haven't seen them,' Cal said. He looked at the butt I had dropped when I was choking. 'What say I do tell Dad you were smoking? He'll chase you, I bet.'

'Another blackmailer!' I cried. 'All right, you can have a fag. I'll keep look-out.'

'I'll come with you,' Dibs said.

'No, you stay here with this kid,' I said.

So I left them there and climbed to the cliff-top and looked across the bay. There was no sign of the *Emma Cranwell*. I didn't mind. Actually, the ship was not why I'd left the cave, it would have taken more than a couple of blackmailers to make me go on look-out if I hadn't wanted to. What I had remembered, back in the cave, was that Susan Prosser liked being at the wharf to see the *Emma Cranwell* berth. If Susan turned up early today, I thought, I would go down to the wharf and talk to her about her mother's crazy budgie. Even though Mrs Prosser lived right next door, the only time we saw her was when she peeped through her bathroom window; this was not often, but it was more often than we saw her budgie. I only knew about the budgie because of what Susan told me. She told me if you said 'Joey is a naughty boy' to this budgie, it would sometimes reply 'Jesus is a naughty boy'; other times it brooded and said nothing. I had not seen Susan for a week or so, she seemed to have picked up her mother's habit of keeping out of sight. I was hoping she would think the *Emma Cranwell* was a good reason to leave the house. Going by what I could see from the cliff-top, she had not done so yet. Sam Phelps and Sydney Bridge Upside Down were the only ones on the wharf.

I decided I would keep looking for about twenty minutes. This would give Cal plenty of time to have a cigarette and get sick.

Whoops whoosh groan groan, I thought, remembering what Dad had said at breakfast about the time I got sick while aboard the *Emma Cranwell* with him. We were on our way back from a holiday (my mother, who liked the city better than Dad did, was following later with little Cal), and Dad must have thought it would be fun to go the last part of the trip in the *Emma Cranwell* instead of in a bus. As he said at breakfast, he hadn't allowed for rough seas. 'My word, Harry, we struck it rough as soon as we left Wakefield,' he said. 'I thought the tub was going to turn turtle, she was tossing and turning so much. I wasn't surprised when you threw up, I remember thinking it was as well you had the bottom bunk. And you had to stay in it because there was little I could do for you, not me with my one leg and that ship trying to turn turtle, it was all I could do to stay in my own bunk. The seas didn't calm till well after midnight, then I was able to inspect the damage. I mean the damage where you were, my boy. What a mess! "It's you for the deck," I said, and up we went. Not a soul in sight when we got there. Only the night, black as pitch, and the sea, just as black. "Take off that jacket," I said. Then the other smell hit me and I knew what had happened. You had pooped yourself! There was still a wind, and it was blowing the smell straight at me. I turned my head, it did no good. Anyway, I couldn't leave you in those pyjamas. "Take them off," I said. And of course you know what happened after that—' I knew, sure enough; I had heard all this before, I was used to the shame of it. In fact, I no longer felt any shame; it was something horrible that had happened to some other kid, one black night on the high seas in years gone by. 'You threw them away,' I said. 'I threw them as far away as I could, out into the ocean,' my father said, 'and left you standing there without a stitch on.' 'I remember,' I said. 'It was the only thing to do at the time,' my father said, 'but you wouldn't have thought so when your mother heard about it. Those new city pyjamas, where were they? Thrown away! Oh, I heard all about that night's mistake, your mother didn't see the funny side of it. Nor you either, I dare say.' 'Yes, I did,' I told him. 'It was pretty funny,' I said, 'how you held your nose when you threw them away.' 'You remember that?' he asked. 'Yes,' I said, aware of Cal watching me, knowing he wished he had that sort of memory to share with Dad. 'More likely you *think* you remember because I've told you about it so often,' Dad said. 'I only mention it now,' he said, 'because I hope your cousin doesn't have the same sort of voyage, it was thinking of her in the *Emma Cranwell* that reminded me of our own adventure. Well, I rely on you boys to make her welcome, let her see that country people know how to

23

treat visitors. Meet her at the wharf, bring her home, tell her I'm looking forward to seeing her when I get in from work. You can leave the dinner to me. But it would help if you peeled some spuds.' 'Yes, Dad,' I said. 'Yes, Dad,' Cal said.

When the twenty minutes were up I gave myself ten more because I was certain I would see Susan Prosser walking along the track beside the railway line at any second. If I headed back to the cave she was bound to appear, I had often just missed her and I would make sure I didn't this time. What I mean by just missing her is this: I would be waiting for her, sitting by the road or leaning against a tree or lying in the shade of a hedge, and as long as I kept watching she would not appear; but if I got busy with something, like trapping an insect, sure enough she would be past me and too far down the road towards home for me to pretend, once I caught up, that I hadn't been waiting for her. It was mad of me to bother, of course. I mean, Susan Prosser did not like me, not nowadays. She used to like me, in the days when she seemed to enjoy telling me about the budgie, but ever since I accidentally killed our wonderful Muscovy drake she had changed towards me, as if, unlike everybody else, she did not believe I hadn't really meant to kill Kingsley. Couldn't she realise, I asked her plenty of times, that I had been as fond of Kingsley as anybody else in Calliope Bay? Was it my fault I landed on him after jumping from the shed roof? But it was no use, Susan Prosser did not like me any more; no matter how often I tried to be friendly, she sniffed and turned away.

Heck, I thought, I'm not chasing her just because I don't

want her to go on thinking I'm a fibber. What do I care?

So I turned, meaning to go back to the cave. I had a last look over my shoulder, and that was when I saw the *Emma Cranwell*. She was coming round the heads, dipping and rolling.

Soon I would meet my cousin for the first time in years. I could not remember her from when we had met long ago in the city, I had been too young to take much notice. According to Dad, who went by what my mother said in her letters, this Caroline was a shy girl who sat in corners and seldom spoke. Her mother, my mother's sister, reckoned it would do Caroline good to be away from the city for a while, the country air would work wonders. Not that we should take her to be a wet blanket, warned my mother. Once Caroline got to know people she apparently had rather interesting things to say; being a city girl, her interests were different from those of country girls, but what she said should entertain us, since we met so few city girls. Anyway, said my mother, make her feel welcome. 'So I rely on you boys to do that,' Dad said. 'Show Caroline that country people know how to treat visitors.' 'Yes, Dad,' I said, 'I heard you before.' 'Well, don't forget,' he said. 'I won't forget,' I said.

But I knew there was no sense in being at the wharf an hour before the *Emma Cranwell* berthed, so I headed for the cave.

When I got to the cave mouth and looked in I saw that Dibs had tied up Cal and was pointing a lighted cigarette at him. When Cal saw me he yelled. He must have yelled a good bit while I was on look-out, I knew he wouldn't let

25

himself be tied up like that without making a fuss. It was a wonder I hadn't heard him yelling, I thought.

'Don't make so much noise,' I told him. 'I want to ask Dibs something. Hey, Dibs, remember when Mr Dalloway asked us about the holidays and said for all the kids who were going away to stick up their hands? Were you there that day?'

'I stuck up my hand,' Dibs said. 'I thought Buster would give me a ride out to where he's working. That would count as going away, I reckoned.'

'Did you notice if Susan Prosser stuck up her hand?'

He closed one eye and twisted his face, trying to remember. He put the cigarette in his mouth and sucked it, but he was too late, it was out.

'She must have gone away,' I said. 'I haven't seen her for a few days.'

'I haven't seen her,' Dibs said.

'I saw her,' Cal said.

'When?' I asked.

'Yesterday,' he said.

'Untie my brother,' I told Dibs. I looked down at Cal. 'Where did you see her yesterday?'

Cal was rubbing his wrists, where the rope had been. 'Not out the front,' he said, frowning at Dibs. 'It wasn't out the front of her place behind that bush.'

'He's always hoping he'll see her there,' Dibs said.

'I'm not!' Cal shouted. 'I don't care!'

'Never mind that,' I said. I knew Cal did hope to see what Dad said he had once seen—Susan Prosser piddling behind that bush—but I wasn't going to blame him for

26

it now, I'd rather know if Susan was still around. 'If you didn't see her there,' I said, 'where did you see her?'

'In Mr Wiggins' van,' Cal said.

I was surprised.

So was Dibs. He said: 'I bet you didn't, boy!'

'I did!' Cal shouted.

'Doing what?' I asked, feeling strange.

'She was just sitting in the van,' Cal said.

'Waiting for Mr Wiggins?' I asked.

'He was driving,' Cal said. 'The van was moving. Going towards the river.'

'What do you know?' I asked Dibs.

'What do you know?' he asked back.

We sure were surprised.

'Dibs is not allowed to tie me up,' Cal said, moving to the cave mouth. 'I didn't do anything to him. This is not his cave, anyway.'

'When he brings cigarettes it makes him a special guest,' I told Cal. 'You had one of his cigarettes. You shouldn't complain, boy. And don't tell Dad, either. We don't like tell-tales.'

'Tell-tales are creepy,' Dibs said.

'You're not perfect,' I told him. 'Who was going to tell Buster about the pistol? And next time I catch you roping up this kid I'll bop you.'

'You should have bopped him already,' Cal said.

'I didn't bop him because you're always wanting to play with him, you got to look after yourself if you chase him like you do,' I said. 'Anyhow, I haven't got time to bop him. We're going down to the wharf. The ship's on her way in.'

'Boy!' said Cal, trying to get past me.

I held him. 'Follow me,' I said. 'You'll only get into trouble, like you did with Dibs. We don't want any trouble with Sam Phelps. Not today. We have to be very careful.'

I led them down the hill track to the clearing beside the railway line, not far from the wharf. This clearing was a good place for picnics if you wanted a change from the beach. Near the cliffside it had trees for shade; across the line was an easy way to the beach in one direction and an easy way to the rocks and the wharf in another direction. We had a lot of picnics there when we were small.

'Mr Wiggins certainly must have something,' I told Dibs while we waited in the clearing for the *Emma Cranwell* to get nearer. 'I didn't think Susan Prosser would go driving with him. What do you know, eh?'

'Mum says he's very obliging,' Dibs said. 'He lets us have big roasts.'

'We do all right from him,' I said.

'Mr Wiggins makes good sausages,' Cal said. 'That's what Dad says, doesn't he, Harry?'

'Yes,' I said, staying friendly with Cal so that he wouldn't run off across the rocks. 'We always have a lot of sausages when our mother's away. What do you reckon about Mr Wiggins' sausages, Dibs?'

'They're all right,' Dibs said. 'Let's go to the wharf. The ship won't take long now.'

I checked to make sure Susan Prosser wasn't coming along the line, then I ran across to the rocks. If we went along the rocks as far as the wharf piles, Sam Phelps wouldn't see us until we got to the top of the funny steps, he wouldn't have time to turn angry and order us back to the woolshed, where he reckoned the official waiting-area was.

So we did that. We moved quickly across the rocks and were soon under the wharf. It got a bit riskier then because we had to work along the slippery wharf timbers towards the steps, and the water below us was very deep. Dibs and I were good swimmers, but Cal wasn't much good.

'You all right, Cal?' I asked, leading the way across the timbers. 'Cal?' I said.

There was a splashing sound.

I looked back.

'He fell in,' Cal said. He nodded to where the water was disturbed. 'He wasn't watching where he was going. How did I know he was right behind me?'

I waited till Dibs surfaced. 'Better hurry,' I told him.

'I'll get you!' Dibs yelled to Cal.

'I didn't do anything to him,' said Cal, beside me now. 'How did I know he was going to jump?'

Dibs swam to the steps. He was waiting for us when we reached them.

'Lucky you weren't caught in the current,' I said. 'You know how dangerous it is.'

'That kid pushed me,' Dibs said, taking off his shirt.

'I didn't,' Cal said. He was already half-way up the steps, moving in his squirrel style because of how each step was placed—tipped up instead of flat.

'You can dry out in the sun,' I told Dibs. 'See you at the top.'

Cal was waiting for me at the top. So was Sam Phelps.

'I know what you're going to say, Mr Phelps,' I said. 'But you better not get angry and make us wait by the wool-shed because we got a special reason for being here. We're waiting for our cousin. Dad said to wait here on the wharf so she'd know she was welcome and not be frightened. Be a sport, Mr Phelps. We haven't seen Caroline for years and years. We're wondering what she looks like now. We're going to show her everything in Calliope Bay. I bet you wouldn't like to be shy and turn up in a strange place and find nobody waiting to welcome you, you'd think nobody cared what happened to you. Caroline will feel awful if we're not right here to welcome her. It's what Dad wants us to do. He'd get pretty angry if you made us go to the woolshed where Caroline wouldn't notice us. He'd be after you to find out how come you wouldn't let us stay. You know what Dad's like when he's angry. I wouldn't want to make *him* angry. So how about it, Mr Phelps? Can we stay here and wait for Caroline and make her feel welcome?'

Sam Phelps said nothing. After I had been talking a while, I was sure he did not see me. But I had gone on talking in case the faraway look in his eyes meant he was wondering what would be the best way to get us off the wharf.

'It's not his wharf, anyhow,' Dibs said when it seemed certain Sam Phelps wouldn't speak.

'No cheek,' I told Dibs. 'Mr Phelps is in charge of this wharf. He's the one we got to make sure doesn't mind us being here. Isn't that right, Mr Phelps?'

Sam Phelps, who was wearing a black shirt and crummy blue overalls and dirty sandshoes, did not answer. He went slowly to Sydney Bridge Upside Down and began stroking the hollow.

'Looks like he doesn't care about us,' Cal said.

I thought of trying to yarn to Sam Phelps about his horse, but he might still be wondering what to do with us. Best to keep out of his way.

'Not long to go now,' I told Dibs.

We strolled to the end of the wharf for a better view of the *Emma Cranwell* coming in.

'Doesn't seem as if Mr Wiggins brought Susan Prosser back,' I told Dibs. I had been keeping an eye on the railway line; nobody had been along it since we got to the wharf.

'She might be hiding,' Cal said. 'Remember the time she was up the cabbage tree—'

'He's always hoping!' shouted Dibs. He ducked when Cal aimed a slap at his bare chest.

'I'm not!' shouted Cal. He pushed Dibs, who didn't hit back, then came across to me. 'I was thinking she went into hiding after that time too,' he said. 'That's all I was thinking, Harry. I wasn't thinking about seeing her bum through the holes in her bloomers. Dibs thought I was going to talk about that, but I wasn't, I was—'

'You've got a good memory,' I said. 'That was years ago. You wouldn't see Susan Prosser climbing a cabbage tree nowadays.'

'He's always hoping,' Dibs said.

'Want another swim?' I asked Dibs.

Dibs nipped behind a bollard as I moved towards him. 'I'll yell to old Phelps if you touch me,' he said. 'He'll boot you off this wharf.'

31

'Quit picking on my brother then,' I said. 'You're only our guest, boy. It's not your cousin who's arriving. We got a right to be here. If we tell Sam Phelps we don't want you hanging around when Caroline arrives, he'll run you off the wharf.'

Dibs waved his hand to show he understood. Then he half-turned and kept waving, this time at the *Emma Cranwell*, now about a hundred yards away.

'Why is he waving?' Cal asked me.

'I know the skipper,' Dibs told Cal.

So did we know the skipper, Captain Foster, but we didn't usually wave to him, he couldn't fool us with his old tub. We knew the *Emma Cranwell* was not much of a ship, not compared with the liners and other ships we saw in books and heard about from Dad. Even so, it was all right to see her getting nearer, dipping now and then, rolling a bit. She came on through what were said to be tricky cross-currents that were apparently as important for Captain Foster to remember as the rocks jutting up here and there. Bigger ships had once called at Calliope Bay, but the ship I mostly remembered was the old *Emma Cranwell*, dipping and rolling among the currents and rocks. I never wanted to sail in her again, but I did not mind watching her come in, bringing our shy cousin.

'I can see Captain Foster,' Dibs said. 'Ahoy there!'

He ran to the edge to catch the rope the *Emma Cranwell* sailor threw across the gap between the ship and the wharf. Other times I had helped to put the rope around the bollard, though this was one of the things Sam Phelps did not seem to like about us being there. This time, anyway, I let Dibs do it on his own. I was looking for my cousin.

I saw her five minutes after the *Emma Cranwell* tied up. This beautiful girl in a yellow dress appeared on the deck near the gangway and I couldn't think why she had appeared so suddenly, then I realised it was because three sailors carrying suitcases had hidden her from me. They let her go first up the gangway. Looking down the gangway from the wharf was Captain Foster, who had been talking to Sam Phelps since stepping ashore. Everybody was looking at my cousin.

After my first thought—that she was beautiful— I thought she was chubby, but quickly decided this was because I was comparing her with skinny Susan Prosser.

Captain Foster went down the gangway and took my cousin's hand. He guided her very carefully; by the time they were at the top of the gangway he had one arm around her. I saw why when she stepped on to the wharf; she was wearing high-heeled white shoes. She was a city girl; sure enough.

What happened next, before Dibs and Cal and I had a chance to get near Caroline, was that she kissed the skipper. We heard her say: 'Thank you very very much.'

Then she kissed the three sailors who had carried her suitcases ashore. 'Thank you,' she said to each of them.

Then, while Dibs and Cal and I were still waiting for a chance to get near her, she walked to Sam Phelps and kissed him too. We heard her say: 'Hello, Uncle Frank.'

My turn next, I thought. I beat Dibs and Cal in the race along the wharf.

3

I WAS thinking, soon after the storm broke, about the scar on the old man's left cheek. I was also thinking about his horse. In fact, when the first of the thunder and lightning stopped and the rain began, I was thinking about everybody in Calliope Bay, one after the other. This was because of what Caroline said about Sam Phelps. She made me think about him in a different way, then I wondered if I could see the other people in Calliope Bay as a stranger like Caroline would see them. Where we lived, there were five houses—five left out of all the houses from the old days, the days when the works had plenty of jobs and there were plenty of men to take them. I thought of these five houses and of the people in them. First in the row, at the end nearest the works, was the house where Mr and Mrs Knowles lived. I did not spend much time thinking about Mr and Mrs Knowles because even if they were different from how I had always thought of them, I could not believe it really mattered, since they were so old; I mean, their sons and daughters had grown up and gone away, and all Mr and Mrs Knowles did was sit in the sun, or walk round their backyard a few times, or call to their cat, nothing much at all. The next house along the row was ours, and I knew about us, so I didn't look for anything different in this house either. But I did think about the Prossers, our neighbours on the other side. I thought about lonely Mrs Prosser and about skinny Susan, and I wondered if Mrs Prosser was actually a happy woman who maybe sang to her budgie all day long, and if Susan actually didn't mind me and might only be teasing when she seemed to run from me. I even imagined that Mr Prosser, missing for years, would unexpectedly return with a fortune and make Susan and her mother show their true feelings. The next house along was where Dibs Kelly and his family lived, but it must have been a mistake for me to start thinking of how Dibs actually was, because I just couldn't think of him differently and it seemed to put me off thinking of the rest of his family as any different from what I had always thought of them as, except that I couldn't be sure about Mrs Kelly, I could probably imagine all sorts of things about her if I tried. I did not try; I moved on to the last house in the row and thought about Mr Dalloway. Well, I didn't get far with Mr Dalloway either. Because it seemed wrong to be thinking about a teacher during the holidays. So soon I was back to thinking about the person I had started with, the one Caroline made me think of first, saying what she did. Hadn't she noticed his scar? Hadn't she noticed how he stared without seeming to see? What about his spiky grey hair, never combed, and his cheeks that always seemed to need shaving? If these things didn't matter, then maybe it didn't matter about Sydney Bridge Upside Down; maybe he was a different horse from the one I thought he was. Maybe Mr and Mrs Knowles—no, I would not go through the others again. The best thing, I thought while the rain pounded on our roof, would be to ask Caroline what she had meant.

Dad smiled. He told Caroline: 'You brought it with you.'

Caroline looked surprised. 'Did I, Uncle Frank?'

'First storm of the summer,' he said.

'It's been sunny all the holidays,' Cal told Caroline. 'We've had good fun.'

'This will soon pass on,' Dad said. 'Tomorrow will be sunny.'

'Do you really and truly think so?' asked Caroline. 'It seems so wild out there now.'

Dad laughed. 'Not like city storms?'

'This one seems louder,' Caroline said 'But I must be imagining it. Storms are all the same.'

'Did Harry tell you about *his* famous storm?' Dad asked her. 'The one when he sailed in the *Emma Cranwell*.'

Caroline, who was certainly the most beautiful girl I had ever seen, smiled at me. 'He told me so many other things on the way from the wharf,' she said. 'But not about his voyage in the *Emma Cranwell*. What happened that time, Harry?'

'Dad will tell you,' I said. 'He likes telling it.'

'You tell me, Harry,' she said.

'No,' I said, very sulky. I had been sulky for several minutes. I didn't know why.

36

'You tell me then, Uncle Frank,' she said, not seeming to mind my sulkiness.

Dad told her. And while he told her I remembered what a damned chatterbox I had been in the wagon with her and Cal and Dibs and the suitcases, and I thought it was strange how I was such a chatterbox then and yet now I did not want to talk, I did not want to stop looking at her but I did not want to talk to her, or to anybody. I had been like this since dinner, since Dad had started talking. He was certainly talking, you would think Caroline had been sent especially for him to talk to, all she had to do was listen to him. And Cal. Cal talked too. Not me, though. Not since dinner. In fact, not since the trip from the wharf. I had talked all the time then. I couldn't stop.

What had started me off was the kiss. I had never been kissed like that before. I was still excited when we were in the wagon, waving good-bye to the *Emma Cranwell* while Sydney Bridge Upside Down plodded ahead along the wharf, then past the woolshed and on to the line round the cliffs. I told Caroline how we had watched from the cliff-top for the ship to come in, how we had secret caves up there, how there was a dangerous tree on the cliff-edge ('He pushed me off the cliff!' said Dibs, but got no chance to say more), how we could come down that path there and go to the beach or the wharf, how we liked playing on the beach and the wharf and the rocks, how we fished from the wharf and Dibs was once bitten by a barracouta he'd caught, and how there were plenty of other places where we could play, especially the ruins of the works that we would soon be passing, and of course the swamp, where we caught frogs, and the river, and across the river there was a store and other things, like a mysterious house without chimneys, and paths that went off into the bush and took you to rather amazing places, like a cliff-ledge where you could stand and watch a great waterfall, or a burial-ground, or a redoubt, or a broken-down windmill, and I told her we would show her all these things while she was on holiday, she would have a lot of fun, we liked having fun. And it must have sounded all right to her because she gave me another kiss, then kissed Dibs and Cal—to keep it fair, I supposed. Her way of kissing sort of took you by surprise. You could see what she meant to do and you had time to turn your head if you wanted to, but you couldn't move, and suddenly she was kissing you. This, I decided, must be a city habit we would just have to get used to, unless there was a rule saying how often you needed to kiss before you moved to some other way of showing you were pleased, like shaking hands maybe. I noticed the second time how very close she came when she kissed, her body was right up against you; it was as if she had to be sure that now she'd found your mouth she did not lose it. Anyway, I also told her, while we were in the wagon, how our teacher reckoned we lived on the edge of the world, and how you could believe this was so if you went out to the heads and looked at the horizon, and how there were people in Calliope Bay who felt lonely and faraway, especially Mrs Prosser ('Harry chases Susan Prosser,' said Cal, but didn't get another word in), and how there were others, like Mr Dalloway, who sped off as soon as the holidays came and were not seen in Calliope Bay for many weeks, and how the rest of us did not mind staying because there was plenty of fun if you knew where to look. And I probably would have told her of the pistol and a few other secrets if Sydney Bridge Upside Down had gone any slower or the trip had been longer. And all this was only a few hours ago. Yet now I did not want to speak. Now, while the rain pounded away, I just wanted to look at her.

Why did she seem beautiful? Because, for instance, her skin was smooth and sort of creamy, and she had no rashes or pimples or scars, and her hair was also smooth and sort of creamy or buttery-looking, and her nose was straight and small and without any bumps or veins, and when she smiled her teeth looked very white, not crooked and not green, and her eyes were good because they were very clear and blue, they were eyes you could stare at and see right through. Next time I was close enough, I thought, I would look hard at her eyes and see right through them. Of course she was not as chubby as I'd first imagined; she simply wasn't skinny, that was all. Or nearly all. Like, when I thought of Susan Prosser's I thought of tits; when I thought of Caroline's I thought of breasts. I felt sort of polite when I thought of anything to do with Caroline. I did not feel polite when I thought of Susan or of the girls who came to our school from back-country places. Caroline was nice. My mother had said she was shy, almost as if this was peculiar, but I could see there was nothing peculiar about Caroline, my mother must have mistaken Caroline's niceness for shyness, and this didn't surprise me because my mother often got the wrong idea about people at first and had to change her mind later, like with Mr

Dalloway, saying at first he would be a better teacher if he didn't have such a high opinion of his own good looks, then not seeming to mind him at all after he'd called on her a few times to talk about our progress at school. Dad was better at seeing what people were like. You could tell he had seen right away that Caroline was nice. He would have seen this, I was sure, even if she hadn't kissed him. Now, very nicely, she said to me: 'You look dreamy, Harry. Are you tired?'

I found my tongue at last. I said: 'I'm not tired. Would you like to try our ginger beer?' I left the sofa, meaning to get a bottle for her.

'Caroline would rather have a cup of tea,' Dad said. He hopped to the stove and picked up the kettle before I could get to it. 'You can try the ginger beer tomorrow, Caroline,' he said, hopping to the sink. 'You'll appreciate the ginger beer after you've been in the sun,' he said, filling the kettle. He put the kettle back on the stove, shoved in some sticks and asked me: 'What will you show Caroline tomorrow?'

'Maybe the waterfall,' I said.

'Too far away,' he said. 'Something nearer for the first day would be better.' He smiled at Caroline. 'Do you walk much in the city?'

'Not very much, Uncle Frank,' she said. 'But I'd love to walk to the waterfall with Harry and Cal.'

'Climb, more like it,' said Cal. 'It's a steep track to the waterfall.'

'Along the river-bank is good,' I said, thinking we would really take her to more interesting places, like the works, only we wouldn't tell Dad.

'River should be high tomorrow,' Dad said. 'All this rain.'

'Be plenty of logs in it,' Cal said.

'Once we saw a body floating by after a big storm,' I told Caroline. 'This old tramp had drowned.'

Caroline looked sad.

'Mr Kelly fished him out,' I said.

'Enough of that,' Dad said, hopping across to make the tea. 'Caroline doesn't want to hear of such unhappy things. Do you, Caroline?'

'I don't mind, Uncle Frank,' she said, looking less sad. 'We all know people die. We know death is not unusual. So many people are dying all the time. Many thousands every minute of the day and night. Many, many thousands.'

Suddenly our house seemed very quiet.

We looked at Caroline. Her voice had been calm, soft—it had been nice. Not only that. Something in it had made me chilly, and I could not decide what this was. Anyway, I could tell that Dad and Cal had also noticed it. Dad had stopped by the stove, the teapot in one hand; Cal, who had been fiddling with a teaspoon at the table, had also stiffened. We were silent. It took a loud knock on the back door to wake us up.

'We're not expecting visitors,' said Dad, hopping to the table with the teapot.

Cal beat me to the door.

Mr Wiggins stood there. He was flicking his sou'wester against his streaming oilskin.

'It's Mr Wiggins!' I called over my shoulder. I dragged back Cal so that Mr Wiggins could get by. Rain whisked into my face.

'Come in, Chick,' said Dad. 'You timed it right. I've just brewed up. Take off your gear.'

'Not staying long, Frank,' said Mr Wiggins, taking off his oilskin. 'I brought the Prosser lass home, thought I'd pop in to see if you wanted to up your order this week. Heard you had an extra mouth to feed...'

All the time he was speaking, he was looking at Caroline. She had left the table when he came in and I'd wondered for a moment if she was moving forward to kiss him. But she settled for smiling at him.

'Yes, my niece will be staying with us for a while,' said Dad. 'Chick, this is Miss Caroline Selby. She's from the city. Mr Wiggins brings our meat every week, Caroline. A very important man. Pull up a chair, Chick.'

'I won't stay,' said Mr Wiggins, still looking at Caroline. 'Well, perhaps I'll have a quick one.'

While Dad poured the teas, I watched Mr Wiggins. In fact, ever since I had heard Dad call him a lady's man a few months back, I had been watching Mr Wiggins whenever I had the chance, which was about once a week when he kept to his regular delivery day, oftener when he made special trips for some customer or other, usually Mrs Kelly. I had decided I did not like Mr Wiggins very much, mainly because of the way he treated kids. He didn't hit kids and he wasn't actually bossy to them; it was just that he obviously didn't think kids were as interesting as grown-ups, he would never yarn to a kid the way he would yarn to grown-ups, especially women. The women must have liked his jokes because they certainly laughed a lot at what he said. Maybe they liked his appearance too. He was short and hairy (he had a moustache, long side-boards, swished-back black hair), and his behind stuck out when he walked, as if he was pretty tough. I wouldn't have said his appearance was all that great, but after what Caroline had said about Sam Phelps I couldn't be sure my opinion of people's looks mattered much anyway. It struck me that Caroline, now back at the table, had been studying Mr Wiggins. I could ask her later how she thought *he* looked.

'Staying long in our part of the world, Miss Selby?' he asked, taking a seat opposite her.

'A little while,' she said. 'I mustn't outstay my welcome.'

'You can stay as long as you like, Caroline,' said Dad. He was sitting at the stove end of the table.

'You couldn't have picked a better time, Miss Selby,' said Mr Wiggins. 'Don't let tonight's downpour mislead you. We're in for plenty more sunny weather this summer.'

'So I was telling her, Chick,' said Dad. 'Storms are rare this time of the year. Don't expect we'll—'

'If there's any particular place you want to see, I'd be glad to give you a lift,' Mr Wiggins told Caroline. 'I'm the only taxi in these parts.' He laughed.

'You can leave it to the boys to show Caroline the beauty spots, Chick,' said Dad.

'We're going to the waterfall,' Cal said.

'Places further afield, I mean, Miss Selby,' said Mr Wiggins, not looking at Dad or Cal. 'Be glad to give you a lift to the store, for instance.'

Dad laughed. 'Doubt if Caroline will find the store exciting, Chick.'

'Well, it's where the nearest telephone is,' Mr Wiggins said. 'Suppose Miss Selby wants to put in a call to her people in the city? She'd have to ring from the store. Be glad to take her there.'

'That's very very kind of you, Mr Wiggins,' said Caroline. 'But I don't think I'll need to ring home. They know where I am. They won't expect a call.'

'Be glad to give you a lift,' he told her. 'Say you want to go shopping at Bonnie Brae. Have they told you about Bonnie Brae?'

'Not yet,' said Caroline, smiling at Dad.

'Give us a chance,' Dad told Mr Wiggins. 'Caroline only got here this afternoon.'

'Bonnie Brae's where I operate from, Miss Selby,' said Mr Wiggins. 'Nearest thing to a town in this part of the country. What about the carnival? There's the anniversary carnival soon. You might appreciate a lift to the carnival.'

'Sandy Kelly usually takes us in the Reo,' Dad said. 'There'll be room for Caroline.'

'Bumpy ride in the Reo, Miss Selby,' said Mr Wiggins. 'Road's rough, some risky bends, long drop to the sea if a driver doesn't watch out. We've lost a few drivers off that road.'

'Sandy's done the run for years,' Dad said. 'He hasn't struck trouble yet. I think we can risk him again. But thanks for the offer, Chick. Very generous of you.'

'Any time,' Mr Wiggins said. 'What about the races, Miss Selby? You interested in racing? Meeting at Bonnie Brae on

44

Saturday week. You might appreciate a lift to the races.'

'I'm not fond of racing,' Caroline said. 'I went once. I've never been again.'

Mr Wiggins, looking enormously interested, leaned over the table. 'Is that a fact? What didn't you like about the races, Miss Selby?'

'I can't remember,' she said. 'I do remember that I didn't enjoy being there.'

'Is that a fact?' said Mr Wiggins. 'Is that a fact?'

'Drop dead,' said Caroline.

At least, that was what I imagined she said when I saw her mouth open twice while Mr Wiggins gazed at her. She did not speak, she just shaped the words. I must have been mistaken about the words she chose, of course. Because she was smiling and still looking nice. I wouldn't have blamed her for being angry because I thought Mr Wiggins was damned cheeky with his talk of taking her places, and I could see Dad was annoyed at him too, anybody would think Caroline didn't have relations eager to show her around, anybody would think we needed Mr Wiggins and his rattly van.

Dad asked: 'Who told you Caroline was here, Chick?'

Mr Wiggins said: 'You can't keep a pretty girl to yourself, Frank. Word soon gets around. No secrets in Calliope Bay, eh?'

'I wonder,' Dad said. 'Take Dalloway the teacher. Lot we don't know about that fellow. Manages to keep things to himself.'

'What do you want to know about him?' Mr Wiggins asked. He grinned. 'Reckon I know what makes him tick.'

'Dare say,' Dad said. 'You get to hear more gossip than I do.'

'Which of his secrets would you like to hear about?' asked Mr Wiggins, winking at Caroline.

'Don't get the idea I care what he's been, what he does,' Dad said. 'I was only using him as an illustration of people keeping things to themselves. It's not that I *care* where he goes for his holidays.'

'Well, that's no secret,' said Mr Wiggins. 'He always heads for the city. Everybody knows that.'

'Of course we do,' Dad said. 'That's not what I meant. But never mind. Care for another cup, Chick?'

'No, that should do,' Mr Wiggins said. 'I've got a long drive home. River might be bad too.' He stared at Caroline.

'Give us a shout if you get stuck,' Dad said. 'We'll see what we can do.'

'I'll make it,' Mr Wiggins said, keeping his gaze on Caroline.

'See you again then,' Dad said. 'What were you saying about my order?'

'Your order?' asked Mr Wiggins, turning from Caroline, frowning at Dad.

'Thought you wanted to know if I was going to up it this week,' Dad said.

'That's right,' Mr Wiggins said, not seeming to care. 'What about some steak? Something tender for Miss Selby, eh? I'll add a couple of pounds of steak. All right, Frank?'

'That should do,' Dad said. He hopped to the door to

hand Mr Wiggins his sou'wester and oilskin. 'Glad you looked in, Chick. I might have forgotten about the order.'

'Any time,' Mr Wiggins said. He glanced at Cal and me, looked longer at Caroline. 'Don't forget the carnival. Don't forget what I said, Miss Selby.'

'Thank you, Mr Wiggins,' Caroline said.

She spoke nicely and maybe I was only imagining that her eyes showed she didn't really think much of his offer, maybe I was only imagining that the look she gave me meant she agreed about Mr Wiggins being damned cheeky. Anyway, she had not kissed him; this must be a good sign.

'He doesn't often show up so late,' Dad said when Mr Wiggins had gone off into the storm.

'Catch me going to the carnival in his old van!' Cal said. 'It breaks down. We saw it in the river—' I was glaring at him, he stopped.

'Mr Kelly will take us,' Dad said. 'We can trust the Reo.'

'Would you like some toast?' I asked Caroline. She was looking at me, and I said it for the sake of something to say.

'It's not my hungry look, Harry,' she said. 'It's my wondering look. I was wondering about the name Dalloway.' She smiled at me, then at Dad. 'I heard you mention a Mr Dalloway, Uncle Frank, and I wondered when I'd heard that name before.' She looked at me. 'Perhaps you mentioned it, Harry?'

'Sure I did,' I said. 'On the way from the wharf. I told you how he reckons we live on the edge of the world.'

'That must be it!' she said. 'I knew I'd heard it before. I couldn't remember.'

Dad was serious. 'But you might have heard it before today? Is that what you mean, Caroline?'

She considered. 'Perhaps I do, Uncle Frank.'

'How do you mean?' asked Dad. 'Can't you remember?'

'It does seem longer ago than this afternoon,' she said. She was silent for a moment or so, then she said: 'It's been such a long day.'

'Yes, you'll want a good sleep tonight,' Dad said. 'Not often we're up this late. All our talking!'

His talking, he meant. He had not given Cal and me much chance before Mr Wiggins arrived, and Mr Wiggins had been as bad, you would think Caroline was meant for him to talk to and make silly suggestions to. I'd catch up tomorrow, it would be my turn then to talk to Caroline.

'I'll pull down your blind,' I told her. 'In case the lightning scares you.' I sped to her room at the front of the house before Dad could say he would do it.

Cal followed me along the passage. He didn't like to miss anything, that kid.

'She's better than Susan Prosser, eh?' he said when we were in the bedroom where our parents usually slept (now Dad would have the smaller spare room next to the kitchen).

'Bit soon to tell, boy,' I said, knowing very well he was right.

Outside it was still raining; it was black too. I pulled down the blind.

'Thank you very very much, Harry,' Caroline said from the doorway.

'If you want to use the dunny, you can have first go,' Cal told her. 'I showed you where it is, eh?'

'Yes, and thank you very very much too, Cal,' she said.

Dad had come hopping up the passage. He told Cal: 'Now Caroline is here, you'd better start calling it the lav.'

Caroline didn't seem to mind. She said she would go out to it right away.

While she was gone, Dad said: 'You fellows must watch your language now there's a young lady in the house. Not so many *damneds* from you, Harry. And don't say *dunny*, Cal. Try to be polite. We mustn't give your cousin a wrong impression. She's a nice girl.'

We promised to watch our language.

'See you do,' he said. 'Now off to bed!'

'I want to go out there after her,' Cal said. 'I always go to the dunny before I put on my pyjamas.'

'I'll go after him,' I said.

'Just wait for Caroline,' Dad said.

When she got back, her yellow dress was splashed with rain, she was brushing her hair with her fingers.

'Sorry, Caroline,' Dad said. 'I should have given you the oilskin.'

'Don't worry, Uncle Frank,' she said. 'Not many drops hit me.' She smiled at us. 'Good night, everybody. Thank you for the marvellous welcome.'

Then she did what I had been hoping she would do. She kissed us. She kissed Cal first, then me, then Dad. My turn seemed to last longer than Cal's, but I didn't get a chance

49

to look through her eyes—because she shut them. When she got to Dad, his crutch slipped and he had to hold her tightly to keep his balance. It was unusual for Dad's crutch to slip.

Cal and I raced to the kitchen. I let Cal go outside first.

Later, when Cal and I were in our pyjamas and bouncing on the bed, I remembered that Dad had looked dreamy as he crossed the kitchen to the spare room, he hadn't noticed me watching.

4

THE FUNNY thing is I forgot what Caroline said about Sam Phelps. I mean, I forgot for more than two days. Then I remembered on her third morning with us. It was just after we had been running around with nothing on that I remembered. We had been running from her room to our room and back again, up and down the passage, in and out of the kitchen, and we were getting puffed, I was not surprised when Caroline dived on to her bed, pulled a sheet over herself and said from the pillow that she'd had enough. Cal and I didn't mind stopping; we'd had our share of smacks.

Cal, who was still shy about Caroline seeing him wearing nothing, went off to get dressed. I sat on Caroline's bed, near the end.

'I've remembered something,' I said, looking straight ahead in case she sat up and let the sheet slip and thought I was staring. 'Remember what you said about Sam Phelps the other night? About him being handsome.'

'I remember,' Caroline said, keeping her head on the pillow. 'Why, Harry?'

'Do you still think he's handsome?' I asked. 'Now you've seen him again.'

'Don't you think so, Harry?' Her head stayed on the pillow, she spoke sleepily.

'What about his scar?' I asked.

'Doesn't matter,' she said.

'What about him being grubby?' I asked.

'Being what?' she said softly.

'Grubby,' I said.

'What?' she said, very softly.

I could tell she was nearly asleep, so I said no more. I guessed I should go and put my clothes on, but I didn't want to leave her, I wanted to be near her a while longer. I told myself she might suddenly sit up and tell me why she thought Sam Phelps was handsome. I knew she wouldn't, but it seemed a good excuse for staying there.

Now she was asleep.

She likes being in bed, I thought. I remembered how she had said the afternoon after her arrival that she was going into the bedroom to change her dress, and how when I looked in there half an hour later she was asleep on the bed, still wearing the dress she had worn for our climb up the small hill across the road from our house. She had gone to bed pretty early the past two nights too, even though Dad wanted to keep telling her about his city experiences (he kept describing buildings and streets he thought she knew, but she didn't know many of them, maybe because Dad was talking of how the city was a long time before). I also remembered that she had not wanted to climb the stairs at the works yesterday because she said she was feeling rather tired, she would prefer to climb them another day, quite early if we didn't mind. I had thought for a moment she might be scared of those ruins and was recalling what Dad had told her about the accidents that had happened there and how dangerous it was (with a warning look at us). Then I decided she was not scared, it was just that she was a city girl and not yet used to running and climbing the way we were. And I told her to sit down while I chased Dibs Kelly up the works stairs, I said I would wave to her from the top floor. She said she would keep looking and would wave back when she saw us. Well, I beat Dibs to the top, but when I looked down I couldn't see Caroline or Cal. That damned Cal must have taken her inside the old killing-room, I thought; he was probably showing her where we had found the pistol, not caring about it being secret. But he had not taken her there, after all. Because then I noticed that they were with Sam Phelps and Sydney Bridge Upside Down. They must have gone to the railway line quickly because it certainly hadn't taken Dibs and me long to get to the top of the works. 'What do you know?' I said to Dibs. I was so annoyed about what had happened I felt like giving Dibs a good push, they would come running back to the works if I did that, if I shouted to them as I did it. I didn't push Dibs, though; it wasn't his fault. I didn't chase across to them, either; if Caroline preferred talking to Sam Phelps, that was her business, she would soon get tired of Sam Phelps and his old horse. 'Going down?' asked Dibs. 'Think I'll look at the scenery a while,'

I said. 'I'm going down,' he said. 'See you,' I said. I knew the scenery too well to look at it long. Instead, I looked at the group by the railway line, and now at Dibs (I should have pushed him!) cutting across to be near her, near *my* cousin. And now at Dibs speeding up because Caroline and Cal had climbed into the freight wagon and Sydney Bridge Upside Down was moving. Sam Phelps was in his seat at the front of the wagon, holding the reins loosely, heading for the wharf with Caroline and Cal. What a dirty trick! Cal could have called me, *he* knew I'd like a ride. Caroline might think I didn't care, but Cal knew better, he could easily have yelled to me. That kid played some dirty tricks, I thought. And what right had Dibs, jumping now into the wagon, to be travelling with my cousin? When I remembered how often I had tried to get a ride on his big brother's Indian and how often I had been turned down, I reckoned it was damned cheeky of Dibs to help himself to a ride with my cousin. I got sulky, up there at the top of the works, while Sydney Bridge Upside Down plodded on. I stayed there. Eventually they rounded the bend, the cliff would hide them till they were nearer the wharf. At least, I took it for granted it would hide them that long. But they stayed hidden for longer than they should have, and at first I thought Sydney Bridge Upside Down must have stopped for a rest, being so bony and old, then I wondered, when they still didn't appear near the wharf, if they'd been derailed, maybe Caroline had been tipped out. She might need help, I thought. I moved a few steps towards the stairwell before I reminded myself that no wagon could be derailed at the speed Sydney Bridge Upside Down went.

So what were they doing? Where were they? I waited and watched. Nothing. It was no use, I would have to go down. I went down slowly, kicking the footholds to make them more dangerous. Serve her right if I crash, I thought. Poor Harry, she would think when they found my body. And all she could do then would be to give me a last kiss. Cal and Dibs would not be sad for long. Trust them to go on having fun, they would think themselves lucky to have got rid of me, they wouldn't care if I fell. And of course I didn't fall, I didn't miss a foothold, not one. In the works yard I thought of heading for home, of leaving the others to whatever fun they had found. I would just walk to the line and look along it—but not walk along it, I certainly wouldn't follow them, if they'd wanted me around they would have yelled to me. So I did that. And I had not been standing long near the line when I saw Dibs and Cal. They were on the line, walking towards me. I didn't move. It seemed a good while before they reached me. 'Where's Caroline?' I asked when they were still a few yards from me. 'Looking at his house,' Cal said, sounding annoyed. 'What house?' I asked, knowing that Sam Phelps lived in a shack in a clearing not far from the wharf woolshed, and nobody could call it a house. 'Looking at his shack,' said Dibs. 'He's got nothing to show her, that shack's not worth looking at,' I said. 'That's what we thought,' Dibs said. And they told me how Caroline had suggested that they come back to play with me because she wanted to accept Sam Phelps' invitation and she said she knew they would rather play than look at a house. 'She'd have let *me* go with her, it was Dibs being there that made it no good,' Cal said.

'Yes, boy,' I told Dibs, 'you've got a cheek chasing her. She's *our* cousin.' 'I wasn't chasing her, I only went for the ride,' Dibs said. 'Get your own cousin,' I told him, and I aimed a punch, but he dodged and ran off and I couldn't be bothered following him. Cal said: 'Mr Phelps said he'd make her a cup of tea. That's why she went with him. How about we go to the works, Harry?' I said: 'You didn't care about the works a while ago, not when you went off with her like you did.' And I wouldn't play with him, he had lost his chance. I waited for Caroline. I had to wait an hour. She came back in the freight wagon, and she waved to me from the seat beside Sam Phelps as soon as she saw me. She would have seen me sooner if she hadn't been listening to what Sam Phelps was saying, and it was strange to see Sam Phelps talking like that. When the wagon stopped I kept a fair way off, and I didn't speak to Caroline until she quit listening to Sam Phelps. 'What a skinny horse, eh?' I said, watching Sydney Bridge Upside Down move off. 'He's a dear,' Caroline said, and I couldn't be sure whether she meant Sam Phelps or his horse, I had a feeling she hadn't heard what I said. That was when I could have asked her what she meant by saying Sam Phelps was handsome, but I clean forgot she'd said it, and I didn't remember till this morning. And now that I had asked her, I was no better off. I would not ask her again, I thought, looking at her, listening to her breathing. I would not bother her, I would let her sleep.

I went to my room and got dressed. Then I made the bed. Cal must have gone outside. He was a funny kid, he hadn't minded playing the running game with me, but now that Caroline joined in (after looking into our room and surprising us on her first morning) he seemed to think it was a rude game and I wouldn't be astounded if he said tomorrow that he would rather not play. This was all right with me, except that he might tell Dad, and I was certain Dad would not like us seeing so much of Caroline's body. I would warn Cal, I would tell him I would think up a revenge if he spoiled our fun.

I looked into Caroline's room on my way to the kitchen. She was still asleep.

Out in the kitchen, I stacked the breakfast dishes and ran the water into the sink. Here I am again on my own, I thought; no help from Caroline. Not, of course, that I expected her to do the dishes; it was just that, before she arrived, I'd figured I would have a rest from doing the dishes. I did not mind doing them, I would not complain about doing them. If she did offer to do them, or to sweep up or anything like that, I would refuse to let her, I would tell her she was on holiday and we wanted her to enjoy herself, we did not expect her to do any damned house-keeping. If she insisted, it would probably be polite to let her do something. So far she hadn't insisted.

No, I didn't mind Caroline not helping. But this didn't mean Cal could stop wiping up.

I went to the back porch to yell to him. I could not see him. The one I did see was Susan Prosser. She was looking over the fence. I waited, expecting her to bob down out of sight. But she kept looking.

'Have you seen my brother?' I said, walking across to her.

'He went down the back,' she said, pointing, sounding friendly.

'When was that?' I asked, surprised by her attitude. She usually acted as though I gave her the pip.

'About ten minutes ago,' she said. 'He was intending to pick some passion-fruit, he said. But he didn't stay long at the vine. He must have changed his mind.'

'Must have,' I said, wondering why she was so friendly. 'Probably after frogs. He puffs them up through straws, then pops them—' She was pulling a face. 'Suppose he'll be back soon,' I said. 'I only want him to help with the dishes.'

Now she looked surprised. 'Oh, do *you* do the dishes?'

'Yes,' I said. 'Dad goes to work too early to do them.'

'I mean, you *still* do them?' she asked.

'I always do them,' I said, puzzled by her smile. There had been nothing to smile about.

'You must like doing the dishes,' she said.

'I don't mind,' I said. I watched her a moment, thinking what a plain face she had. Then I asked: 'How is your mother's budgie? Has he said anything interesting lately?'

'Not particularly,' she said.

I had the feeling there was something on her mind. She was pretending to be friendly because she was curious about something. Well, so did I have something on my mind—about her. About her and Mr Wiggins. I would not mention it now, though. Like her, I would pretend to be friendly.

'So Joey's said nothing interesting, eh?' I asked, making my eyes twinkle so that she would not guess I was suspicious. 'Does he still say "Jesus is a naughty boy"?'

'Sometimes,' she said.

'Anything else?' I asked.

'Oh, he says "Guess what?" rather often,' she said.

'I wonder why?' I said. I didn't, I was only being friendly.

Susan Prosser shrugged. 'I haven't the faintest idea,' she said. 'By the way, what was that noise in your place?'

'Noise? What sort of noise?'

'Like people running around.'

'That's odd,' I said. My insides seemed to flutter, I was sure my face had turned red.

'Were you all running around?' she asked.

I got over my fright, or whatever it was. 'Oh, you must mean when I was chasing Cal,' I said. 'I always chase him in the mornings. He chases me too. It's our morning exercise.'

'Sounded rather louder than your usual noise,' she said. 'Sounded more like three people.'

'No, just us,' I said offhandedly. I looked towards the swamp. 'I wonder if Cal went with Dibs. Did you notice if Dibs was with him?'

'He was on his own,' she said. She frowned, apparently not sure whether to stay friendly. 'Why doesn't your cousin do the dishes?'

'Caroline?' I said. 'Caroline's on holiday.'

'I shouldn't think helping with the dishes would spoil her holiday,' Susan Prosser said. She smiled quickly, apparently deciding to go on seeming friendly. 'What does she do while you're washing up?'

Now she was getting too nosy, I might not stay friendly. 'Tidies up her room,' I said. 'Writes in her diary. She has things to do.'

Susan Prosser looked astonished. 'Does your cousin keep a diary?'

'Sure,' I said. Actually, what Caroline was writing, she said, was her autobiography; but this was none of Susan Prosser's business.

'Is she enjoying her holiday?' asked Susan Prosser.

'Why don't you ask her?' I said, suddenly realising that I no longer cared what Susan Prosser was like beneath her dress; I knew her body wasn't as great as Caroline's, and for the first time in years I did not want to look at it, she could keep her skinny body covered up for ever, see if I cared. Now I was sorry for her. I told her: 'Caroline wouldn't mind meeting you. We haven't noticed you about lately. Have you been hiding?'

'I've been too busy to meet anybody,' she said.

'Busy doing what?'

'Studying.'

'In the holidays?'

'People don't stop studying merely because of the holidays. Some people.'

'Why? What's wrong with leaving it till school starts again?'

She moved back from the fence. 'I don't believe you'd understand. You're not studious.'

'I do all right at school,' I said. 'Even if I'm not one of Mr Dalloway's pets.'

'I don't study because of Mr Dalloway,' she said. 'I study

for my own sake. Some day I'll leave Calliope Bay. I want to know how to do something when I get somewhere else. I won't know unless I'm properly educated. Do you understand?'

'Sure I do,' I said. Best to stay friendly. 'I didn't mean *you* were one of Mr Dalloway's pets.'

'It wouldn't matter to me if you did,' she said. 'Not that it would help me to be one of his pets.'

'I think he likes you, Susan,' I said.

'That scarcely matters now, does it?' she said. When she saw that I didn't understand, she added: 'You do know he won't be coming back next term?'

'Gosh!' I said. 'I never heard that!'

'It's true,' she said.

'How do you know?' I said, not believing her.

'I merely happen to know,' she said with a look that was obviously meant to show how sorry she felt for a kid who could not believe his teacher had left for ever.

'Who told you?' I asked.

'You don't *have* to believe me,' she said. 'Oh, I can't stay here chatting. I have some studying to do.'

I watched her go inside. I don't like her now, I thought. Why is she so nosy? Why does she make up fibs about Mr Dalloway? Who cares if she studies during the holidays? Who cares about her stupid budgie, anyway?

I went to the end of the yard and looked for Cal. I couldn't see him. That was another bop I owed him. I went back to the kitchen.

The water in the sink had cooled. I didn't care. I sloshed the dishes quickly, then dried them, using the tea-towel

61

to get rid of the parts still greasy.

I had wondered if Caroline would hear the rattle of the dishes and come out and insist on helping. Evidently she hadn't. Better get on with the sweeping. I would do the kitchen first, then the passage, then our room, then maybe I would go into Caroline's room—

Should I go to her room first? After looking so long at Susan Prosser, I wouldn't mind looking at Caroline. It would be a nice change.

I forced myself to keep to the first plan. I swept the kitchen quickly, then began on the passage.

'Harry!' called Caroline.

I dropped the broom and sped up the passage. I stopped in her doorway.

She was sitting up in bed. The sheet had slipped. After a moment or so I noticed that she looked more beautiful than ever.

'I've been dreaming, Harry,' she said. 'How long have I been asleep?'

'Only an hour,' I said. 'It's all right. There's no house-work to do. We don't want you doing housework while you're on holiday.'

She yawned and stretched her arms above her head. Then she said: 'Pull up the blind, Harry dear. Seems it's another sunny day.'

'Yes, it is,' I said. I kept my back to her while I was at the window. The road was clear, it usually was. I heard her bed creaking, but I made myself look at the road.

'Think I'll wear this today,' she said. 'Do you like this dress, Harry?'

So of course I had to turn round. She was by the corner wardrobe, holding up a flowery orange-and-green dress.

'It looks good,' I said.

'I'll wear this one today,' she said.

She put on the dress. It was all she did put on, though I figured she would probably put on other clothes when I wasn't there.

'Cal's gone to the swamp,' I said. 'Shall we go and see if he's caught any frogs?'

'All right,' she said. 'A quick wash, then I'll put on some lipstick. In case we meet anybody.' She smiled at me. 'Do you prefer girls to wear lipstick, Harry?'

She moved towards me and I had a good idea what she would do. 'I like lipstick,' I got in before she kissed me. It was a small kiss.

'There,' she said after it. 'Good morning again, Harry.'

She ran to the bathroom while I was taking a deep breath. I went to the kitchen and checked that there were still ten bottles of ginger beer in the sink cupboard. Should I offer her one? Or should I wait till we got back from the walk?

Dibs Kelly turned up just then, so that settled it. I would not mention the ginger beer.

I had not seen Dibs since I'd chased him by the railway line yesterday, but he didn't look as if he remembered how angry I had been, he looked friendly, ready for fun. He was grinning.

'I got something for the cave,' he said. He brought a square biscuit tin from behind his back. 'How about this?'

'What do we want a tin for?' I asked.

'Not only a tin,' he said. He took off the lid, showed me what was inside—a small paraffin lamp, glass funnel and all.

'Hey, that's good,' I said. 'Where did you get that? Did you pinch it?'

'Dad gave it to me,' Dibs said. 'Too small for him, he reckons. So we can use it to light the back of the cave, eh?'

'Be all right for night-time,' I said. 'We can use the cave at night.' I thought about it. 'If I can dodge Dad,' I said. 'Or if he's away some night and there's only Cal and me at home.' I recalled there were nights, once every month or so, when Dad and Mr Kelly drove in the Reo to Bonnie Brae, to smoke concerts or something. We could go to the cave on one of those nights. Good old Dibs!

'Coming up then?' he asked. 'I don't want to leave this at our house. One of the kids will find it and bust it.'

'We'll go up there this morning,' I said. 'I'll see if Caroline wants to come.'

'I don't mind,' Dibs said. He ran his tongue over his lips, but I ignored that.

I had heard Caroline going from the bathroom to her room and I guessed she would have had time to put on the lipstick and anything else she wanted to put on. Sure enough, when I reached her room she was just turning from the dressing-table mirror. She had lipstick on. She was also wearing a pair of brown flat-heeled shoes.

'What say we leave the swamp till another time?' I said. 'Would you like to see a cave today?'

'Is it far, Harry?' asked Caroline.

'Not far,' I said. 'No further than the wharf, going round the back way. It's not a very steep track. It won't make you tired, Caroline. And you can see the wharf and the bay from up there.'

'That sounds nice,' she said. 'We might even have time to call on Mr Phelps, do you think?'

'Well, he's usually busy about now,' I said. 'He stores things in the woolshed for farmers. They have different days for collecting stuff. He keeps things there for the store too—'

'Anyway, we'll have a nice walk,' Caroline said.

Dibs was waiting for us in the kitchen. If he expected Caroline to kiss him, he fell in; all she did was give him a smile. She didn't care who she smiled at.

I looked down the yard as we left in case Cal was there; he wasn't. Served him right that he was missing this fun, he shouldn't have dodged wiping the breakfast dishes.

I saw Susan Prosser on her front veranda when we were up on the road, but pretended I hadn't seen her. She couldn't be studying very hard. Unless the book in her hand was a textbook.

'You know what Susan Prosser reckons?' I said to Dibs when we were down the road a bit. 'She reckons Mr Dalloway won't be here next term.'

Caroline, who was walking between us, gave me a look when I said Mr Dalloway's name, but she did not speak.

'Susan Prosser doesn't know,' Dibs said.

'She's dippy,' I said. 'She makes up things.'

'Mr Dalloway would have told us,' Dibs said. 'He wouldn't tell her and not tell us.'

'She says she stays inside because she's studying,' I said. I glanced at Caroline, but she was looking at the works—or maybe the railway line.

'Susan Prosser is like her mother,' Dibs said.

'That's what I reckon,' I said. 'Heck, who wants to study in the holidays?'

Dibs made a disgusted noise. He couldn't be bothered with Susan Prosser.

I went on thinking about her for a few moments, mainly because I was still puzzled at the back of my mind about her and Mr Wiggins driving off in the van the other day, but also because I had not liked the way she snooped this morning, asking questions about our running around in the house, wanting to know why Caroline hadn't helped with the dishes. Susan Prosser had better watch out, I thought.

Caroline stopped when Dibs turned from the road towards the hill track.

'This is the way we go,' I told her. 'It's not very steep.'

'Can't we go on the line?' she asked.

'There's a track to the cave further along,' I said. 'But it's much steeper than this one. You'd get very puffed, Caroline.'

'That settles it then,' she said, smiling. 'I'll follow Dibs.'

'I'll catch you if you slip,' I said.

'Dear Harry,' she said. I was probably close to getting another kiss, but she must have decided to save it for me. She followed Dibs.

Just before we went over the first rise, I looked back at the houses. Susan Prosser was still on her front veranda, she seemed to be looking up at us. I could not see Cal. We went over the rise. Now we couldn't be seen from the houses.

It didn't take us long to reach the cave, even though Caroline made us stop a few times so that she could look across the bay. She seemed to screw up her eyes to look, then she said how blue the bay was, she said what a wonderfully sunny day it was, she said she could not see much of the wharf. I told her we'd take her to where she could get a good view of the wharf—after we had been to the cave.

She liked the cave. She did not hang back and say it was scary, as I was sure a girl like Susan Prosser would have.

'And what do you boys do in here?' asked Caroline. She sat down, not far in from the cave mouth.

'We have a good talk,' I said, sitting opposite Caroline.

'And what else?' she asked. She was partly shadowed, but the light from the cave mouth fell across her legs.

I hesitated, then decided it was safe to tell her about the cigarettes. 'Sometimes we have a smoke,' I said, watching her legs.

She laughed. 'That must be exciting.'

'Don't think we've got any today,' I said. 'How's the fag supply, Dibs?'

'We've run out,' said Dibs.

'Just as well I don't smoke,' said Caroline.

'My mother smokes a lot,' I said. 'But I don't take her cigarettes. I like the ones Dibs makes.'

'Perhaps I could try one next time you have some,' Caroline said. 'Would you let me try one, Dibs?'

'Sure I will,' said Dibs. He had taken the lamp from

the tin, had stood it near the fireplace. 'I should have got some paraffin for this thing. How about we go down and get some?'

'Let's sit here a while,' said Caroline. 'Isn't it lovely and secret in here?'

'It's good,' I said. 'This is where we waited for the *Emma Cranwell*. The day you arrived.'

'What a wonderful idea!' she said. 'And what do you boys discuss when you have a good talk in here?'

'Different things,' I said, noticing Caroline draw up her legs. Her legs were now out of the light. I was used to the darkness, though. I could see that she had her chin on her knees, that she had let her dress fall back from her knees, that she was gazing across the cave at me.

'One time we talked about getting some gun-powder and blowing up the works,' Dibs said. 'We could hide the gun-powder here until it was dark, then go down and blow up the works. That was one thing we talked about, eh, Harry?'

'Yes,' I said, deciding Dibs had not really given away a secret because we weren't sure we should blow up the works, they were so good for playing in.

Caroline straightened one leg. 'Where would you get the gun-powder?'

'My brother Buster could get it for me,' Dibs said. 'He works in a quarry. He uses a lot of gun-powder.'

'Would he mind if you blew up the works?' asked Caroline. 'Think of the explosion!' She straightened the other leg, but did not bother to straighten her dress.

'Buster wouldn't care if there was a big explosion,' Dibs

said. 'Buster likes big explosions and going fast on his Indian and everything like that.'

'He must find Calliope Bay very quiet,' Caroline said.

'That's why he goes away a lot,' Dibs said.

'Do you think it's too quiet?' I asked Caroline. Should I move closer to her? Could she tell I was staring at her knees?

'I like a quiet holiday,' she said. 'I like this holiday, Harry.'

'I can show you a lot of other places,' I said, sliding across the cave. 'You haven't seen the waterfall yet, Caroline.'

'I'm looking forward to the waterfall,' she said.

'Harry, can I tell Caroline about the pistol?' asked Dibs.

'What?' I said. That was the moment when the light in the cave seemed to change and I saw more of Caroline and was certain she wore only the dress, the shoes, the lipstick. I looked into a blacker part of the cave.

'Can I tell her about the pistol?' asked Dibs.

'Tell me about the pistol,' Caroline said.

'No,' I said, realising what Dibs had said. It could be dangerous, I thought. 'No, we haven't got the pistol now,' I told Caroline. 'We found a pistol, but we threw it away. We knew we couldn't keep it. So we threw it away, that's what we did.'

'That's right,' Dibs said. 'I remember now.'

'So you can't show it to me?' said Caroline.

'We threw it away,' I told her.

'What a shame,' she said. 'I'd like to see a pistol.'

'We'll show you the next one we find,' I said. It was too

warm near her now, I must leave the cave. I said: 'Would you like to see the view from the cliff-top, Caroline?'

'Mmm,' she said.

She followed me from the cave, then went ahead, straightening her dress as she went.

Dibs, who was last out, nudged me and nodded towards Caroline, grinning. I took no notice of him. He had better not say anything cheeky about my cousin, I would fix him if he did.

On the cliff-top overlooking the wharf, Caroline got excited because she could see Sam Phelps and Sydney Bridge Upside Down. She seemed to have to stare hard to see such a short distance.

'Would they hear me if I shouted?' she asked, running to the dead tree near the edge.

'Sure,' I said, wishing they wouldn't.

'Yoohoo!' she shouted. But it was not a very loud shout. Even though he was just below us, Sam Phelps did not look up.

I saw that Caroline had one hand on the tree. 'Be careful of that tree,' I said. 'It might fall if you touch it. You could slip over the edge.'

'You know what Harry did to me—' Dibs began.

I turned to him, my fist to my nose. 'We have good fun up here,' I said loudly. 'So far no accidents.' I took my fist from my nose as I turned back to Caroline. 'What say we go home and have lunch? Or do you want to look at the view some more?'

'Oh, I think that will do for the time being, thank you, Harry,' she said.

I led the way along the track. I made sure I led them away from the start of the other track, the one that went down to the clearing beside the railway line; I did not want Caroline to suggest that we visit the wharf. When I got to the last rise and had first look at the houses, though, I saw something that made me change my plans. I saw Mr Wiggins' white van outside our house. I turned before the others could see.

'I remember,' I told Caroline. 'You were asking about the other way. You know, the quick way to the railway line. Yes, we could go down it and maybe visit the wharf.'

'What about your lunch?' she said.

'It's early,' I said. 'We've got time to visit the wharf. Eh, Dibs?'

'I don't care,' Dibs said. 'I got nothing else to do.'

'Come on then,' I said. And I led them to the other track, then down it to the clearing.

Caroline sat on the grass in the shade as soon as we were there. 'It's a lovely spot,' she said.

'We used to have picnics here,' I told her.

'I've never been on a picnic,' she said.

'Never!' I cried. 'Never in your whole life?' I wasn't really amazed, of course; I just wanted to stop her thinking of lunch and heading home, the longer we talked in the clearing the more chance Mr Wiggins would be gone when we got home.

Caroline laughed. 'Never, never, never!'

'What do you know?' I said to Dibs.

'What do you know?' he said back.

We wasted some more time in the clearing, talking of

picnics and what we liked best about them. Because of the way she sat, I had to keep trying not to look at Caroline; she sat with her knees up and the light was much better here than in the cave. It would have been good, I guessed, if I'd been the only one looking; Dibs being there too made it different. I was a bit relieved when Caroline got up and strolled towards the railway line. She must be wondering about Sam Phelps and Sydney Bridge Upside Down. Well, I wouldn't mind her being with them—not as much as I would mind her being with Mr Wiggins. So I decided we could now go to the wharf.

I pointed out that one way to reach the wharf was to go across the rocks and along the timbers under the wharf as far as the funny steps. The other way, I said, was to walk along the track beside the line.

'What say we have a race?' I said to Caroline. 'You go along the railway track, Dibs and I go across the rocks.'

'That sounds like fun,' she said.

Dibs and I did not move very fast because he agreed with me that it would be polite to let Caroline win.

'She's a good sport, eh?' he said as we went across the rocks. 'Likes having fun, eh?'

'I bet Cal will wish he hadn't missed this fun,' I said. 'Wonder where he got to. Hope that kid doesn't fall in the river. I'll get the blame if he does. Dad will chase me with his whip.'

'I wouldn't like to be chased with a whip,' Dibs said.

'It doesn't happen often,' I said, sorry now that I had used Dad to stop Dibs from thinking about Caroline. Dad was all right, he'd understand that it would be Cal's own fault if he was washed out to sea.

By the time we were at the top of the steps, Caroline was chatting to Sam Phelps and stroking the horse's hollow. Sam Phelps looked hard at Dibs and me, but didn't tell us to beat it. We praised Sydney Bridge Upside Down and agreed with Caroline that only a very strong-hearted horse could keep it up the way he did.

In fact, the horse was what Sam Phelps and Caroline chatted about for the next fifteen minutes. I was disappointed, I thought they'd chat about other things.

Maybe they saved the other things for when we were heading back along the line, Caroline up front beside Sam Phelps, Dibs and me inside the wagon.

All the way along, I kept hoping Mr Wiggins had gone.

Sure enough, when we reached the road I saw that his van was no longer outside our house. I was so pleased I began to whistle.

I stopped whistling when I reached our front gate. Because I saw Susan Prosser staring at me from her veranda. It was the meanest stare I'd ever seen.

5

THERE WERE several reasons why the picnic Mrs Kelly held in Caroline's honour was different from the picnics my mother used to hold. One reason was that my mother was not at Mrs Kelly's picnic. Another reason was that Caroline was not at my mother's picnics. I thought of more reasons while Sam Phelps was drinking Mrs Kelly's lime juice in the clearing, but those two were enough to be getting on with. What started me thinking of differences was the memory of something that happened at one of my mother's picnics. I remembered we were sitting in the clearing, the Kelly family and us, when Sam Phelps and Sydney Bridge Upside Down appeared, and Mrs Kelly called to Sam Phelps that he was welcome to a drink, and Sam Phelps came across from the line and had the drink, and he drank from a cup that had been lying on the picnic rug, and it turned out this was one of my mother's cups because as soon as Sam Phelps went on down the line my mother threw the cup into the bushes and blackberry and said, 'We can't let anybody else use it now. Not after that dirty old man's been drinking from it.' This had surprised me. Mrs Kelly had seemed surprised too; she had looked towards the spot where the cup had landed, then at my mother, but she had not spoken. Now, at this picnic years later, she did nothing special with the cup Sam Phelps had drunk from; she put it in the basket with the other cups. Mrs Kelly, of course, was different from my mother. I did not think, for instance, that my mother would have held a picnic in Caroline's honour. And I bet Caroline wouldn't have much fun at all on her holiday if my mother was around, my mother had a way of frowning that could spoil everything. It's a good job she's missing this picnic, I thought.

We had been at the clearing since mid-morning, Mrs Kelly saying a picnic was best if you made a proper day of it. Since it was a Saturday, Mr Kelly was home with his Reo, and he drove us all down as far as the beach just across the line from the clearing. He and Dad stayed with us for an hour, then they discovered they were short of beer; they drove off in the Reo and said they would be back later. I didn't mind how long they took, they had spent most of the time talking about ancient visits to the city, glancing at Caroline to make sure she was listening. It was odd how even Mr Kelly tried to impress Caroline; you'd think he would realise she was too young to care what happened when he was last in the city. He was probably fooled by her smile; she should frown, I thought, when old fellows like Dad and Mr Kelly tried to impress her.

I had been afraid the small Kelly kids would spoil the

picnic with their shouting and fighting. But they were all right. Mostly they played in the bush, or over on the rocks and the beach. I did not have to take any more notice of them than I usually did.

'Why don't you boys run off and play?' Mrs Kelly asked after we had finished the meat pies, sandwiches and fruitcake. She was looking at me as if she thought I was stopping Dibs and Cal from playing.

'I'm having a swim as soon as my food goes down,' I told her. 'It's dangerous to swim after a big meal.'

'You'll come to no harm after a meal that size,' Mrs Kelly said. She was trying to get rid of me, sure enough.

'Best not to take risks,' I said. I knew that sooner or later Caroline would be going for a swim. She had her swimming costume on under her dress; I knew this because I had seen her putting it on.

'Off you go, Dibs,' said Mrs Kelly, probably thinking I would follow Dibs. 'It's not like you to linger after a meal.'

'What an old bitch!' Dibs whispered to me.

'Dibs!' shouted Mrs Kelly, very purple.

'Come on, boy,' I said to Dibs. 'We don't want to spoil the picnic.' I looked at Caroline. 'Coming with us?'

'Never mind her,' said Mrs Kelly. 'Caroline and I are going to have a chat. You boys run off and play.'

I couldn't be sure if Caroline's smile was for Mrs Kelly or for me. Anyway, I thought, she'll soon get sick of Mrs Kelly, she'll soon want to swim.

'I'll come back for my togs,' I told Mrs Kelly.

She shook her head at me. I guessed she was rather

crabby with all the work she had done for the picnic; my mother, at any rate, got crabby if she had been doing much work, like making a big supply of ginger beer, not that her last lot had been big enough to keep us going all through the holidays, we were now down to five bottles.

'Let's look for crayfish,' said Cal, who seemed glad to be away from the clearing. 'The kids said they saw some out on the rocks.'

'I bet they didn't,' I said, not wanting to get too far from the clearing.

'No harm in looking,' Cal said. 'Come on, Dibs.'

They ran off across the rocks, so I followed them. But I was not thinking of crayfish; I was thinking of Caroline.

I was thinking of our time at the beach the day before. It had been exciting, but also strange. I mean, when I looked back I knew which moment I would always remember, but there were other moments that were important for me nowadays, right now in Calliope Bay, even if they did not move into the for ever part of my memory like the main moment. One of these other moments was when Dibs told Caroline and me (Cal was over on the dunes) about his discovery that Susan Prosser was in the habit of going for night walks. He knew it was a habit, he said, because he had checked for three nights, and every night she had walked along the road towards the beach soon after eight o'clock. She stayed away about half an hour, he said. What did we think of this for a habit? I was late in telling him what I thought because I had only just noticed a curly hair sticking out from beneath Caroline's white swimming costume. Of course, I should not have been surprised to see it, since I knew she had a lot of curly black hair on that part of her body, but it seemed different seeing the one hair and I would have gone on staring at it if I hadn't heard Dibs telling, somewhere in the distance, about Susan Prosser's new habit. Caroline, anyway, was first to answer him. 'That's the girl who studies so much, isn't it?' she said. 'So she says,' Dibs said. 'Well, I imagine she goes for walks to clear her head,' Caroline said. She looked at me, asked: 'Do you think that's the reason, Harry?' I said it might be, though it was pretty strange for Susan to go out alone at night, seeing how she usually hurried along in daytime, as if scared of being spoken to. You would think a person who was scared in daytime, I said, would be even more scared in the dark. 'She's not scared, she thinks she's clever,' Dibs said. Clever people, I said, could be scared as easily as those who weren't clever. Caroline agreed with me. 'Perhaps,' she said, 'the reason is that Susan is shy. After all, she hasn't talked to me yet. I saw her looking over the fence one day and she turned her head when I smiled at her. She must be lonely.' 'That's what my mother says about Mrs Prosser,' Dibs said. 'We never see Mrs Prosser,' I said. I reflected. 'Well,' I said, 'only when we catch her looking from her bathroom window.' We all reflected then; nobody spoke for some minutes. During the silence I looked out to sea; I forced myself not to look at Caroline or at any part of her. Susan Prosser worried me, I reflected. I could not be sure, for instance, how much she knew about our running game. I didn't think she would be cheeky enough to sneak into our yard and maybe peep through a window while I was chasing Caroline, or Caroline was chasing me, but I took no chances, I pulled down all the blinds and made sure the back door was shut before we began running. Would the lowered blinds make Susan Prosser even more suspicious? You could not be sure with a girl like that. I had found her looking over the fence several times, and we had talked for a while, both pretending to be friendly, and I had not liked the way she looked at me, there was nothing more scary than a person who pretended to be friendly but could not keep the meanness out of her eyes. I knew she guessed we were having fun in our place, and I could imagine what she would be like if she knew Caroline and I ran around with nothing on (Cal had a way now of keeping on his pyjamas and watching); if Susan knew what our fun was really like, she would be so angry she would be bound to tell Dad. I could scare Cal into not telling Dad, but it would be harder to get Susan to stay quiet. I shouldn't worry; Susan would never find out. To keep things easier for her, I made sure I ran quietly, and I told Caroline to go on tip-toes too. I noticed that Caroline did not get so tired now, the last couple of mornings she had not gone back to bed after the run, she had a shower while I did the dishes, Cal wiping for me. Caroline had swept the house two or three times, but she was not very good at sweeping; she had cooked the dinner two or three times, but the stove had given her trouble and Dad had told her not to bother, he said he did not want her to be a housekeeper, he said he was used to getting the evening meal and would continue getting it, he said he didn't mind at all. Anyway, lying there on the beach yesterday, I had reflected so much about Susan Prosser that I hadn't noticed Dibs running across to Cal on the dunes.

79

He'd probably said he was going, but I hadn't heard. The first I realised that Caroline and I were on our own was when she kissed me, one of her small kisses but pretty good even so. I fell back on the hot sand, and this was when the for ever moment arrived. Before I could sit up or twist away, Caroline laughed, pointed to my swimming shorts and said, 'Harry's naughty dingdong,' and I certainly knew what she meant because on her first morning of playing the running game she had said Cal and I had 'sweet little dingdongs', and what had happened to mine then was what had happened to it there on the beach. Well, I did what I usually did when this happened—I thought of the river on a cold day. It worked again, though I had noticed that my cock, which was what I called it, had been harder to fool lately. I told Caroline I would see what Dibs and Cal were doing over there on the dunes, and I heard her laughing as I shot off across the sand. I hadn't minded her talking like that, it was only that I got embarrassed and was shooting off across the sand without thinking. If I had given myself time to think I'd probably have stayed there near her and chatted to her about it, I might even have told her about the escaping curly hair. Still, it was better for me to go to the dunes, I guessed; much as I liked what Caroline said, it did make me feel trembly, as if I was doing wrong.

So that was what I was thinking while I followed Dibs and Cal across the rocks. I was thinking Caroline was the most beautiful girl in the world and I didn't care how often she pointed to my dingdong—and there was nothing wrong with this.

'It's funny on Saturdays,' I said, not realising Dibs was so near.

'Eh?' he said. 'What's funny?'

'Nothing,' I said, thinking how close I had been to saying that Saturdays were funny because Dad was home and we couldn't run around after breakfast. Then I said: 'It's funny you kids thinking you'll find crayfish. You won't find any here.'

'I know,' Dibs said. 'I'm only filling in time. Then I'm going for a swim with Caroline.'

'How do you know she wants to go for a swim?' I said. 'She didn't say she was going for a swim.'

'She's wearing her togs, isn't she?' he said.

'How do you know?' I said, grabbing his arm.

'I saw them,' he said. 'It's the way she sits, boy.'

I held his arm, wondering if I should tip him off the rock, if I should give him his swim a bit sooner than he expected. Then I decided he hadn't said anything cheeky, and I let him go.

'You shouldn't be looking,' I told him.

He laughed. 'Who's talking!'

'What do you mean?' I made my voice fierce.

'I've seen you looking,' he said. 'I bet she has too.'

'I bet I haven't looked any more than you,' I said.

'You get more chances than me,' he said. 'Anyhow, she'll be changing her way of sitting after this. You see.'

'Why?' I said. I reached for him, but he dodged me and jumped to the next rock.

'Because Mum's noticed, and I bet that's what she's telling her about now,' Dibs said. 'Mum notices that kind

81

of thing, she's always telling my sisters not to show their bloomers. And another thing—she reckons Caroline wears too much lipstick. I heard her saying that the other day.'

'Your mother better watch out,' I said, jumping to his rock. 'My father won't like it if she's a stickybeak.'

He was on the next rock before I could grab him. 'She only gives friendly advice,' he said. 'That's the way women talk. They're allowed to.'

Well, he had sisters and I hadn't, and I guessed he knew what he was talking about, he had seen more naked girls than I ever had, he knew more about them than I did, though I was catching up. It might be best if I made no fuss; I had enough to take care of, what with the danger of Cal or Susan Prosser saying something to cause trouble.

I looked towards the clearing and saw that Mrs Kelly had moved close to Caroline. Yes, she was very likely talking to her. I hoped she didn't make Caroline unhappy.

Dibs was moving on across the rocks. He glanced back at me several times.

I wouldn't chase him. I wouldn't stay on the rocks, either. Cal had gone nearer the shore and would not be in trouble even if he did fall into the sea, so I could move to the beach. I would keep an eye on the clearing, and if I saw Caroline waving or jumping I would know she wanted help. She might even yell out to me. I would race to the clearing if she did.

'Harry!' shouted Cal.

I looked back from the beach. He was waving with one hand and pointing to a rock with the other.

He had evidently found something, maybe a sea-chest full of silver coins.

He was too far away. I waved to him, pointed to the dunes and walked towards them. I would sit up there and look at the clearing, and blow Cal and his treasure.

I heard him calling some more, to Dibs now. I knew Dibs would go to him.

I paused half-way up a dune. Everything looked peaceful in the clearing.

It was the same when I looked from the top of the dune. Mrs Kelly and Caroline seemed calm.

I sat in the sand, glanced towards the works, then downward. And there was Susan Prosser. She was in the hollow on the other side of the dune, only about ten yards away, and she was looking up at me. She was wearing a pink frock; on the sand beside her were three books.

Seeing her there gave me a fright. I wanted, the moment after I saw her, to dive back to the beach. I might have done so if she had not been looking at me.

I grinned as I walked towards her. 'Doing some studying?' I asked. 'You must be keen—studying on Saturday.'

'I'm not really studying,' she said, looking at me suspiciously. 'I'm really sunbathing.'

I squatted on the sand, decided against saying it was a good idea to wear togs for sunbathing. Better to be friendly. I said: 'You could have come to our picnic. We've been here for hours.'

'I knew about the picnic,' she said. 'Mrs Kelly invited me.'

'You should have come,' I said. 'We've been having fun.'

'Naturally,' she said. That had a nasty sound.

'Naturally what?' I said.

'You're always having fun,' she said.

'It's the holidays, isn't it?' I said.

'You don't save your fun for the holidays,' she said.

'Better than studying and being gloomy all the time,' I said, knowing I would soon be very angry if I didn't hold myself back. '*Why* didn't you come to the picnic?'

'Because I had other things to do,' she said. Now she did not seem suspicious, she sounded sort of superior, as if she believed she was better than a kid who always wanted fun.

'What's clever about going for walks at night?' I asked. The question popped out, I hadn't realised I was going to ask it.

She gave me her famous mean look. Then she said very quietly: 'Have you been spying on me, Harry Baird?'

I was shocked. '*Me* spying! Gosh, *I'm* not the one who—' I stopped just in time. I was nearly going to say she was the one who did the spying. That would certainly have made her think there was something worth spying on. In fact, I might have said too much already. She seemed to be waiting for me to go on, to give myself away.

'What did you say?' she asked presently.

'Actually, *I* haven't seen you going for walks at night,' I said, feeling all right again. 'I only heard about it from another kid. Doesn't worry me if you go for night walks.'

'I can guess who told you,' she said. 'If he didn't have such nasty habits, he wouldn't notice when somebody goes for a private stroll in the evening.'

I didn't know what she meant by that, but I certainly would not ask her to explain, it was bound to make either her or me angry. 'Suppose these walks help to clear your head,' I said. 'After you've been studying so hard.' I said this very pleasantly, I made it seem that I envied her for being clever enough to study until her head got cloudy.

She looked rather surprised. 'Yes, it helps,' she said slowly.

'By the way,' I said, 'have you heard any more about Mr Dalloway?'

'I have no idea what his plans are,' she said.

'You still reckon he's not coming back?' I asked.

'It's not what I *reckon*,' she said. 'It's what I understand to be true.'

'And he won't be here next term?'

'So I understand.'

'Why won't he?'

'I haven't the faintest idea,' she said. 'I imagine it's because he prefers the city.'

'I wonder why?' I said, acting stupid so that she could go on thinking she was clever.

'Why what?'

'Why he would prefer the city.'

'You know who to ask about that,' she said. '*I* don't know the city.'

I guessed she meant Caroline. I said: 'I'll ask her.'

'How often do you write to her?' she asked. When I stared, she added: 'Your mother. Do you *ever* write to her?'

'Oh, her!' I said. 'She doesn't expect me to write. Dad tells her the news.'

'All of it?' Though she spoke nicely, I knew she wanted to worry me. 'I'd be surprised if your father told her all the news.' She paused, but I thought it best to say nothing. 'I used to talk to your mother a good deal,' she said. 'I think she might like to hear from me. If she's staying long in the city. Do you know how much longer she'll be there?'

'No,' I said. Then I thought how terrible it would be if Susan Prosser wrote tell-tale letters to my mother. 'Dad says she'll be back any day,' I said. 'He says she might be back by—oh, by the end of the week maybe.'

'You don't sound very positive,' she said. 'I think I'll write her a letter.'

'Don't do that,' I said.

'Harry, you look frightened,' she said. She laughed.

I was annoyed at myself for letting her see. 'Heck, I don't care if you write to her,' I said. 'I don't care if you tell her about Cal and me playing at the works when she told us not to. I don't care if you tell her we're not weeding the garden like we should. I don't care.'

'I hadn't intended mentioning those things,' she said. 'I did think of mentioning your cousin. Would that be all right, Harry?' Now she was pretending to be sweet, or half-pretending, wanting me to understand that she could make trouble for me.

'You haven't even met Caroline,' I said. 'What can you tell my mother about her?'

'I can put two and two together,' she said.

'Why don't you like Caroline?' I asked. 'How can you be jealous of somebody you haven't even met?'

'I'm not jealous,' Susan Prosser said, reaching for her books, standing.

'You are,' I said, putting out my hand. I thought I should pull her back, make her tell me why she was jealous of Caroline. But she dodged my hand.

'I can see her, I can hear her,' she said. 'I know what she's like. She's insincere. She's the insincerest person I've ever seen or heard.'

This amazed me so much that I shoved my hands over my ears and fell back on the sand. I closed my eyes and kicked my legs in the air. 'Yee-ow!' I shouted.

When I looked up, Susan Prosser was off the beach and going through a fence gap. She turned towards the track across the paddocks beside the works. She was walking very quickly.

I ran after her. Near the fence I jumped because of a sudden terrible pain in the heel of my right foot. Watching Susan Prosser, I had not noticed the piece of barbed wire in the grass, I had stood on one of the barbs. I flopped on the grass and looked at the puncture. There was a blob of blood on it, my foot was throbbing. The barb had been rusty, I might be poisoned.

I hobbled back to the dune, and I said angry things about Susan Prosser to myself on the way. Going up the dune, I tried to keep the heel out of the sand; every time I did lower it, I left blood spots in the sand. As the poison spread, I thought, the foot would get stiffer and stiffer. Already it seemed stiff.

I hobbled along the beach and across the railway line towards the clearing. Back on the dune, I had thought how I would ask Caroline to bandage my foot. Then, on the beach, I saw that the Reo had returned and that Dad and Mr Kelly were in the clearing, and I guessed it didn't matter whether it was Caroline or Mrs Kelly who did the bandaging, Mrs Kelly would probably do it better anyway, it was not something you could expect Caroline to do well. I could not see Caroline from the beach, but supposed she was hidden behind Dad and Mr Kelly. I could not see Cal or Dibs or any of the other kids.

Although I said 'Ouch ouch' several times when I was near enough to the clearing to be heard, Caroline did not run to see what was wrong, as I had hoped she might. In fact, Caroline was not there. The only ones there were Dad and Mr and Mrs Kelly. This was a shock. I forgot my foot and looked in every direction. Caroline was nowhere in sight.

'What's the fuss?' Dad asked.

So I had to show my heel, and Mrs Kelly agreed that such an injury might cause complications if it wasn't attended to; she bandaged it.

I felt dizzy about then, maybe because of the sun. Mrs Kelly, who said I had gone so pale my freckles were sticking out like currants, made me lie in the shade. And I still did not know where Caroline and the others had gone.

I felt gloomy, mad at myself, sick of everything. Everything was in a mess.

What might happen now was that everything would turn black for me. Off and on, maybe twice a year, I had black times; these had gone on for as long as I could remember. Things would go wrong, I could do nothing or think nothing that seemed right. Nothing seemed fun. At these times I would want to bop everybody I saw, and I wouldn't care if they bopped me back and went on bopping me until I couldn't feel a thing or see a thing or think a thing. I would say dirty words over and over to myself, and sometimes I would shout them out loud, provided Dad was not around, it didn't matter so much if Cal or Dibs heard. At these times, too, nobody believed anything I said, my parents picked on me, my father kept threatening to use the whip if I didn't stop telling lies, I hated them all, I hated myself, I even thought of jumping off the wharf or from the top of the works. Every black time lasted two or three days, and I reckoned I was lucky to get through it; when everybody else in the world was satisfied with everything it was terrible to be lonely (what did Susan Prosser know!) and furious and guilty and shitshitshitshit. Lying there in the shade on this sunny day, I certainly hoped I was not in for another of the black times.

Dad and Mr Kelly were drinking beer and listening to Mrs Kelly.

I had not been listening to Mrs Kelly. Then I heard her say, 'a terrifying situation for any poor girl to find herself in' and I began to listen. She was saying: '—brought up sensibly, but not of course to know what dangers to expect or how to protect herself. I believe she shared a flat with another girl, but this young lady proved to be not as respectable as she originally seemed, being addicted to wanton pleasures. Indeed, promiscuous. It seems Tilly returned one evening from a Tabernacle social to discover her flat-mate joined to a young man on the lounge rug and was thereupon invited by the young man to await her turn. She locked herself in the bedroom, but was presently tormented by heavy blows upon the door, the visitor threatening loudly, the flat-mate cajoling between-times. Fortunately for Tilly, there was a fire-escape outside the window. But what an ordeal for a girl as strange as she was to city ways! She could have been forgiven if, there and then, she had left the city. No, Tilly had spunk, she didn't give up easily. She found another place to live—a boarding-house where the landlady was unusually considerate and, indeed, motherly. Or so it at first appeared—'

'Don't tell me the landlady turned out to be a hard nut too,' said Mr Kelly, rolling a cigarette.

'I see they've talked Sam into it,' said Dad, who was nearest the edge of the clearing and had a better view along the line than the rest of us.

'Young people often make the mistake of expecting their elders to behave consistently,' said Mrs Kelly. 'I don't suppose the landlady was *un*motherly, more that her depravity did not show—extraordinary visitors— drawn curtains—furtive footsteps and creaking doors at all hours—terrifying for poor Tilly—nobody to turn to—'

'Talked Sam into what?' I asked, hobbling to Dad.

'See?' Dad whispered, raising his glass.

I could not see.

Mr Kelly laughed. 'It's a wonder she ever left home. Or was there nobody to warn her?'

'Has there ever been a time when girls on their own have *not* been in that kind of danger?' asked Mrs Kelly. 'Would they ever go to such places if they knew what dangers awaited them? Of course, there is a decadence about city life—like walking from sunshine into a dark cobwebby room—brush them off but they keep clinging—'

Now I could see the group along at the end of the beach, in from where the railway line finished near the works. I could see Caroline and the kids. I could see Sam Phelps. And, surprisingly, I could see Sydney Bridge Upside Down. He was unhitched from the wagon, and I could not remember when I had last seen him like that.

'What do you know!' I said.

'I'd treat that foot gently,' Mrs Kelly told me. 'Stamping with it won't help.'

'Anyway, Sandy,' said Dad, holding out his glass to Mr Kelly, 'I reckon I'll start on the house next week-end. Get it painted before the wife turns up. The boys can help. I'll do the climbing, they can do the low bits.'

'I'll give you a hand with the roof, Frank,' said Mr Kelly. 'Don't like to think of a fellow with one leg scampering about on the roof.'

'Never notice it,' said Dad. 'Never notice it.'

The kids were moving back from Sydney Bridge Upside Down, as if to give him room. Caroline was talking to Sam Phelps. Dibs left the other kids and went across to Caroline and Sam Phelps. Caroline stood beside the horse, put her arms into the hollow. Dibs bent down, grabbed Caroline's leg and lifted her. He helped her to sit in the hollow.

'Hey!' I told the others in the clearing. 'Caroline's riding Sydney Bridge Upside Down.'

Mr Kelly laughed. 'Thought they'd talk Sam into it.

He's got a lot of time for those kids.'

I moved towards the line.

'Hold on!' Dad told me. 'Want you to help us pack up the picnic things soon.'

I waited by the line. 'Can't I see what they're doing?'

'You heard what Mrs Kelly said about your foot,' Dad said. 'Do you want to lose it? Do you want to be like your old man?' He laughed after he said it, but I knew he was serious, his voice had a threat in it.

Heck, it was no use Mr Kelly saying Sam Phelps had a lot of time for kids. Sam Phelps had never let any kid ride Sydney Bridge Upside Down.

'When I remember Tilly,' said Mrs Kelly, 'I'm reminded of old tales about pure maidens pursued by black-hearted rascals. Usually a castle, bats flapping in corridors, weird happenings at midnight. No telling if anybody will arrive to help the heroine escape. Indeed, I believe Tilly did have an employer who pursued her one day in and out of offices, around desks and filing-cabinets, very much in the old manner. Of course, we have no castles, and such things as black magic and mad monks are scarcely commonplace nowadays—our terrors are different—another fire another abyss, as they say—'

Now Sydney Bridge Upside Down was cantering along the beach. I saw Caroline's yellow hair. I saw her white bathing-costume. She was bouncing in the hollow.

The kids were several yards behind the horse. Sam Phelps had not moved.

'I've been watching that cloud,' Dad said. 'We could be in for some rain, Sandy. Another summer storm, eh?'

'Could be, Frank,' said Mr Kelly. 'Could be.'

I saw Caroline and Sydney Bridge Upside Down turn towards a dune. I saw them go a little way up it.

Then I saw Mr Wiggins' van move past Sam Phelps and move on till it was near the dune where Caroline and Sydney Bridge Upside Down were. I saw Mr Wiggins leave the van and cross to the bottom of the dune. I saw him looking up at Caroline.

'Time to load the Reo,' said Mr Kelly.

I hobbled to the beach with him and Dad. I was damned angry.

6

THE NOISE of the hooves is so loud that I am running frightened even before I see Sydney Bridge Upside Down galloping through the dusk towards me. The noise gets louder as I run it is as if there are many horses stampeding towards the works trying to get there before I do and the faster I run the further away seem the works and all the time the hooves get closer and I keep taking frightened looks over my shoulder to try to see if it really is only Sydney Bridge Upside Down making all that noise. Until suddenly I am in the works and going up the stairs still running still hearing the hooves (We begin on the ground floor, dear Caroline, because this is where the animals were delivered. Most came in lorries, some came by rail from the wharf, picked up by ships at Port Crummer down the coast. Dad said there was seldom much noise on the ground floor because the animals didn't know what they were in for when they arrived, and by the time they were downstairs again they were carcasses, ready for the cold chambers that are now like spooky dungeons. Up on the other floors, the killing-floors, was where you heard the squealing and groaning, where you saw the pools of blood. Even now, when you walk across those concrete floors, you can imagine stains, and some days on the top floor I've heard squeals and groans below me and I've thought it is not the wind I can hear. Now the wind blows through broken walls, cement chips fall, the stains are sprinkled with cement dust. I stayed up here in the rain one day because I was annoyed at Dad. He had chased me with the whip, and although I knew he soon stopped being angry after these chases I guessed I had better keep out of his way a while longer and too bad for him if I got pneumonia through not being able to shelter. Actually, I could have sheltered in the dungeons, or in the lower-floor killing-rooms, or even down in the yard where there is the furnace they used for burning leftovers, like eyes and ears and hairy bits. The furnace-house is not so easy to hide in because there is only one way of getting in now that the doors are rusted shut; you drop through a hole in the top, down to the black bricks on the floor, and unless you have dangled a rope there is no way of getting out. If you forget the rope and nobody comes along to lower one you could stay in there for ever, and it wouldn't be much use shouting for help because the brick walls are so thick and the hole at the top is so small. You could die in there. I kidded Dibs into dropping in there once, I said it would be easy for me to reach down and grab his hand if he jumped, but I knew it would not be easy, I knew it would be impossible. So he had to stay in there until I got a rope and it took me an hour to do that. Dibs said later it was awful waiting for me to get back, he said it seemed much longer than an hour, and even though it was a fine day and he could see the piece of blue sky through the hole he said it was chilly and quiet and creepy in there and he had the feeling he was buried, he said he had felt like shouting but when he tried to shout nothing happened because his voice seemed to have dried up, he said he would never go in there again no matter how often I promised to save him, he said he did not trust me. I told him he should think himself lucky the furnace hadn't been lit, what say barrows of leftovers had been tipped on him and set alight? Don't blame me for the bad time you had, I said. Nobody forced you to go in there, I said. Remind me not to drag you out next time, I said. And all he said was there would be no next time, not for him. He said I could get Cal to jump in, see how he liked it. But I wouldn't frighten Cal like that. I know he's a pest of a kid sometimes and I shout at him and throw things at him, but I wouldn't want to scare him to death, it's better to have a brother than not to have one. I can tell him things even when I don't care if he hears me or understands what I'm saying. What matters is that I am not on my own and I don't have to go on thinking and wondering and worrying, I can talk. So I don't care when he climbs the chute, doing what Dad warns him not to do, he's a good climber and he won't fall, he moves like a squirrel. When we get to the top floor I'll show you where he pops up out of the chute. That's how he always goes to the top floor, not like me, I always go up the stairs, I reckon the chute would collapse if I went up it too often, though it's not so bad going down because you go so fast the chute doesn't have time to collapse. But don't you try it, dear Caroline. It's best to wear pants when you're whizzing down that. Thick pants. And sandshoes for the braking. I don't think any girl would want to try it, I can't imagine Susan Prosser for instance being brave enough to even look down the chute, supposing she was ever brave enough to go to the top floor. One of these days I might ask her to go up there, to test her, to see if she's brave as well as clever, not that she doesn't know the works, she knows this place sure enough, I mean in the secret way of people who do more than notice that a place is where it is, they go to it as well, they visit it when they want to be on their own, when they have something special to think about. I followed her in the moonlight the other night. I waited by the side of Dibs' house for her to leave, I waited there because I still wasn't sure what she meant about Dibs' nasty habits and I thought I might clear that up while I was waiting, and when I saw what he did from the veranda in the moonlight I knew what Susan Prosser meant, and it was not long after the dirty dog had done it that I saw Susan going along her side-path and out into the road, and I waited till she was a good way along the road, before I followed her, and this is where she came, she came to the works. But she did not come to this floor or to the ones above or even to the stairs. She sat in the moonlight on the concrete steps at the front, and that was all she did. I watched her from behind the furnace-house. I heard the swamp frogs and, a long way away, the waves that reached the rocks and the funny steps. I didn't know what Susan Prosser was thinking, she was just sitting there in the moonlight, staring. I could have called to her. I could have watched her jump and run. I could have chased her. I could have made her so frightened she wouldn't dare write to my mother. But I didn't. I just waited in the moonlight and watched her. I hoped she wouldn't learn from Mrs Kelly, who knows everything, that my mother still isn't saying how long she reckons on being away. You know, my mother surprised Dad in her latest letter by not even mentioning how much she misses us or how she's looking forward to seeing us all again soon, not even asking how we're off for ginger beer, so it seems she is enjoying the city and is in no hurry to end her holiday, though we know she'll be back for the start of school, mothers are always home then. Of course, Dad doesn't mind if she stays away another week or two, because he hasn't started painting the house and I know he wants to have this under way before she gets back. Anyhow, dear Caroline, that was what I was thinking while I watched Susan Prosser sitting in the moonlight on the works steps. Don't you dare write to my mother, I kept thinking. Then I thought: Please please don't write to her, Susan, I'll be your friend if you don't write, I'll stick up for you whenever other kids pick on you, I'll say you are pretty and not skinny and snoopy, I'll bop anybody who says you're dippy. And I kept behind her when she went home in the moonlight. I don't know if following her did me any good. I don't suppose it did. Because she still worries me) still hearing the hooves still running still going up the stairs and now I know I will never get to the top before Sydney Bridge Upside Down reaches the works. I haven't been able to go fast enough

Sydney Bridge Upside Down will be right behind me right on top of me at any second now. Now the noise of the hooves stops and there is another noise and the blind is rattling and I think the other noise must be little spurts of thunder another summer storm has come but the other noise can't be thunder the sounds are sharp and there are too many of them to be thunderclaps I must be awake because I know I am sitting up and I know Cal is lying beside me and I can hear him breathing and I can hear the blind rattling and I am trying to decide what the other noise can be other noises I realise the noise of running feet the noise of a crutch stomping along the passage the noise of a cracking whip, all those noises and the wind rattling the blind now moans round the corner of the house then whines then suddenly screams and I am awake aren't I because I can hear Cal breathing still hear the blind rattling now the blind stops rattling Cal stops breathing our house is quiet not a sound I can't be awake I am asleep or dead. Then far away a small sound then I hear the hooves and I am running again and the noise of the hooves is louder Sydney Bridge Upside Down must be near the furnace-house now galloping closer while I try to reach the next floor if I turn I'll see him but I can't turn I have to get to the next floor and suddenly I am there I am lying on the floor face in a stain fingers scratching the cement dust choking still hearing the hooves (And this, dear Caroline, is the killing-floor with the interesting room. It must have been the room where they did special things, because it has an iron door with large bolts, strong enough to keep out anybody while they did the cutting-up. It also has a

99

peep-hole. I found it one day. Well, why make a peep-hole unless what went on in the room was something special? You can imagine all the big killers busy with their knives and sledgehammers, then one of them looks at the others and says he wonders what is happening in the special room today, and how about he takes a peep, and the others tell him to go ahead but to be careful because it's against the rules to peep, so he strolls over very carefully, makes sure nobody in charge is looking, then he reaches up like this and takes out this brick, then he reaches in like this and takes out another brick—and there! He can look into the room. What does he see? Say he sees a body stretched on a table and a man with a knife bending over it, making fancy twirls with the knife before he sticks it into the body, you can hear him humming as he twirls the knife, chuckling as he sticks it in. Or say he sees something funny, like three killers playing cards with chops and kidneys, having bets and pretending to hide their cards when the others in the game are staring at them, giving nothing away, bluffing like Dad says he used to bluff when he played poker, like the time he won his whip off a stockman who thought Dad must have a great hand, he was sitting so calm and sure, the stockman too scared to have a go at keeping the whip he'd thrown on the table, then losing it because he hadn't guessed Dad was bluffing. Or say he sees a battle between an angry animal and some killers armed with all sorts of weapons, because this is the room they keep for the animals that won't give in even after they have been bashed with sledgehammers and stabbed with knives, where any animal that won't give in is taught a real lesson, by the time it has been shot at and slashed and whacked in here it wishes it had given in quickly like the other animals, no animal has a chance in here, this is where it must end. Or say he sees something sweet, like the men who are not strong enough to be killers making sausages, long strings of them, hanging them round their necks, making skirts of them, turning them into fancy costumes, dancing and singing in this special part of the killing-floor, maybe the only happy ones in the place. Or say he sees say he sees say he sees) still hearing the hooves scratching in the dust and trying to get up and make for the next lot of stairs because I am sure this is not a safe place I must go higher in the works I must get to the top nobody can get me up there I can hit back from up there I can throw bricks at Sydney Bridge Upside Down from up there teach that mad horse a lesson. Now the noise of the hooves is so loud I tell myself I might as well give in I will never make it to the next lot of stairs. Then I do move an inch or so and I try harder and at last I am moving inch by inch towards the stairs clawing my way through the stains and the dust expecting at any moment to hear the hooves thunder into the works knowing the noise will be much greater then because of the echoes like when I called to Cal through the chute and the Cal-Cal-Cal echoed on the great echo of the hooves might even bring down the walls but I can't go back now I must get to the top I must get to the next lot of stairs (I fooled the other kids one day last summer, dear Caroline. I came up here and I was puffed that day, like you now. I was tired from running up and down hills. I was the hare in the annual paper chase. Mr Dalloway picked me for hare because he said he'd noticed

I was a good runner, but I think it was because he'd noticed in earlier years that I took my time as a hound and left it to the other hounds to pick up the trail, this year he wanted to be sure I was kept busy. Anyhow, I gave them a good run. I shot up the hill behind the school, ducked through the trees and along the valley to the line of hills up from the houses, and I went along the top for a while, then down again through the trees and along to the high parts up from the wharf, where our caves are, then down the track to the picnic clearing and over the rocks to the beach, along the beach to where the river crosses to the sea, and that was when I reckoned I was due for a rest. I stopped scattering paper and came across here and sat on the top floor and waited. My first idea had been to go along the river-bank as far as the crossing, then head for the school. What I had done instead was to make the trail end at the river. This would puzzle the hounds. They might reckon I had swum across the river to be awkward, and if they tried to pick up the trail on the other side they would be all the more puzzled, they might even begin to wonder if I had been swept out to sea. This would worry Mr Dalloway, sure enough. Anyway, they had given me ten minutes' head-start and I had wasted no time on the run, so I could have a good rest and check on how they did. I saw three hounds on a hill above the houses, but they were going so slowly I knew they must be stragglers. I didn't see the leaders until two of them shot out from the clearing and began sniffing along the beach. There was no wind that day, the paper hadn't shifted from where I'd dropped it. The two leaders were going pretty fast and there were other hounds not far behind. I couldn't see Mr Dalloway, he must be rounding up stragglers. What I must decide soon, I thought as I watched the leaders moving along the beach, was when to sneak away from the works and drop more paper. I could keep out of sight of anybody on the dunes by cutting across the paddocks behind the works and then through the trees beside the swamp to the river-bank. I would do this, I thought, when I had seen what happened at the end of the trail. What happened was that the leaders sniffed around so long, trying to pick up the trail, that all the other hounds arrived, even the slowest stragglers. Mr Dalloway arrived too. I saw some of the kids pointing across the river, but it seemed none of them wanted to take the risk of going over, or maybe Mr Dalloway warned them not to try. I waited no longer. I sneaked across the paddocks and through the trees beside the swamp, and when I got to the river-bank I began dropping paper again, and I dropped it all the way back to school. I was at the school maybe twenty minutes before Mr Dalloway and the other kids arrived. Apparently one kid had finally gone far enough along the bank, he had picked up the trail and called to the others. Mr Dalloway was annoyed. How come there was a break in the trail, he wanted to know. I said a sudden breeze must have swept the paper into the river. He said there had been no breeze. I said it might have been a river breeze that had not reached anywhere else. He didn't believe me. I didn't care, I'd only done what I had to do. I thought when he called at my home after school next afternoon that he would tell my mother about the paper chase mystery, but she said nothing to me about it later, so I guessed he had called about something else, probably about Cal being such a dud at sums. Anyway, dear Caroline, if what Susan Prosser says is true I won't have to worry about this year's paper chase, because Mr Dalloway won't be here next term, he's left the bay for good. I don't care, I'm glad he's gone, I'm glad I won't see him again, I'm glad he's escaped) if I get up this lot of stairs and up the next and scramble up the footholds to the top I'll escape I'll be safe. The sound of the hooves is in the works now thundering like I'd imagined they would the echoes shaking the walls and spilling cement dust on me as I scratch my way up the stairs nearly to the next floor nearly there. I look down and I see a rider somebody is in that mad horse's hollow somebody is forcing Sydney Bridge Upside Down to chase me (Why sit like that, dear Caroline? Why not come to the edge and look across the bay? Don't you care about the scenery? What are you looking at? What do you want me to do? Do you want to grab my hand and do what you did when we were running the other morning? You know, when you held it down there between your legs and wouldn't let me take it away. I can't, dear Caroline, I can't, I can't) I can't get there I can go no higher no matter how loud the hooves are thundering up the stairs now thunder all around me and I can only wait for the horse to reach me to crash upon me and I watch. I watch Sydney Bridge Upside Down leap flying hooves and foam from the stairs and land on the floor below me. I watch Mr Wiggins jump clear. I watch Mr Wiggins run with a knife to Sydney Bridge Upside Down and stab and slash until blood spouts everywhere. *Caroline!*

7

THERE WAS a skinny, snoopy girl who lived on the edge of the world, and her name was Susan Prosser and she died during the summer holidays I'm telling you about. It was Sam Phelps who found her body. Sam Phelps lifted her body on to Sydney Bridge Upside Down and brought it to Mrs Prosser. This was on a Monday afternoon.

I start with Sam Phelps and Sydney Bridge Upside Down and the body of Susan Prosser, but now I go to our wash-house on the morning of that day. I was there with Caroline.

'Cal should be helping, eh?' I said, giving the wringer handle an extra push so that a lumpy sheet would go through.

'He's only a little fellow,' said Caroline, guiding the sheet from the rollers to the laundry basket.

'All he did was fetch some driftwood,' I said. 'Now he's off. I bet he's playing with Dibs Kelly. But I don't care.'

I did not want to complain too much in case Caroline

thought I was getting at her. I wouldn't get at her. I didn't mind lighting the copper and boiling up the clothes and putting them through the tubs and wringing them and pegging them out. Better for me to do all that than Caroline. I certainly didn't want her to do any more than she was already doing, which was mostly watching me and catching the clothes when they came through the wringer and pegging out socks and hankies and other small things. That was enough for Caroline to be doing. Especially since she had said she was a bit off-colour today.

'I know why you're grumpy, Harry,' she said, patting the sheet into place in the basket. 'Because we didn't play our game this morning.'

'I'm not grumpy,' I said. 'I don't care if that kid doesn't help.'

'You didn't look happy when you came to breakfast,' she said. 'You must have had a restless night, I thought. Then you scowled, you did scowl, when I told you I couldn't run.'

'I didn't scowl,' I said. Actually, I hadn't felt much like running up and down after breakfast; the way I pretended to be disappointed, so she wouldn't think I was relieved, had apparently fooled her.

'It's not for ever,' Caroline said, leaning towards me, smiling into my face. 'I'll be all right in a few days.'

I wondered momentarily how she knew she would be all right in a few days, then I told myself a rest from running around wouldn't be so bad, I did not enjoy the game as much these days as I had at the beginning. I would enjoy it more if Cal played too. But Cal did not even watch now. He got dressed straight after breakfast and went off on his own. You would have thought Caroline wasn't worth looking at! Myself, I reckoned she was worth looking at all the time, naked or not. Today, for instance, she wore black slacks and a black sweater, and she looked as beautiful in these as she did when she wore a frock and not much else, if anything. I guessed Cal was simply too young to appreciate having a girl like Caroline around the house; when he was older and remembered these days he would be annoyed at himself for missing the fun.

So why, at this moment, didn't I care that I had missed the usual fun? I knew. I frowned.

'Harry, *did* you have a restless night?' asked Caroline, her face so close to mine I could see into and through her eyes. 'You're pale. You need cheering up.'

'It's this washing,' I said, stuffing a towel between the rollers and pulling away my fingers just in time. 'Too much washing. Like Dad said, it mounted up too much.'

'Let me wring, Harry,' she said, grabbing my hand from the wringer handle.

'No!' I said, pulling away my hand before she could do anything with it. 'No, it's all right, Caroline. I'll soon be finished.'

She looked unhappy. I must have offended her.

'I'm sorry,' I said. I held out my hand. 'Here.'

She did not take it. She turned from me and walked to the wash-house doorway, stood there with her back to me. 'Think I'll go for a walk this afternoon,' she said. 'I might walk to the store.'

'Don't go there,' I said. I was certain Mr Wiggins would

be near the store some time this afternoon. 'How about going to the cave instead. Or we could go to the wharf—'

'Not today,' she said, still with her back to me. 'I feel like going somewhere different today.'

'What about the waterfall?' I said, figuring if we left early enough we could be across the river and on our way up the waterfall track before Mr Wiggins arrived.

'No, I think I'll go to the store,' she said.

'Why?' I asked. 'Why go there?'

'Might make a phone call,' she said. 'Somebody said I'd have to go there to ring up.'

'Mr Wiggins!' I said, shocked into saying his name. I was shocked because I thought the phone call could only mean that she wanted to leave Calliope Bay.

'Mr Wiggins?' She turned to look at me, and my face must have seemed strange because her expression changed. She was smiling when she turned; she stopped smiling when she looked at me. 'Harry?'

'It was Mr Wiggins who said about the phone,' I said quickly as she walked towards me. 'That night when he was talking about the carnival. Are you going to the carnival with him, Caroline?'

'You mustn't worry about Mr Wiggins,' she said, taking my hand. 'I won't go with him.'

'We don't mind if you want to,' I said, going warm as she kissed my hand. 'Dad says it's for you to decide. He says you must please yourself whether you go with Mr Wiggins or in Mr Kelly's Reo—'

'Your hand's so cold, Harry,' she said. 'You can't be well. You should lie down for a while. I know,

I'll make you a hot lemon drink.'

'It's because I've had my hand in the water,' I said. 'There's nothing wrong with me. Soon as I've finished the washing I'll feel better. Honest I will.'

'We'll hang out these, then go inside for a while,' she said. 'A lemon drink and a rest are what you need, Harry.'

This was all right, I thought. I felt better already, it was good to have Caroline holding my hand and worrying about my health. Not since my mother left had anybody cared how I felt, and my mother's way of caring had been sort of crabby; she thought it was a pest when kids were sick but had to pretend she cared, being a mother.

We put out the rest of the clothes and went into the house. I sat at the kitchen table while Caroline made the lemon drink. I was being looked after, and I liked it.

'Won't be any good when you go,' I said sadly. 'I wish the holidays would last for ever and school would never start again.'

'So that's why you've been grumpy!' said Caroline. 'You've been thinking about school.'

'Not much,' I said. 'Not as much as thinking what it will be like when you go. Are you really going soon? Is that why you want to ring up?'

'Poor Harry,' she said, putting the lemon drink in front of me. She kissed me. 'No, that wasn't why I wanted to ring up. It wasn't because I was thinking of going. But I suppose I should be thinking of it. I can't stay here for ever, can I?'

'You can if you like,' I said. 'We don't mind. You ask Dad. He doesn't mind.'

'Aunt Janet might,' she said. 'But we'll see. I won't go to the store, after all. I can ring up another day.'

'This lemon drink is pretty good,' I said. I usually turned down offers of lemon drink, I preferred ginger beer any time.

'I was very fond of lemon drink when I was a little girl,' Caroline said. 'Especially when Uncle Pember made it for me.'

'Who is Uncle Pember?' I asked.

'Uncle Pember was a nice old man,' she said. 'He had a big black beard and a black cloak, and he wore dark glasses. He took me for walks when I was a little girl. Would you like me to read you something about Uncle Pember? I mention him in my autobiography.'

'Gee!' I said. She had never shown me her auto-biography, not even after I had shown her my cigarette cards, and I had figured it would be rude to ask her for a look since it was probably so private.

'We'll go into the bedroom,' she said, taking my hand and leading me up the passage. Caroline's hand was very warm; all of her was warm, I could feel her warmth whenever I was near her.

She led me to her bed and I sat there and waited while she got an exercise book from a suitcase, and the unhap-piness I had felt in the wash-house had vanished and I told myself I was lucky to have Caroline for a cousin, she was the best person in the world.

'Sit here beside me, Harry,' she said, her back to the pillows. 'We'll be cosy. Now what part shall I read you?' She turned a few pages. 'What about when Uncle Pember took me to a parade? Like to hear about that?'

I said I would. I could see the writing in the exercise book, but made myself look straight ahead. The window was up, but no noises came from outside. The sun shone on the wall I gazed at, but I did not care about the sunshine. All I cared about was my warm cousin beside me.

Caroline read: 'I'll mumble mumble you to the big parade, declared Uncle Pember. Mumble mumble, he added. I was very little and did not always hear what he said. Mumble mumble is what I often thought he said. Ponk ponk, I would say back to make him chortle. Would there be toffee-apples at the big parade, I inquired. Uncle Pember said there would be no toffee-apples because toffee-apples were only for the summer show. Besides, he said, pretty little girls in nice frocks should not eat toffee-apples. Why not, Uncle Pember? Because their frocks got sticky, he said. Mumble, he declared, mumble mumble. Oh, ponk ponk, Uncle Pember, I said. I knew a number. The number was seven. Look at the seven, I kept saying to Uncle Pember when we walked to the parade. There were sevens on front gates and motor-cars. Look at all the sevens, I said. At last he said: Child, no more sevens, please. I see a five, I said. Mumble, he said. The parade was for Christmas. Uncle Pember said it was a month early because mumble mumble. All the people watching the parade were huge. I could not see. Uncle Pember held me up. I saw an elephant. A brown man with long thin arms and a lovely hat threw little things from on top of the elephant. Children ran to catch the little things. Uncle Pember said the little things were lollies. I did not get any lollies because the elephant would have stamped on me. Uncle Pember let me sit on his shoulders. His beard tickled my legs. I saw a band playing loud music. The music made me pull Uncle Pember's beard. Mumble mumble, he said. The band went by. I saw a seven. It was on a palace of flowers. I told Uncle Pember I could see a seven. He inquired: Is that all you can see up there, child? I yelled: No no no! I saw a monster. The face was squashy. It was red and yellow and green and black. It was staring at me. It frightened me and I weeweed on Uncle Pember. He cried: Mumble mumble mumble! I was too frightened to say ponk ponk—'

She had reminded me, and her warmth was no longer all I cared about. I turned from her, but I had not been able to stop the choking sound, I could not stop the tears.

'Oh, Harry, I didn't mean to make you sad,' Caroline said. She shut the exercise book and put her arm round me. 'You mustn't feel sad, you mustn't cry.'

'I'm not crying!' I told her, the damned tears rolling. 'I'm not crying!'

I go now to the morning of the day before. This, of course, was when Susan Prosser was still alive, still snooping.

Since it was a Sunday and Dad was home, I didn't know what Susan Prosser expected to see by looking over our fence. That was what she was doing when I went out into the yard, and she did not bob down when she saw me, it was as if she had been waiting for me to go out.

'Good morning, Susan,' I said. 'What's new in your place? How's your budgie? Has he said anything clever lately?'

'You wouldn't like what he says,' she said. She seemed friendly, but I knew better than to trust her. 'I don't think I should repeat what he says. You might be distressed.'

'I'm tough,' I said, gulpy. 'Tell me what Joey says.'

'If you insist,' she said. 'He says: 'Write a letter write a letter write a letter.' That's all he says.'

I knew I had gone pale. But I said calmly: 'That's a clever thing for a budgie to say.' I was sure my voice was very friendly.

'I warned you,' she said. 'I said you might be distressed.'

'I'm not distressed,' I said. 'What do you mean, Susan?'

'Ha ha,' she said.

'Honestly, I'm not distressed, Susan,' I said. It was hard forcing myself to stay friendly when I felt like reaching over the fence and bopping her.

'Why pretend?' she said. She had such a mean look I wouldn't have been surprised if icicles had shot from her eyes. 'You know you're distressed. You know you're wondering if I took the budgie's advice. Own up, nasty Harry.'

'Why do you call me nasty?' I asked. 'What have I done to you? I don't call you nasty, do I?'

'That's scarcely the point,' she said, rolling her eyes as though I had said the sort of stupid thing she had expected me to say.

'Have I ever called you skinny and snoopy?' I asked. 'Other kids have, but I haven't. I stick up for you.'

'Don't bother,' she said. 'I mean, don't bother to say such things. I know you wouldn't stick up for me. Not that I believe other children do call me skinny and snoopy.'

She did not sound too sure. 'Ask Dibs Kelly then,' I said.

'That dirty boy!' she said. 'Ask *him*?'

I pretended to be puzzled. 'I don't understand why you think you're better than kids like Dibs and me,' I said. 'So you're clever. So you do a lot of homework. So you don't like fun. So why should that make you better than us? That's what I can't understand.'

'I know you're only saying that,' she said. 'You're only pretending you don't know what I mean.'

'I was trying to be friendly,' I said, hating her.

'Sometimes I wonder what a boy of your type will be like when he's older,' she said. 'What sort of grown-up will you be? I imagine a large, coarse person who thinks only of his own pleasures. Not caring about other people's feelings, not being generous unless he thinks he'll get something in return. Spiteful as well.'

'And Dibs too?' I asked, making myself grin.

'He won't be as bad as you,' she said. 'Because he's not as cunning as you. Cunning people are the worst. They don't care who they hurt.'

'I haven't hurt you,' I said. I was beginning to feel I didn't care what she did about writing to my mother or what else she did to make me feel bad; I would rather not go on listening.

'You've hurt other children,' she said. 'I've seen the way you play. You enjoy hurting others.'

'Like Dibs, you mean?' I said.

'Even your own brother,' she said. 'I've seen you throwing passion-fruit at him.'

'Only in fun,' I said. 'He doesn't care.'

'I've heard him crying,' she said.

'All kids cry,' I said. 'The Kelly kids cry and it's nothing to do with me when they cry. I don't make them cry. So I don't know what you're talking about. Honestly, I don't.'

'Ha ha,' she said.

I was more irritated when she said it now than I had been last time. She seemed to be trying to make me hit her, to make me get into trouble. Maybe she figured I'd get into more trouble by hitting her today than if it were a day when Dad was not home. She might even hope he would chase me with the whip. This would be bound to please her.

Well, I knew a way of hurting her without hitting her. Boy, could I make her unhappy!

The trouble was I might make her so angry there would be no chance at all of stopping her from writing to my mother. I still might have a chance of doing that if I stayed friendly, let her go on thinking she was clever.

'What you probably don't understand, Susan,' I said, 'is that kids in families often fight one another. It doesn't mean they hate one another. Like, Cal gets on my nerves sometimes because he touches things in my drawer and messes them up. My cigarette cards, for instance. He knows it's a rare collection and I don't like other people messing it up. Not unless I give them permission—'

'What *are* you talking about?' Susan asked. 'I don't want to hear about your silly cigarette cards.'

'I'm explaining why I might bop Cal,' I said. 'If he doesn't ask me if he can have a look, I might bop him.

But it doesn't mean I hate him.'

'No, only one of your nasty habits,' she said.

What was the use? 'You don't have brothers or sisters,' I said. 'You don't know how kids in families—'

'Oh dear!' said Susan Prosser. 'The excuses! You'll tell me next that Dibs Kelly is your brother.'

'Eh?' I said.

'You hit him too. Is *he* your brother?'

I knew then she really wasn't interested in why I sometimes bopped kids, all she was interested in was my unhappiness. She wouldn't leave the fence until she was sure I was unhappy. And I couldn't leave the fence until I made her see I was not unhappy. Of course, if Dad or Cal or Caroline came into the yard and spoke to me I'd have an excuse to leave. But there was no sign of them.

'Actually,' I said, 'I don't hit other kids very often. I don't get into much trouble at school. Some kids get the strap more than I do.'

'Yes, I've noticed you're rather smart at escaping punishment,' she said. 'I sometimes wondered why Mr Dalloway let you off for things he punished other children for doing. He must have had a reason.'

'Search me,' I said. 'I'm not his pet.'

Susan Prosser looked into the distance. 'It might have been because he didn't want to upset your mother,' she said. 'She might not have had such a high opinion of him if he punished her sons. I suppose that could have been the reason.'

'Search me,' I said.

'Anyway,' she said, 'I'm glad I took our budgie's advice.

It really was time I wrote a letter.' She drew back from the fence. 'I thought it would be difficult to write. But it turned out to be easy. I enjoyed writing it.'

'Is that the one you said you'd write?'

'Oh, did I mention it before?'

'You said you were going to write to my mother.' I noticed how she kept back from the fence, maybe scared I would grab her.

'Did I?' she said. 'I'd forgotten.' She moved further back. 'Yes, I did write, I thought it would be nice for her to hear from Calliope Bay.' Suddenly she was waving a letter. 'Here it is,' she said. 'This will let your mother know what's been happening.' She was smiling; I mean, her mouth was shaped into a smile.

'What have you said in it?'

'Oh, this and that. Only what's been happening in the neighbourhood.'

I took a deep breath. Then I smiled at Susan Prosser. I told her: 'My mother will be pleased to hear from you, Susan. She thinks you're very clever. She likes you.'

'I like her too,' she said. 'Your mother has always been kind to me. That was why I was only too happy to fetch cigarettes from the store for her when you and your brother were away having fun.'

'She often said how good you were,' I said.

Susan Prosser was using the letter like a fan. 'Your mother always offered me a drink of ginger beer when I called on her,' she said. 'Before she went on holiday she said I was welcome to call at your place for a ginger beer whenever I felt like it. She said she

117

was making enough for everybody.'

'Hey, she didn't tell us!' I said. 'She didn't say you could have some—'

'So *you* say,' Susan Prosser said quickly. 'I know how much notice to take of you. Oh, I can imagine who got my share. I can imagine why she needed it too. People become very thirsty when they run around a lot.'

'Honestly, my mother didn't say you could have some,' I said. I sure was surprised it was the ginger beer that had made Susan Prosser so unfriendly. Heck, why hadn't she said she wanted some? She could have had as many bottles as she wanted—as long as she didn't send that letter. Now it was too late. The ginger beer had all gone.

'Not that I mention ginger beer in this,' she said, waving the letter. 'I wouldn't be so petty. It was not important. It was no more than I expected from you.'

'Honestly, I didn't know,' I said.

She shook her head. 'So you say. And your father didn't know? And your brother didn't know?'

'None of us knew,' I said.

'Anyway, it doesn't matter,' she said. 'As I say, it was not important.'

She turned, still waving the letter like a fan.

'By the way, Susan,' I said, making my voice very friendly.

She paused to look at me. 'Yes?'

'I'll post it for you if you like,' I said.

'Ha ha,' she said.

'Save you a trip to the store,' I said.

'I don't intend going to the store,' she said. 'Mr Wiggins

will be calling tomorrow. He can take it to the post-box for me. I certainly wouldn't let *you* take it. I'm not that silly.' She made her voice sarcastic. 'Honestly I'm not.'

She went inside, and she waved the letter all the way.

I go now to the following afternoon, to the time in Caroline's bedroom.

To cheer me up, Caroline said she would read another bit of her autobiography. This, she said, was about a later incident in her childhood, about a girl called Penny who was so poor she had to wear a grey Army jersey as a dress. Caroline explained that Penny was quite short, which was why the jersey fitted her, and very cheerful, which was why she did not complain about being poor. Apparently her parents did not mind when she went for walks in the city at night, her parents being rather rowdy and always having parties where there was much drinking and games it was best for a little girl not to see. There came a night, said Caroline, when Penny met a stranger during one of her walks in the city. This stranger had a black beard and a black cloak and wore dark glasses. 'Now I'll read on,' said Caroline.

This is what she read: 'I say, said the stranger when Penny passed the doorway where he stood, you are too young to be wandering in the city at this hour, do your father and mother mumble mumble mumble? Not if I carry my dolly, said Penny. What difference, asked the stranger, does your dolly make? My dolly's a police-lady, said Penny. Telling me this later, Penny suggested that I might wish to walk in the city with her one night. I said I did not have a police-lady dolly. Penny confided that perhaps her own police-lady dolly did not really make a difference. At least, she said, it had not appeared to make a difference when she met the stranger in the black cloak, for he attempted to put her in his car without further ado. She said the stranger had a big black car. He assured her it was warm in the car and they could sit in it and chat. During the chat, Penny mentioned the lights she enjoyed looking at when she was in the city at night. The stranger remarked that lights were mumble mumble and added that he could show her a chandelier. The chandelier was in a big house, he said. If Penny and her dolly were agreeable, he said, he would take them to see the chandelier and also mumble mumble mumble in the big house. Now, while Penny was telling me this I had a suspicion. Did you say he had a black beard and a black cloak and wore dark glasses, I asked her. Yes, said Penny. That sounds very like my Uncle Pember, I said. Fancy that, said Penny. So this was how I discovered that Uncle Pember sometimes waited in doorways and talked to interesting people who passed by. Penny was interesting because she was very cheerful. One of the things I always remember about Penny is her jersey. Another is her cheerfulness. When Uncle Pember held her up to touch the chandelier she laughed and laughed. She said he was tickling her with his beard. It's funny you should say that, I said when she told me about it. It's funny because I can remember when Uncle Pember's beard tickled me, I said. Later in the story of my life I will tell of Uncle Pember's amazing secret and what became of him. For the time being, I end with this memory of my friend Penny—'

Caroline closed the exercise book and kissed my ear. 'So

wasn't that a coincidence, Harry? Who should my friend meet in the city but my own Uncle Pember!'

'That was very surprising,' I said quietly. I felt awful again, I could not pretend she had cheered me up.

'Harry!' she cried. 'You didn't listen!'

'I listened,' I said. 'I heard what you said about your Uncle Pember and your friend Penny.' I sniffed because I had also heard her say that her uncle had an amazing secret. It was when she said that I felt bad again, and I knew she could do nothing to cheer me up, she might as well stop trying.

She whispered in my ear. 'If you like, I'll chase you down the passage.' She took hold of my shirt.

'Don't,' I said.

She tried to hold me, but I pushed her hand away and rolled off the bed. I shouted: 'I don't want to!'

'Go then,' she said, turning her back to me. 'Go and play with Dibs and Cal.'

'I don't want to,' I said. 'I want to stay with you.' I moved to the bed. 'I'm feeling sad, Caroline. I don't want to—' I had to stop because there was the gulpy feeling in my throat again and I knew I was about to howl.

I sat on the bed, and presently she turned and put her arm around me, and I lay there beside her and neither of us spoke. And all that happened was that she raised her black sweater and let me rest my damp cheek on her breasts.

Now I go to the works the night before. This, of course, was Sunday night. The moon was shining.

I had followed Susan Prosser there because ever since our chat about the letter at the fence in the morning I had been thinking of the way I knew of hurting her without hitting her. She had made me unhappy. Well, I knew how to make her unhappy.

I was watching her from behind the furnace-house. Would she jump from the steps and run if I spoke? Or would she be curious about my being there and listen to what I had to tell her?

She was in the moonlight, I was in the shadows. If I stepped out suddenly without speaking she might be frightened. Or she might simply be angry.

I would have to be careful, I thought.

'Why are you hiding there?' she asked.

I went stiff. I said nothing. She could not see me.

'I can't imagine what you expect to discover by hiding there,' she said. 'I'm talking to you, Harry Baird. Or do you imagine I don't know you're there?'

I stepped from behind the furnace-house and walked towards the works steps. I said cheerfully: 'Hello, Susan.'

'Every time I come here,' she said, 'you follow me. Why? I'm rather interested to know why anybody does such a peculiar thing.' She had not moved from the steps, she was looking up calmly at me.

'Not always,' I said, my voice shaky.

'Not always what?' she said. 'And why are you frightened? You're not frightened of me, are you?'

'I mean, I haven't always followed you,' I said, my voice no longer shaky. I sat on the steps, not too near her. 'Dibs was the one who noticed you went for walks at night. I don't know how many walks you had before he noticed.' She would know from my voice that I was not frightened.

'You've followed me often enough,' she said. 'Don't put the blame on Dibs Kelly. I wish you wouldn't mention *him*.'

I knew this was my chance to do what I had come to do. I would make her unhappy.

I spoke carefully: 'I know why you don't want Dibs to be mentioned. It's because he piddles from his veranda, eh?'

'Is it?' she said.

'I'm surprised you care about Dibs doing that,' I said, noticing a pile of bricks nearby in the moonlight.

'Yes, I imagine you think it's normal behaviour,' she said. She had one hand stuck awkwardly in the pocket of her cardigan. 'Like wanting to read other people's letters no doubt.'

She must have the letter in that pocket, I thought. I looked at the pile of bricks. Those bricks, I thought, should have been taken to the cave.

'Oh, I don't want to read your letter,' I said. I laughed. 'It's Dibs I've been thinking about, Susan. I mean, other people have been seen piddling. He's not the only one. I remember Dad telling me about a girl he saw once—'

Susan stood up.

'He saw her right next door,' I said, standing up too. 'Gosh, he was surprised! She was doing it behind the bush. Can you imagine that, Susan?'

She watched me.

'Very surprising,' I said. 'Nearly as surprising as when the same girl was seen going for a drive with Mr Wiggins. I wonder what she did with Mr Wiggins?'

'I suppose you mean the time he took me to the dentist at Bonnie Brae,' she said. She didn't sound unhappy yet.

'So it *was* you behind the bush that time?' I said. 'So that's who Dad was telling my mother about! I was wondering about that.'

'Why do you tell lies?' she asked, sounding quite calm.

'He did see you,' I said.

'I imagine he did,' she said. 'But you knew that. You weren't wondering if I was the one. So why tell lies about it?'

I did not know what to say. Heck, if what I had told her didn't make her unhappy, what else would?

She sighed. 'Not that I really blame you,' she said. 'I do know why you tell lies. I know who you're trying to protect. It's not you I blame, Harry.' She did not sound stern or sarcastic; she sounded as if she wanted to be my friend.

I lowered my head. 'I'm sorry, Susan. I only wanted to make you a bit unhappy. I don't care what you did. You were only small then, you had to do it in a hurry. I'm sorry.'

'I guessed you were trying to make me unhappy,' she said. 'But I can't be unhappy about something that happened so long ago.'

'I know,' I said. 'I apologise, Susan.'

'I believe you mean it,' she said. 'I accept your apology.'

'Thank you, Susan,' I said. I looked round the yard, then into the works. 'Well,' I said, 'suppose I'd better get the pistol, then go home.'

'What pistol?' she asked as I moved into the works.

I paused. 'Just an old pistol we found,' I said. 'We left it upstairs. Better take it home before the small kids find it.' I walked towards the stairs.

'Does it work?' she asked from a few yards back.

'No, it's broken,' I said, reaching the stairs.

'Where did you find it?' she asked.

I kept walking. 'In one of the rooms here,' I said, not turning. 'It's up on the second floor. I'll just get it, then I'll go home.'

I did not stop to check that she was following me. I knew she was. Her footsteps were echoing in the works.

I go now to the afternoon of the following day. I was back in Caroline's room.

We had been out to see if the washing had dried, and we had brought most of it in. Then we had lunch (Cal was still missing), and after that we went to Caroline's room because Caroline said I looked awfully pale and could do with another lie-down.

This time, though, she did not raise her sweater, which was just as well because Dibs Kelly would have seen us when he threw the passion-fruit into the room.

'Hey, Harry!' he shouted. He threw another passion-fruit and this one hit me. 'Come out and see! Susan Prosser's dead! Sam Phelps found her at the works!'

Caroline was first off the bed. She looked back at me from the doorway. 'I *thought* I heard her name being called during the night,' she said. 'I must have fallen asleep—'

'Dibs is probably having a joke,' I said, slowly getting off the bed.

'I don't think he was joking,' Caroline said, hurrying out the front.

I followed her to the road.

Along the road to the right, plodding from the direction of the works, was Sydney Bridge Upside Down. I could see that somebody, or something, was sprawled across the hollow.

I looked the other way. Along the road to the left, speeding from the direction of the river, was Mr Wiggins' van.

I knew the van would reach us before the horse did.

8

BUT FOR Caroline I wouldn't have been stroking Sydney Bridge Upside Down's hollow. But for stroking Sydney Bridge Upside Down's hollow I'd have been quicker reaching my brother, who was drowning.

I was stroking Sydney Bridge Upside Down's hollow because Caroline had been aboard the *Emma Cranwell* for more than twenty minutes, and I was wondering why it should take her so long to greet the friends she had made during her voyage several weeks before. Even if she kissed every member of the crew, it should not take this long. What was she doing? Why didn't she come ashore?

So that nobody would notice how worried about Caroline I was, I concentrated on stroking Sydney Bridge Upside Down and telling Sam Phelps what a great horse this was. Sam Phelps gave me a look that said he was used to such compliments and couldn't be bothered discussing them, not with me anyway.

We had been looking forward to going to the wharf to

see the *Emma Cranwell*—Caroline because she wanted to greet her sailor friends, Dibs and Cal and myself because the school holidays were running out fast, and we had to make the most of any happening. The carnival at Bonnie Brae was still to come, but it would be the very last special happening before school began and we certainly weren't going to mooch around for another week until then.

It was surprising, too, what a difference it made not being able to play at the works. Ever since Susan Prosser had fallen through the chute hole, Dad had been warning us not to go near the works, and he was so fierce with his warnings that I did not dare disobey him. Before, when he had said how dangerous the works were, I hadn't really believed him, I knew you would have to be pretty careless to come to any harm, which was why I hadn't minded Cal climbing up the chute even though Dad had said he shouldn't. Now Dad was not the only one who said how dangerous the ruins were. Mr Kelly went on about them as well. He and Dad were always telling each other these days that something should be done about pulling down the rest of the works before there was another accident, kids being what they were and liable to do the most scatter-brained things, even such an apparently sensible girl as Susan Prosser who should have known better, they said, than to wander around the works at night. The Bonnie Brae policeman, the one who came to Calliope Bay to write in his notebook about Susan Prosser, had also been very solemn; he had lined us all up, even the smallest Kelly kids, and given us a lecture about the works and, when he saw how carefully we listened, about the dangers of playing on the road, swimming near the wharf, and eating strange berries. So, with all these warnings, I did not dare go near the works. And the holidays were no longer such fun.

Luckily, in a way, Dad decided it was time he started painting the house. He told us about his decision at breakfast the morning after he'd had a letter from my mother. This was the letter in which she said how sorry she was to learn that Susan Prosser, such a nice girl, had died, and how sorry she felt for Mrs Prosser, collapsing after Susan vanished into the night and recovering only to be handed her dear daughter's body. My mother told Dad to extend her sympathy to Mrs Prosser. She was a bit late, though; Mrs Prosser had gone to Bonnie Brae with Susan's body for the funeral and had not returned to Calliope Bay, her house was empty. 'Your mother doesn't say when she'll be back,' Dad told me. 'She doesn't say she expects to see the house painted, either.' He saw Caroline looking at him, and he smiled. 'But that doesn't mean she won't suddenly arrive without warning, it doesn't mean she won't expect to see the place painted. So we'd better get started. We'll put those ladders up in the morning. Sandy Kelly will help me with the roof. Would you boys like to start on the tankstand in the morning?' We said we would, and we did. And Dibs came along with his father later, and soon we were all splashing the paint around. Except Caroline, of course. Nobody would expect a girl like Caroline to help with painting a house. It was enough if she simply looked on, which she sometimes did. She said it was marvellous how Dad got up a ladder with his one leg. She said it was marvellous how smoothly Cal and I had painted the tankstand. I enjoyed painting, it took my mind off a lot of things. It was better, for instance, than being alone with Caroline in her bedroom; I mean, better than when I was feeling gloomy and she was holding me and telling me to cheer up. Because somehow this did not work, I went on being gloomy. At other times, when I was happy, I was glad Caroline talked to me and sang to me and went for walks with me. So how I felt had nothing to do with Caroline, not when I felt gloomy anyway; it was my own damned fault. I still thought Caroline was the most beautiful person in the world.

Actually, she was watching Cal and me painting the back porch—Dad and Mr Kelly were off at work—when Dibs came to tell us that the *Emma Cranwell* had rounded the heads. Because of this bit of a wind, he said, the ship was dipping and rolling even more than usual, she might hit a rock.

'We have to finish painting,' I said, in a way not wanting to go to the wharf, yet also wanting to go very much. The trouble was that when he mentioned the *Emma Cranwell* I remembered how Susan Prosser had often liked seeing the ship come in, and the memory of Susan Prosser seemed to put me off wanting to go.

But not for long. Because Caroline got excited about the news and said she would love to go to the wharf, she said she was going inside to change her dress, then she would hurry to the wharf, and the last one there was a rotten egg.

'I'm going,' Cal said. 'Paint makes me feel sick.'

'I won't be the rotten egg,' Dibs said, making for

the side-path. 'I'll wave to Captain Foster.'

'I don't mind being a rotten egg,' I said. 'I'll wait for Caroline.'

'You sure you're coming?' asked Dibs. He was staring at me oddly. His mother had also stared at me like that lately. I wondered if they talked about me and, if so, what they said. Well, they had better watch out; what I did was none of their business.

I told Dibs: 'I'll catch you up. Don't suppose it matters if Dad gets angry because I haven't done enough painting.'

This seemed to satisfy him. He ran off with Cal.

I decided I would wait out here for Caroline. If I went inside she would want me to help choose a dress. I couldn't be bothered doing that today.

Staying outside did no good, though. Because soon I heard 'Harry?', and there she was on the porch, wearing a petticoat I could see through and holding up a yellow dress. The petticoat made me more excited than if she had been wearing nothing. I stared at her, I could not speak.

'Would this be a nice one to wear?' she asked.

'Eh?' I said presently, forcing myself to think of the river on a cold day.

'Harry, shall I wear this one?' she asked.

I concentrated on the dress. 'Don't forget it's windy today,' I said, remembering how this dress behaved last time she wore it. It had been a windy day then too.

She eyed the dress. Then she said: 'Oh!'

'Eh?' I said, looking at the petticoat again.

'I wore this when I came ashore,' said Caroline. 'I can't wear it today. That settles it. I'll wear the blue one.'

'Good idea,' I said. Gosh, I thought. The blue one showed so much of her throat and more; if she leaned forward only slightly you could see right down.

Anyway, it was the blue dress she was wearing when we got to the wharf, and this dress was no better behaved in the wind than the yellow one, besides having what I reckoned to be the other disadvantage.

Like Dibs had said, it seemed a rough trip in for the *Emma Cranwell*, and seeing her rolling and dipping as she dodged the rocks made me remember the pongy voyage I'd once had in her. I looked the other way. I only hoped Caroline was not reminded of what had happened to me aboard the *Emma Cranwell*. Better for her to think of her own times aboard the ship, whatever they were like.

She, at any rate, did not mind watching the ship plunging nearer. Dibs and Cal were having a good look, too.

I turned—and found myself face to face with Sydney Bridge Upside Down. I had not heard him coming up behind me.

What old eyes he had. They were looking at me sadly and knowingly. He must recognise me.

Then I saw that Sam Phelps, standing beside the horse, was also looking at me.

I preferred to stare back at Sydney Bridge Upside Down.

I told him in my friendly voice: 'Sorry I didn't bring any sugar, old fellow. Maybe the sailors will have some.'

'Ahoy there!' shouted Dibs.

'Hello, Captain Foster!' called Caroline.

'He can't hear you,' Cal said. 'The wind's the wrong way.'

'And I can't see him,' Caroline laughed.

The horse's old eyes were beginning to make me nervous. Also, it was hard to stop glancing at Sam Phelps. I knew why he was looking at me, he wanted to be sure I kept out of the way when the *Emma Cranwell* berthed, he was probably wondering if Caroline was enough of a reason for him to let us stay as well.

'Better let Mr Phelps catch the rope this time,' I told Dibs. I said this loudly enough for Sam Phelps to hear; he would know I was on his side.

Dibs ignored me. 'Ahoy there!' he yelled.

'Ahoy, Captain Foster!' called Caroline.

I could see the sailor waiting to throw the rope as the gap narrowed between the ship and the wharf.

I moved nearer Dibs. This time, I thought, I would help to wind the rope round the bollard.

Dibs tried to shove me aside when the rope came flying towards us. I gave him a push.

I was the one who caught the rope, I was the one who put it round the bollard.

I glanced at Caroline to see if she had noticed. She hadn't.

She hadn't noticed me because she was too busy waving to the ship. She was waiting for Captain Foster when he stepped from the gangplank, and he looked pleased to see her and to get one of her kisses, but I didn't hear what they said to each other. I felt that Caroline had forgotten me, I was only a kid who had helped her to have a little fun while she waited for the *Emma Cranwell* to return to port, and now I did not matter. I was gloomy.

I was even gloomier when Caroline went aboard the *Emma Cranwell*, not bothering to glance back at the wharf to see if we would be allowed aboard too.

We weren't, of course.

Dibs had a try. He reminded Captain Foster, who began chatting to Sam Phelps as soon as Caroline was out of sight, how he had once been allowed to see the engine-room and said he would certainly like another look.

'Not just yet, lad,' said Captain Foster. 'We'll be unloading some packing-cases and I wouldn't want you youngsters ending up under *them*. Best to stand back until Mr Phelps gives the all-clear.'

'What about Caroline?' asked Dibs. 'How come you let her go on?'

'She'll be out of harm's way,' said Captain Foster with a wink at Sam Phelps. I didn't like that wink and Sam Phelps couldn't have either because he did not wink back.

So that was how I came to be stroking Sydney Bridge Upside Down's hollow and telling Sam Phelps what a great horse he had. Although I didn't want him to see I was worried about Caroline being so long aboard the *Emma Cranwell*, I was rather hoping he would tell Captain Foster it was time she came ashore, Captain Foster would listen to him even if he wouldn't listen to me.

But Sam Phelps did not speak. That was his trouble. He hardly ever spoke. Not these days. Apparently in the old days, before his daughter ran away and his house was pulled down, he used to speak a fair bit, though Dad said he was always a moody fellow and you never knew where you stood with him. Still, I reckoned he got on all right with Caroline (he talked to *her*, he also let her ride his horse), and it was possible her being on the ship was a good enough reason for him to make a speech. An angry one maybe. I'd like to be near when he made it.

I was so busy thinking about Caroline and the sailors and what Sam Phelps might say that I didn't realise Cal and Dibs had crossed the wharf to the funny steps, keeping out of the way like Captain Foster had told them to.

At first I went on stroking the hollow when I heard the cries for help. It was as if somewhere inside me a tiny frightened voice was calling 'Help! Help!'

Then I saw Sam Phelps move across the wharf. The cries were louder, they were certainly not my own.

I was right behind Sam Phelps when he reached the top of the steps. He stopped, but I didn't. I went on down as fast as if they were ordinary steps, skimming over them the way I could skim over the footholds high in the works when I had to.

I knew I must go fast because I had seen from the top of the steps what was happening. Dibs had his left foot jammed in the steps near the bottom and was trying to tug it free; he was the one calling for help.

Cal was in the water. All I could see of him was his white face. It bobbed down. It bobbed up again. His eyes seemed puzzled, his mouth was opening and shutting, but he was making no sound. His head bobbed down again as I reached the dinghy at the bottom of the steps. I knew I could grab his hair if he bobbed up again.

The strange thing was that Cal was not being swept

away by the dangerous current. He was in the one spot, his head bobbing down, then up.

For a while, as I reached out from the dinghy, I did not think his head would bob up again. Then there it was, and I stopped myself from jumping in; instead, I grabbed his hair and dragged him to the dinghy. I pulled him into it.

Lying there, he looked at me, and his face was very pale and he said nothing.

'You were drowning,' I told him.

He just looked at me.

'Why didn't you try to grab the dinghy?' I asked. 'Why did you let yourself—'

'Are you all right, son?' It was Sam Phelps talking. He was steadying the dinghy with one hand while he leaned across to look at Cal.

Cal nodded.

'He was drowning,' I told Sam Phelps. I saw Dibs still trying to free his foot and I called to him from the dinghy: 'What happened? Did you push him?'

'He tripped,' Dibs said. 'He went too fast into the dinghy and fell out.'

'If you pushed him, boy—' I said.

'I didn't push him,' Dibs said. 'Did I, Cal?'

Cal breathed in quickly a few times, then said: 'I tripped.'

'You were lucky,' I said. 'You nearly drowned.'

Sam Phelps took Cal up to the wharf. I stayed behind to help Dibs free his foot, which was cut and swollen, then I went up the steps. Dibs crawled after me.

The packing-cases Captain Foster had mentioned were being unloaded from the *Emma Cranwell*. Cal was sitting on a box. Sam Phelps stood beside him. They were watching the sailors.

Sam Phelps looked hard at me. 'Now you know why I don't want you boys on the wharf,' he said. 'After this, you'll stay by the woolshed.'

He said this very firmly, it was the angriest I'd ever heard him speak. I was the one he looked at when he said it. He must think I was to blame for Dibs trapping his foot and Cal nearly drowning.

'It was an accident,' I said. 'I didn't do it.'

'There'll always be accidents with you about,' he said, keeping up this hard look which seemed meant to frighten me. 'You stay off the wharf.'

'He was drowning,' I said. 'I saved him.'

'Stay off this wharf,' he said, turning away.

'What do you know?' I asked Dibs. 'He's blaming *me*.'

Dibs was sitting on the wharf, rubbing his ankle. 'Must be because you're the eldest,' he said. 'Or because he doesn't like you.'

'I've done nothing to him,' I said. 'Where do we have fun now? They won't let us play anywhere. See what you kids have done!'

'Don't blame me,' Dibs said. He pointed at Cal. 'He's your brother. You should look after him.'

'I got other things to do,' I said.

'Like goofing about with your cousin, eh?' Dibs said.

'Be careful, boy,' I said. Then I saw that Cal was very pale. I put my arm around him. 'Are you feeling sick, Cal? Want to go home?'

'I'm watching for a while,' Cal said. 'Mr Phelps said I could watch.'

'All right,' I said, looking at the ship, looking for Caroline. 'We won't tell Dad about this,' I said. 'He'll only get angry.'

'I won't tell him,' Cal said.

'I'm telling somebody,' Dibs said. He looked up at me cheekily. 'Guess who?'

'Don't tell your mother,' I said. 'She'll tell Dad.'

'Wrong guess,' Dibs said.

'Can I have a turn?' Cal asked.

'If you like,' Dibs said. 'Three guesses. Harry's already had one of his.'

'I'm not playing,' I said.

'I guess Buster,' Cal said.

'Right first time!' Dibs said, looking amazed. 'You're smart, Cal. Smarter than Harry. Guessing right first time! What do you know, Harry?'

'I wasn't playing,' I said.

'I guessed Buster because I knew about him coming home,' Cal told me. 'Dibs said before—'

'Don't tell him,' Dibs said. 'You know what I said about a ride on the Indian. You know who'll want a ride if he sees Buster first.'

'I wasn't going to tell him, Dibs,' said Cal. He spoke as if *he* shared secrets with Dibs, which was pretty odd because *I* used to share them. A good many times lately, I now realised, Cal and Dibs had been off having fun together, and I was too busy thinking of Caroline and being with her and listening to her to notice that Dibs was no longer as annoyed about Cal as he used to be. They were only kids, of course. Even so, Cal was a traitor to say he wouldn't tell me about Buster, especially since I had just saved him from drowning.

'You said you'd let me know when Buster was coming,' I told Dibs. 'So we could ask him about some ammo. What about that promise, eh?' I did not speak angrily, I was more sad than angry that they had kept such a secret from me.

'I haven't had much chance to tell you,' Dibs said. 'You don't play with us now. If you'd been in the cave yesterday I could have told you. That's when I told Cal.'

'What about the pistol?' I said. 'Have you kids been looking at it?'

'Only once,' Dibs said. 'Just to make sure nobody had pinched it.'

I didn't believe that. I bet they'd had more than one look at the pistol. It had been hidden under some rocks at the back of the cave ever since we had found it; nobody would pinch it. I could see through Dibs. He hoped to get some ammo from Buster and use the pistol without telling me. That was why he did not want me to know Buster was coming home after so many weeks.

I had given up asking when Buster was due back. I used to ask Mrs Kelly whenever I saw her, then Dibs told me one day that Buster had had a row with his father and nobody in the family knew for sure when they would see him and his Indian again, and his mother was sick of being asked about him. Dibs promised to tell me whenever he had news of his big brother. I believed him. I stopped annoying Mrs Kelly with questions.

Now I wished I had kept going to the cave with them, I wished I hadn't missed so much of the fun. But even as I wished this, I looked at the *Emma Cranwell* to see if Caroline was in sight. She wasn't.

'Anyway,' I said to Dibs, 'why tell Buster about Cal nearly drowning? Why would he want to know that?'

'So he'll give Cal a ride,' Dibs said. 'Bet he gives him a long ride when he hears about it.'

'He'll probably take me to the store,' Cal said. 'Probably buy me some toffees.'

'Seems pretty strange to me,' I said. 'I save you from drowning, yet you get the reward!' But if it stopped him from telling Dad about his narrow escape I didn't care how many toffees he got.

'Think I'll look at the packing-cases,' Cal said, getting off the box. 'Mr Phelps doesn't mind if *I* look.'

'What do you know?' I said to Dibs. 'He thinks he's everybody's favourite. I bet nobody would make a fuss of me if I nearly drowned. I bet nobody would dive in and save me.'

'You can say that again,' Dibs said, jumping up and following Cal before I could bop him.

Those two kids certainly annoyed me. I forgot Dibs' broken promise, though, when I sneaked along for a look at the packing-cases two of the sailors were lifting into the freight wagon.

Written on each case was:

THIS SIDE UP
MR D. S. NORMAN
℅ SCHOOLHOUSE
CALLIOPE BAY

I knew what this meant. It meant Susan Prosser had

been right. Mr Dalloway would *not* be back next term. We would have a new teacher.

Before she died, of course, I was getting around to believing Susan Prosser when she said Mr Dalloway had gone for good. It was after she died, when I discovered what a fibber she was, that I decided she must have been fibbing about Mr Dalloway. She had fibbed about the budgie ('What budgie?' asked Mrs Prosser when Dad, at my suggestion, offered to look after Joey), and she had fibbed when hinting at what she would write to my mother about Caroline and me (the letter said nothing about our running game), but the packing-cases showed that she had not fibbed about Mr Dalloway. This all suggested that she really had been pretty dippy, she certainly wasn't as clever as she pretended to be. How could I feel sorry for her? I did not feel sorry for her, I did not care now.

And now I did not mind waiting for Caroline, either. It was right for her to meet her old friends. They would let her go eventually. After all, one of these days she'd go for ever; that day, at any rate, had not yet arrived.

I moved from the wagon and sat on a bollard to wait for Caroline, and I did not follow Dibs and Cal when they went aboard the ship to look at the engine-room.

I was glad I waited. For, when the sailors at last guided Caroline and her presents up the gangway, I was the one she hurried to, I was the one she kissed.

And why should I care about the dirty looks Sam Phelps gave me, as if warning that I could not expect a ride behind Sydney Bridge Upside Down? Caroline would make everything all right.

9

I T WAS not until we were aboard the Reo that Mrs Kelly, old purple face, had her idea. She said we should have invited Sam Phelps to come to Bonnie Brae with us, it would be a big treat for a man who lived such a lonesome life. Dibs groaned and so did I, but this only seemed to encourage her. She left her seat beside Caroline—Mr Kelly had put two long stools on the Reo's tray—and pushed past us to the cab. She leaned round the driver's side of the cab to tell Mr Kelly about her idea. He said it was a mad idea.

'It must be years since Sam was last at Bonnie Brae,' she said. 'What a treat for him to see the place again!'

'Come off it,' said Mr Kelly. 'You'll want us to give his nag a lift next. I hear there'll be a gallop or two. What about it, Frank? Would you put your money on Sydney Bridge Upside Down?' We could hear him laughing with Dad along there in the cab.

'I hope you haven't forgotten what happened to Mrs Prosser,' Mrs Kelly told Mr Kelly. 'People were content to let her live a lonely life, afraid to leave the house, hiding. And see what happened to her!'

For a few seconds there was no sound from the cab. Then Mr Kelly got out and came round to the back of the lorry. He put a hand on the tailboard, looked along the road towards the wharf.

Mrs Kelly worked her way to the tailboard.

'We'll be late, Mum,' Dibs said as she went by.

'Late for what?' she asked. You would think there was no carnival at Bonnie Brae and we were all sitting in the Reo for the fun of it.

Dad hopped along and stood beside Mr Kelly.

'What do you reckon, Frank?' asked Mr Kelly after they had looked down the road together.

Dad glanced at Mrs Kelly. 'I don't reckon he'll want to come. He was saying yesterday how the horse seemed out of sorts. He won't want to leave that horse alone all day. You know what he thinks of Sydney Bridge Upside Down.'

'There you are then,' said Mr Kelly, looking up at Mrs Kelly. 'Do we try to save Sam from being lonely? Or do we leave him here so his horse doesn't get lonely? Which is fair? What do I do now?'

'I suppose you'd better not bother,' she said, looking at Dad as if she didn't believe what he had said.

Dad looked up at her as if he had simply been telling the truth. Then he followed Mr Kelly back to the cab.

'He would have come if we'd asked him in plenty of time,' Mrs Kelly told Caroline as the Reo moved off.

'Not if his horse was sick,' Dibs said. 'Mr Baird was right about that.'

'I'm talking to Caroline,' Mrs Kelly told Dibs. She said to Caroline: 'Mr Phelps has few pleasures nowadays. I understand he was once a keen reader. Now, my husband tells me, he never opens a book. His main interest in life is his horse.'

Caroline nodded. 'He's a dear old horse.'

'Boy, he had to pull some big loads the other day,' Dibs said. 'All those cases for the new teacher. Must have a large family, eh?'

'A large library, very likely,' Mrs Kelly said. 'It's books that take the room and make the weight. It will be interesting to have a well-read man in the bay. For a teacher, Mr Dalloway was surprisingly ill-read.'

'Cut talking about school,' I whispered to Dibs. Monday, when the term began, was much too close. I wanted to forget about it. I would forget about it by having a great time at the carnival.

Mrs Kelly gave me another of her looks when she saw me whispering to Dibs. I'd had many of these looks lately, which was why I never called on her nowadays; I had the feeling that if I turned up expecting a piece of bread and some of her plum jam, she would tell me to clear off. I couldn't think why she looked at me like that; I used to reckon she was friendly, much more interesting than Dibs to listen to.

She said nothing right now, maybe because I forced myself not to look at her. I looked over the side at the road. Then we were at the river crossing and the other kids were looking over the side too, reaching down to see if they could stir the water, wondering if the lorry would

144

get stuck. But the river was shallow today and Mr Kelly whizzed the Reo across.

Even so, there was one bad thing about it—I was reminded of how Mr Wiggins' van sometimes got stuck in the river, and this reminded me of Mr Wiggins, which of course was the bad part. Trying to cheer myself up, I thought there was also a good part—Caroline was coming to the carnival with us and not with Mr Wiggins. She did not care about the lady's man.

I risked looking at her. The risk was that Mrs Kelly might interrupt the look and make me feel bad.

Caroline was wearing a white dress, also a blue cardigan. The cardigan was Mrs Kelly's idea; she said, when Caroline came out to the Reo wearing only the dress, that although it was a sunny morning the day might very likely turn cool by late afternoon. I thought the cardigan was a good idea too, it seemed to go so well with Caroline's hair and eyes, it helped to make her beautiful.

She smiled at me. And Mrs Kelly did not notice the smile because she was looking at the cab, probably trying to send a warning thought to Mr Kelly not to go so fast, the Reo sure was zooming along now.

We zoomed past the old house without chimneys and if Mrs Kelly hadn't been with us I would have told Caroline about that house and why, according to Dad, it had no chimneys. When I was smaller, Dad had told me the house had no chimneys because the people who lived in it did not believe in God. He meant brick chimneys because I had later discovered, when I did some exploring after deciding his explanation did not sound right, that there was actually a tin chimney at the back, like the one on Sam Phelps' place near the wharf. I guessed Dad had been trying to scare us into going to Sunday school. Now that there was no Sunday school, or church, in Calliope Bay, he did not mention God. This suited me, since I had not been fond of Sunday school. Of course I believed in God, and I trembled when I thought of the huge books in the sky, the ones in which anything you did down here, especially anything awful, was described. I did not think of them often, I could go for many months without thinking of them. Actually, I reckoned some things were not put in the books; it seemed impossible for *everything* to be noticed from so far away.

Next we zoomed past the waterfall track, and I remembered that Caroline had still not been to see the waterfall, something had always happened to stop us from going, like her feeling too tired, and now the holidays were nearly over and we still hadn't been. And now that the holidays were nearly over, how much longer would Caroline stay with us? Maybe until my mother came home, whenever that was. It seemed my mother had become sick in the city and did not think she should travel all the way back to Calliope Bay until she was quite well. Naturally, I did not want her to be sick too long, but if it meant Caroline could stay I guessed I could do without a mother for a bit more. Cal was the one who missed her; he kept asking Dad when she would be home. He didn't know when he was lucky, that kid.

Not long after we had zoomed past the store we heard a horn tooting on and on in the distance, then nearer, then right beside us, then behind us. The tooting must have been meant to make us stop, but Mr Kelly slowed the Reo for only a moment before he was zooming on again. From the start, of course, he would have seen who was doing the hooting, but those on the back of the lorry had to wait, though not for long. Because Mr Wiggins' van seemed to flash by, then it was far back down the road as we zoomed on.

Before we turned a bend we had time to see him pull up and change direction. Now he was following us.

'Unusual for Mr Wiggins to be down this way on a Saturday,' said Mrs Kelly.

'I bet he can't catch Dad,' Dibs said. 'He hasn't got a chance now.'

'Your father should have stopped to see what he wanted,' Mrs Kelly told Dibs. She stood, meaning to head for the cab, but the lorry was swaying and she sat down again, almost crashing on Caroline.

I caught sight of the van just before we turned another bend. Mr Wiggins was chasing us, all right.

I looked at Caroline. She didn't notice me looking. Mrs Kelly did; she gazed back at me.

Mr Wiggins chased us all the way to Bonnie Brae. He did pretty well to keep not too far behind, seeing it was mostly such a bendy and narrow road, and we looked into deep and rocky gullies as we zoomed along, we looked at the sea far below, at huge breakers. It was a dangerous road, but Mr Kelly had been over it plenty of times and so had Mr Wiggins. Once or twice I thought Mr Wiggins was catching up, and when this happened I could not help looking anxiously at Caroline, but it turned out all right because the Reo moved ahead again and, like Dibs said, Mr Wiggins didn't have a chance.

Well, I knew why Mr Wiggins had been bound for Calliope Bay and I was more than ever glad now that Mr Kelly had taken no notice of Mrs Kelly's mad idea about bringing Sam Phelps; if we had waited for Sam Phelps, Mr Wiggins would have had time to reach Calliope Bay. And although I was sure Caroline would not have got into his van, I hated imagining how he would have looked as he tried to tempt her into it, I had seen him looking at her plenty of times. I had not always been able to keep Caroline out of sight when Mr Wiggins visited the bay, though I made sure I was near whenever he called at our place, he could never be alone with her. No matter how hard he tried to be alone with her I was always there, watching and listening. I had to admit that he sometimes made her smile, as he made Mrs Kelly and other women smile, and this annoyed me so much I once asked Caroline what exactly Mr Wiggins had said to make her smile, and she told me it was not really what he said, it was the saucy way he said it. I asked her to give me an instance of this, and she thought for a while, then told me he had said he was longing for the day when her slip would show, and she agreed there was nothing funny about such a remark, but she had smiled because of how he said it. I was none the wiser, of course. Heck, I'd been by his van when he had said the same sort of thing to Mrs Kelly and she had smiled too, it must simply be that Mr Wiggins had a secret way of looking at girls and women when he said stupid things, they themselves did not know how he trapped them into smiling. Hypnotism maybe.

We were only about a mile from Bonnie Brae when somebody else joined the chase—Buster Kelly on his Indian. Dibs spotted him first; he saw Buster whizz past Mr Wiggins' van when we were on a straight stretch, then the Indian came roaring up behind the lorry, and there was Buster grinning up at us while we waved. It was fun to see Buster again, he was a decent fellow. I had been very disappointed when he had not arrived home a week ago, as Dibs had said he would, and my disappointment was not only because I couldn't ask him for some ammo for the pistol, or even because I couldn't get a ride on the Indian, it was mostly because he was a decent fellow who did not mind talking to kids and did not get bossy with them.

'Buster, be careful!' Mrs Kelly called when he took both hands off the handlebars to show what a great rider he was.

That only made him clasp both hands above his head as he whizzed along behind us.

'He's a daredevil, that Buster,' Mrs Kelly told Caroline. Caroline smiled. This was the first time she had seen Buster, and I could tell she did not mind smiling when she saw him, she did not try to stop herself from smiling as she did with Mr Wiggins.

Buster was taking risks. The road might be straight here, but it was not very smooth and the Indian did some jumping while he kept his hands above his head. He did not wear a helmet, either. Like all the Kellys, he had ginger hair, and now it was blowing about in the wind, sometimes falling over his eyes. Buster did not care, though; he kept right up behind the Reo, grinning at us most of the time, putting on a horrified look whenever the Indian hit a bump.

He probably would have followed us all the way into Bonnie Brae if his mother had not kept pointing and shouting to him to be careful. Suddenly he frowned back at her, put both hands on the handlebars, took the Indian to the outside of the road and whizzed on past the lorry, out of our sight. We could hear the roar of the Indian fading ahead of us as he sped on to Bonnie Brae.

Back along the road, Mr Wiggins was still in the chase, but not gaining.

'First thing we do at the carnival is look for Buster,' Dibs said. 'Bet I find him first, boy.'

'Bet I do,' I said.

'I'll try that Death Ride place,' Cal said. 'That's where Buster liked going last year.'

'Now we all know where to look,' said Dibs, staring at me as if I hadn't already guessed where to look for Buster, as if he had hoped to keep Buster to himself and Cal.

'Or he might be near the merry-go-round,' Cal said. 'That's where I'll look first.'

He didn't fool me. I had seen the look he gave Dibs. So Cal would rather stay friendly with Dibs than let his own brother get to Buster first! What a brother to have, I thought. Because he did not like Caroline as much as I did, he preferred to be friendly with Dibs. I had been wasting my time ever since that day at the wharf; ever since then I had done my best to be friends with them, going to the caves with them, playing on the rocks with them, looking for swamp frogs with them—and it had made no difference, they still wanted to keep me out of their fun. All right, if they went on like this, I would pay them back. For instance, I could tell Dad about the pistol, I would rather give up the pistol altogether than let those kids have it. Or I might pay them back in another way, there were plenty of ways of paying kids back.

They fell in about the Death Ride, anyhow. Because there was no Death Ride at this year's carnival. I discovered this as soon as we got there, and without running off like Dibs and Cal to look for it. I simply asked a red-coated carnival official how to get to the Death Ride, and he told me there wasn't one because so many motor-bike fellows had crashed last year, there had been a lot of complaints about broken skulls, fractured arms and legs and other injuries.

I decided to wait a few moments at the Reo before looking for Buster. I could check on what Caroline wanted to do. I could be her guide, there was plenty to see in Bonnie Brae at carnival time.

What they did in Bonnie Brae at carnival time was to decorate the town and have something going on in every street. There were seven streets, including the main street, and there was also a paddock at the end of town for horses to race and jump in, so you could reckon that round every corner there would be things to see. Everywhere there were flags and banners and bright posters, and a band played on a platform half-way along the main street. No cars or trucks were allowed in the main street, so the people could wander wherever they wished. People came to Bonnie Brae from miles away at carnival time, from back-country places and from coastal towns like Laxton and Port Crummer and Wakefield.

Mr Kelly had parked the Reo in a side-street, not far from the main street. On the main-street corner was a notice: BONNIE BRAE'S HAPPY DAY. This notice, Mr Kelly told the small Kelly kids before they ran off, could be the landmark for them when they returned to the lorry for lunch. Not that those kids, I reckoned, needed a landmark.

Dad and Mr Kelly did not stay long at the Reo. They said they had to meet some carnival officials and would watch out for us later. Mrs Kelly wanted to know where they were meeting the officials. Mr Kelly said they were all meeting at the Rob Roy hotel, but she must not get the idea that much drinking would be done, only two or three sociable glasses. After all, he said while she gazed at him, he had to keep fit for the drive back to Calliope Bay. He'd better not forget it, she said when he was already on his way, Dad hopping along beside him.

'And what, young man,' she said, turning to me, 'is keeping you here? Aren't you eager to see the carnival sights?'

'Caroline doesn't know her way around,' I said. 'I'll show her where everything is.'

What I *was* anxious about was when Mr Wiggins would find the Reo. He had got caught up in the traffic and we had lost him. But I knew it would not be for long.

'What a splendid plan!' Caroline told me. 'I mustn't miss anything.' I was sure that if Mrs Kelly hadn't been there,

Caroline would have kissed me for being so thoughtful.

Mrs Kelly, who was getting to be as crabby as my mother, seemed about to say what she thought of the plan. Luckily, two excited-looking women greeted her at that moment, and the three of them began gossiping.

'Come on,' I said to Caroline. 'She can catch up with us when she wants to.'

We hurried to the main street where quite a few people were strolling already, enough of them at any rate to make it hard for Mr Wiggins to spot us.

'Did I hear somebody calling you?' Caroline asked as we turned the corner.

'I didn't hear anything,' I said, not looking back. Anyway, plenty of kids were named Harry.

Now that I was with Caroline I was not so keen to look for Buster Kelly. Eventually, I thought, I would meet him. I no longer cared what Dibs and Cal told him, I would easily put him right about their fibs later.

The fellows in charge of the hoopla stalls in this part of the main street were certainly sharp-eyed; not one of them, no matter how busy he was lifting hoops off the things on his table, missed noticing Caroline and me as we went by. 'Come along!' they cried. 'Try your luck! Prizes for everybody!' One of them called to me: 'Come on, young fellow! Bring your sister over! Win a prize for your sister!' That was when I wished I had a sack of money. I would spend it all on Caroline, I would win the biggest prizes and give the lot to her.

With what I did have, even at a penny a throw, I could not hope to win many prizes. Best to hurry on.

Unfortunately, Caroline seemed to want to linger at every stall. And she kept clicking the catch on the little red-and-gold purse that was one of her presents from the *Emma Cranwell* sailors. Her doing that, of course, only made the stall fellows try even harder to tempt her to have a go. If I had not pulled her along by the arm she would not have got past the first stall. She would have made it too easy for Mrs Kelly or Mr Wiggins to find us.

'We can come back here later,' I kept telling her. 'Plenty more things to see.'

This worked for a while, almost to the end of the first block. Then we reached the stall where there was a big fellow with curly yellow hair and very tanned skin and the whitest teeth I had ever seen, and he held out the hoops to Caroline with a smile that was so goofy I felt like snatching the hoops from him and throwing them away.

'We can come back later—' I began.

'Oh, what a lovely vase!' Caroline said, moving to the stall before I could grab her. 'That would make a nice welcome-home present for Aunt Janet.'

She had her purse open. She was holding out a note to the stall man.

'A little suggestion,' he said as he handed her six hoops. 'Try for one of the smaller prizes first. That way you'll get your hand in.'

'You hold this, Harry,' Caroline said, giving me the purse. 'Then you can have a turn.'

'Don't be too long,' I said, looking along the street.

Some of the strollers moved to the stall when they saw Caroline with the hoops. I saw nobody I recognised.

Well, my beautiful cousin won the vase. She also won a box of chocolates, a plaster puppy, a doll and several trinkets. She was the luckiest thrower at the stall. I didn't see every throw she made, because I was so busy looking up and down the street, but I did notice a couple of times when the stall man seemed to help the hoops settle over items. It was queer too that none of the twelve hoops I threw settled over anything, I was right out of luck.

'A little suggestion,' said the stall man when I at last got Caroline to quit buying hoops. 'I'd be happy for you to leave your prizes here while you're looking at the other attractions. You can pick them up later.'

'That so nice of you,' Caroline said, close to him, smiling up at his teeth. 'We'll call for them on our way back.'

'I'll be waiting,' he said, turning on another of his goofy smiles.

'Wasn't that exciting, Harry!' she cried. She gave me some coins. 'These are for you. For bringing me luck.' Before I could dodge, she kissed me. 'And that as well.'

I knew my face was red. She should not kiss me when so many people were around. Heck, she was so excited it was a wonder she hadn't kissed the fellow at the stall.

I said nothing. I put the coins in my pocket, not looking at them.

'Oh, I must go there,' she said a few yards further on.

I thought she was looking at the Town Hall. The notices said there was a pioneer parade inside, with prizes for the biggest beards.

It turned out she was looking at the *Ladies* place beside the Town Hall.

'Will you wait for me while I have a weewee, Harry?' she said. 'Then we'll look for some more excitement.'

'I'll wait,' I said, keeping my hand in my pocket, jingling the coins. I watched her follow several other women into that place, she would have to queue.

How much had she given me? I couldn't tell by feeling the coins. But I did not want to take them from my pocket because I had seen three tough-looking boys staring at me from not far away. These boys, I remembered, were at the hoopla stall when Caroline was having so much luck; they probably saw her giving me the coins. They might even have seen the notes in her purse and, like me, been surprised that she had so much money. I must keep an eye out for these boys as well as for—

My arm was grabbed. I could not get my hand from my pocket so I could use it to try to struggle free.

I was spun round, still held tightly.

And guess who was holding me. Uncle Pember!

That, at any rate, was who I thought was holding me. I did not think it for longer than a second. Because then I recognised Mr Wiggins behind the big black beard.

Mr Wiggins was so hairy at ordinary times, with his moustache and long sideboards and thick swish-back, that the beard seemed to close up his face altogether, leaving glaring eyes and fierce teeth as all that I could see of what was really him.

'Hello, young fellow,' he said in a friendly voice that made me shiver. 'Enjoying the carnival?'

'Yes thanks, Mr Wiggins,' I said.

He let go of my arm. I rubbed it.

'Waiting for the parade?' he asked, looking past me at the Town Hall. 'Think I stand a chance of winning the beard contest, son?' He looked up and down the street.

'It's quite a large beard,' I said. My voice too was friendly. 'I thought they'd have to be real beards.'

He had not heard me, he was so busy looking around. 'What's that, son?'

'They needn't be real beards, eh?' I hoped Caroline had not reached the head of the queue yet.

'No, no,' he said, looking everywhere except at me.

'I'm waiting for my brother,' I said. 'We're going in to see the pioneer parade. Haven't seen my brother lately, have you, Mr Wiggins?'

'Your brother?' he said. 'No, no.' Then he did look at me. 'By the way, Harry,' he said, 'have you seen your cousin? Where would Caroline be?'

'I think she went to the Rob Roy hotel with Dad and Mr Kelly,' I said. 'Think they wanted her to meet some carnival officials.'

'Is that so?' he said. 'Is that where she is?'

'I *think* so,' I said. 'I think they said they were going there.' Now would he head for the Rob Roy, two blocks back along the main street?

He looked at his watch. 'That reminds me. Some officials I want to talk to. Probably find them along there. Enjoy yourself, son.' He went off quickly in the direction of the Rob Roy.

'Sorry you had to wait so long, Harry,' Caroline told me about three seconds later. 'There was such a big queue. Now where shall we go?'

I glanced across the street, but the three tough-looking boys had vanished. I guessed they had seen me talking to Mr Wiggins and had been scared away.

'How about we go along the end and see what's happening at the jumping paddock?' I said.

'All right,' said Caroline. 'Harry,' she said the next moment, 'was Dibs' brother—you know, the one on the motorbike—was he coming to the carnival?'

'He's around somewhere,' I said. 'We might see him at the jumping paddock. Dibs and Cal went to look for him. They might have found him by now.'

'He's very daring, isn't he?' she said.

'Yes, he is,' I said.

She was walking faster, which was all right since it got us away sooner from the Town Hall part of town.

We were not far from the jumping paddock when I saw six cowboys standing 3-2-1 in a pyramid, the three at the foot of the pyramid pulling faces to show how heavy the others were, the others grinning to show how easy it was.

Caroline went up close to the pyramid. She seemed to enjoy going close to things, like faces.

She clicked her purse. I told her to wait until they began turning somersaults. I said it was not very clever to make a pyramid unless they also turned somersaults.

They did not turn somersaults, though. What they did was wink and grin at Caroline, even the bottom three.

Caroline waved back.

'They'll get tired, standing like that all day,' I said, squeezing her hand and pulling her along through the crowd.

'They weren't doing it for themselves, Harry,' she said.

'They were doing it for the life-saving team. Didn't you see the sign?'

'They should *do* something if they expect people to give them money,' I said. 'What's so clever about standing like that?'

'Poor Harry,' she said.

'Heck!' I said.

'I know why you said that,' she said. 'Because you're not having fun. Why aren't you having fun, Harry?'

'I *am* having fun,' I said, stopping because Caroline stopped. I tugged her hand. She moved only a few steps. What made her stop, it seemed, was the band beginning to play back along the main street. She turned to look.

'We can see them later,' I said. 'They'll be playing all day.'

'Mmm?' she said. She seemed to be forgetting me.

'It *is* fun,' I said, studying the faces in the crowd. 'If you think I'm not having fun, Caroline, it's because—'

'They're playing *Painting the Clouds with Sunshine*,' she said.

'They must have seen the sky,' I said, huffy because she was forgetting me. 'It's not so blue now.'

'My poor Harry,' she said, looking sadly at me. She seemed to have guessed I was too busy watching for enemies to enjoy the carnival.

'It's because school starts on Monday,' I said. 'I keep thinking of it. Wish I didn't.'

'You'll have your schoolmates to play with,' she said. 'Think of me, Harry. I won't have anybody to play with all day.'

159

'We can have fun after school,' I said. 'It's still sunny when we finish school.'

'And during the day I can write more of my autobiography,' she said. 'While you're doing your lessons, Harry, I'll be writing the story of my life.'

I was nearly going to tell her I'd seen Uncle Pember outside the Town Hall, but that would have meant mentioning Mr Wiggins, and I knew Caroline would rather I did not mention *him*.

I said: 'I'd like to hear some more of your autobiography. Especially about your uncle. The one with the black beard.'

Caroline said: 'Uncle Pember? Yes, he had an amazing secret.'

I said: 'I know. You told me. That's what I'd like to hear about. Can't we skip some of the earlier parts of your autobiography and get to the secret bit?'

Caroline said: 'It would spoil it, Harry. You must be patient.'

I said: 'If I told you *my* amazing secret would you tell me Uncle Pember's?'

Caroline laughed. 'No, you'll have to be patient, Harry.'

She did not believe I had a secret. Even if I told her what it was, she would think I was making it up to try to get her to tell me about Uncle Pember.

We had stopped at a tent near the jumping paddock. Caroline was first to stop, and this was because a boxer was on a platform outside the tent. He had a broken nose and oily black hair and a hairy body and he looked very tough.

He was bobbing about and every now and then pretending to give an invisible opponent some hefty swipes with his boxing gloves. A sign on the platform said this boxer, Kid Savage, would accept challenges, and anybody who lasted three rounds with him would get a prize.

Caroline and a few other people seemed to enjoy watching him. I got tired of seeing him hurt invisible opponents, but Caroline did not move when I touched her arm. So I went along to where a kid was hitting a bopping-bag at one end of the platform. Every time he hit the bag it bounced back at him and he had to hit it again quickly or dodge.

'How about a turn?' I asked the kid after glancing along to make sure Caroline was still watching the boxer.

The kid let me have a turn. I began bopping that bag and bopping it harder every time it bounced back at me, and I imagined there was a face on the bag, and you can guess whose face it was, and you can guess how that made me bop it even harder. I ignored the kid when he said it was his turn, I just went on bopping that bag. I got angry at it. I was so angry I missed hitting it properly, and it bounced back and hit me. And this made me even angrier. My nose was bleeding, but I went on bopping. Then the other kid pulled me away and I stood watching him, puffing, wiping my nose on my shirt-sleeve. My nose soon stopped bleeding, but it certainly made a mess of my sleeve. I rolled up the sleeve.

Then I remembered Caroline and I hurried back to where I'd left her, but she had gone. Kid Savage was still in action, other people were still watching him. But Caroline had gone.

I looked for her among the groups outside other side-shows, I went back along the main street as far as the Town Hall, I went down two side-streets before returning to the Kid Savage tent. And all the time I kept asking myself why she had disappeared without telling me, she must have seen me at the bopping-bag, she must have known I was only there because I was filling in time while she watched the boxer. Yet she had left me!

Or maybe she had not seen me at the bopping-bag. Maybe she thought I had gone on to the jumping paddock. That was where I had better look.

When I got to the jumping paddock, though, it was harder than ever to find her. There seemed more people watching from the rails round the paddock than there were back in the main street. I had thought they would be watching horses going over fences and racing; they weren't, they were watching motor-bikes being wheeled into the paddock. When I got there the motor-bikes were silent, as if the fellows wheeling them were going to have a pushing race. Then, one after another, the fellows started up the engines, and suddenly there was so much noise I could no longer hear the band, and more people left the main street and came to the jumping paddock, and pretty soon I was surrounded. I guessed I might as well watch the race, Caroline should be able to look after herself for a while.

The race was fun, sure enough. The four motor-bikes went very fast, and those fellows were good riders because they all got round the paddock several times without falling off or crashing. There was plenty of bumping, plenty of skidding, and all the time I kept thinking a rider was bound to fall and hurt himself, but there was no serious accident until the third race and by then I had forgotten Caroline. I remembered her during the silence that came as the two riders hurt in the accident were carried from the paddock. I suddenly thought: Where's Caroline?

I got away from the crowd by the rails—and met Cal and Dibs. They were running towards the main street, but stopped when I shot in front of them.

'*You* didn't find Buster!' Dibs shouted. 'We found him first, boy.'

'I didn't look for him,' I said. 'Where you going?'

'Buster's on next!' Dibs said, very excited. 'We got to find Dad. Buster says Dad will want to see him ride through the burning hoop. Come on, Cal!'

I ran after them. 'Is that what Buster's going to do?' I asked when I caught up with Dibs. 'Is Buster going to ride through a burning hoop?'

'He's on next,' Dibs said, running into the main street. 'Come on, Cal! I know where Dad will be!'

I ran with them for a block. Then I saw Caroline and I stopped running.

Caroline was hiding from Mr Wiggins.

I could tell this straight away. Because I no sooner saw Caroline in a shop doorway than I saw Mr Wiggins, still with his whiskers, walking slowly along the street, staring everywhere, looking for somebody, looking for Caroline.

He saw me. He walked towards me.

This was all right. It meant he had his back to Caroline.

I had arrived just in time.

'Hello, Mr Wiggins,' I said before he could speak. 'Did you win a prize? I haven't seen another beard as big as yours. I bet it's the biggest beard at the carnival.'

The band was playing nearby, so he probably didn't hear all I said. In any case, he did not mention the beard when he spoke. He said: 'Your cousin wasn't at the Rob Roy, son. Have you seen her lately?' Again his voice was friendly. Again I was not fooled.

I said: 'Buster Kelly is going to ride through a burning hoop.' I pointed towards the jumping paddock. 'Suppose that's where Caroline is, Mr Wiggins. Everybody will be watching Buster Kelly.'

His eyes shone through all the hair and he nodded. He walked a few steps, then turned to ask me: 'Why aren't *you* watching him?'

'I'm getting Dad so's he can watch,' I said.

He moved on up the street. He still looked about him. But now he was past Caroline's doorway. She was safe.

She must have seen how I had saved her, but she said nothing about Mr Wiggins when I went across to her. In fact, she acted surprised when I greeted her, as if I were the last person she expected to be greeted by. She was carrying a plaster puppy that looked very much like the one she had hooped at the stall earlier in the day.

'Harry!' she cried when I was right next to her. 'Harry, where did you go?'

'Where did *you* go?' I asked.

'I met Mrs Kelly and we looked at the stalls, then we went back to the lorry,' she said. 'I collected my prizes on the way. But I forgot the puppy, so I had to go back for it.

It will be a nice present for Mrs Kelly.' She held the puppy up for me to admire, but I ignored it.

'I looked everywhere for you,' I said.

I saw Dad and Mr Kelly go by. They were following Dibs and Cal. Dad was moving as fast as the others; he did not let his crutch slow him.

Caroline did not see them go by. I did not point them out in case she wanted to follow them.

'I couldn't find you anywhere,' I told her.

'Fancy not finding me!' she said, cuddling the puppy. 'Wasn't that strange?'

Yes, it was strange, but I did not say so. Something in her voice made me think she hadn't really minded my not finding her, she had been happy without me.

'Strange, wasn't it, Harry?' she said, and she looked at the puppy more than she did at me.

I said nothing.

'Wasn't it, Harry?' she said.

'Oh, sure,' I said.

The band had stopped playing, so the noise of a motorbike along at the jumping paddock seemed extra-loud. It got louder and louder. Then it stopped, and there was the noise of the crowd cheering. I could guess what had happened, and now I wished I had stayed at the paddock instead of looking for Caroline. Finding her and saving her did not seem to have done me much good, all it meant was that I had missed what was probably one of the most exciting parts of the carnival. Blow Caroline, I thought.

'I wonder why they're cheering,' she said. 'Shall we go and see, Harry?' But she did not move from the doorway.

Was she not really hiding? Was she waiting for somebody?

'It's too late,' I told her. 'That was Buster going through the burning hoop. He won't do it again.'

'You mean Dibs' brother?' she said, looking very surprised. 'You mean the one who followed us? *He* rode through a burning hoop? Why didn't you tell me he'd do that, Harry?'

Now she did move from the doorway.

I did not follow her. I said: 'I told you he'd be at the jumping paddock. I told you that before.'

'Not about the burning hoop,' she said, stopping and looking back at me.

'I didn't know that bit myself then,' I told her, staying in the doorway. 'Too late to see him now. We've missed him.'

'Come on, Harry,' she said. 'He might do it again.'

'He won't,' I said, and my earlier feeling of sadness had turned to something gloomier, almost as though I were in for another of my black times, which would be ahead of schedule.

Would she leave me? Would she find the others?

I looked at her.

She looked back at me, seeming puzzled.

But those questions did not matter, after all. Because that was when the first drops of rain fell, and the drops got heavier, and the rain went on and on and washed out Bonnie Brae's happy day.

Even without the rain, though, the rest of the day would have been awful. In fact, it had turned awful before the rain. And I knew who was to blame. That damned Mr Wiggins.

10

'AND NOW,' said Fat Norman, chalking a cross beside the next word on the blackboard list, 'somebody give me an example of a *catastrophe*.' He stared at us, his stare settled on me.

I put up my hand. 'Please, sir.'

'Yes?' said Fat Norman, nodding to me.

'Please, sir,' I said. 'Please, sir, if somebody didn't like Mr Phelps and wanted to pay him back for doing something bad, he might shift the rails on the wharf and Mr Phelps wouldn't notice and next thing Sydney Bridge Upside Down would pull the wagon off the side of the wharf and it would crash into the sea. Mr Phelps would be drowned and so would his horse, and the wagon would sink to the bottom. Please, sir, all that would be a catastrophe.'

Fat Norman waited, making sure I had finished. Then he said: 'That seems more an example of revenge. What is your name?'

'Harry Baird,' I said. 'Please, sir, *wouldn't* that be

an example of a catastrophe?'

He watched me for a moment or so. 'I suppose it will do,' he said. He turned to the blackboard, chalked a new cross. 'Now who can give me an example of a *predicament*?'

I put up my hand. 'Please, sir.'

Though I was first to answer, Fat Norman did not choose me, he did not even look at me, he waited until another hand went up.

This, I thought, was typical of our new teacher. Besides being forgetful—he had three times asked me my name in the three days since school had started—he acted as if he sometimes did not know the answers to the questions he asked. Spelling, sums, geography—any of these things could seem harder for Fat Norman than they were for me. For instance, I had mentioned in geography class the day before how our previous teacher, Mr Dalloway, had once said that living in Calliope Bay was like living on the edge of the world; many people, Mr Dalloway had said, must have felt they were about to fall off. I asked Fat Norman if he'd had this feeling yet. How long did you have to be in Calliope Bay, I wondered, before you had it? Fat Norman said he hadn't had this feeling. In any case, he said, he did not think it was a geography topic. He took it for granted, he said, that we all knew the world was round. Which, of course, had nothing to do with it. You would never have caught Mr Dalloway hinting at anything like that, *he* knew we weren't dumb.

It was not as if I had been a complete stranger to Fat Norman on the first day at school, either. We had met at his house—it used to be Mr Dalloway's—on the Saturday before school began. I had taken him his mail. His mail was a letter. Dad, who had collected it from the store when we called there on our way back from Bonnie Brae, said it would be a friendly gesture to the new teacher if we delivered this letter, he said the teacher was bound to arrive some time during the week-end, he would have to if he reckoned on starting at school on the Monday. We did not know until we got home, of course, that Fat Norman had arrived while we were at the carnival. He had driven to Calliope Bay in his own car, and he had brought his wife and three kids with him. All the Normans were fat. The eldest kid was a boy about Cal's age, but he certainly didn't look as if he had done as much running around as Cal, he looked too fat to run anywhere. This kid had a good stare at me when I took the letter along, but he said nothing. He was on the front veranda with his father, helping to empty one of the packing-cases, when I got there. Fat Norman thanked me for bringing the letter but did not invite me in out of the rain. Maybe he would have acted differently if it had been an important letter; I knew it was not an important letter because he screwed it up after glancing at it. If it had been important he would have read it carefully, then read it again, several times maybe, the way Dad had read *his* letter. The important thing about Dad's letter, I discovered after tea, was that my mother still hadn't decided when she would return home. Although she was recovering from her illness, she wrote, she did not think she was yet well enough to travel, and of course it was a shame she couldn't be home to see the kids off to school but she knew they would understand the position if he explained it to them. 'So that's the position,' said Dad after he had read the letter to us. 'She's taking her time about it. In no hurry to see us fellows again, eh?' He smiled after he said that, but I knew he was worried, he had not read any of her earlier letters as often as he had read this one, as if hoping every time he read it to find something new, something that might explain why she was in no hurry to see us again. He kept looking at Caroline too; he seemed to expect her to help in some way, yet when she said she was sure my mother would be home soon Dad did not really stop worrying, I could tell he was only pretending to be cheerful. And next morning, Sunday morning, I heard him talking to Caroline in her bedroom (he had taken her a cup of tea), and he was saying things like 'Janet's never done it before' and 'Janet knows how Cal frets for her', so I guessed he was still anxious, and for the first time I felt a bit anxious myself, though I didn't know why I should feel anxious, I didn't care how long she stayed away, I certainly didn't. Especially, I kept reminding myself, if it means Caroline has to go when *she*'s home again. Because by then, of course, I had forgiven Caroline for seeming to act oddly to me at the carnival. I had decided Mr Wiggins was the only one to blame for the carnival not being as exciting as I had expected it to be. I had also decided that I hated Mr Wiggins. I spent so much of Sunday thinking how I hated the butcher that I even forgot how close school was. I later realised, in fact, that I was in a *predicament* over Mr Wiggins and his annoying habits. I realised this when I saw the word on the blackboard and would have given it to Fat Norman as an example (changing the names) if he had nodded to me. He hadn't nodded to me. He had not even looked at me.

Ordinarily, I would probably have gone on thinking how stupid Fat Norman was and no wonder the only job he could get was in Calliope Bay. But I did not go on thinking like this. Because I suddenly thought of a way out of the predicament. The thought was so surprising that I blinked, I could no longer see the words on the blackboard.

Once I got used to this thought, though, I felt better. I didn't mind Fat Norman then. Oh, *Mr* Norman. I wasn't the one who called him Fat Norman the first day of school. It was his own fat son, the kid named Bruce, who called him Fat Norman when we were talking at morning play-time. If it was good enough for his own son to call him Fat Norman, we reckoned, it was good enough for us. 'That's reasonable,' said Bruce Norman, 'but don't let him hear you using that term, he turns maniacal if he hears himself called that.' 'Turns what?' asked Dibs. 'Turns murderously angry,' said Bruce Norman. 'What do you know?' Dibs said to me. I hesitated, then, in the old friendly way, said to Dibs: 'What do you know?' Anyway, once I'd had this thought about my predicament, I didn't mind so much that the teacher was stupid, he could be *Mr* Norman for all I cared. Not that I took much notice of what he said for the rest of the lesson. I was staring at him, I could see his mouth opening and shutting; but I did not hear a word he said.

I was planning on making a quick getaway after the lesson, the last of the day. I would shoot home, see how

Caroline was doing, then keep my promise to go up to the cave with Cal and Dibs.

But Mr Norman delayed me.

'I say, Harry Baird!' he called as I headed for the door. 'I want a word with you.'

'Please, sir?' I said when I reached his table.

'I've been wondering about the example you gave,' he said.

'Please, sir?' I said.

He frowned. 'Your example of a catastrophe. I've been troubled by it. Was it based on something you'd overheard? Is there anybody who would want to take revenge on Mr Phelps in that fashion?'

'I made it up,' I said. 'I thought it would be a good catastrophe.'

'Don't misunderstand me, Harry,' he said. 'I mean, has Mr Phelps done anything bad that you know of? Never mind the nature of any possible revenge. *Has* he done anything bad?'

I reflected. I twisted my face. Then I said: 'I don't think so, sir.'

'Nothing?' he asked.

'I don't think so,' I said. Why was he making such a fuss about something that was none of his business?

'You know, Harry,' he said. 'I am not only a teacher, I am the father of young children. You can understand that I have to consider my own children's welfare, can't you?'

'Eh?' I said.

'I think you're old enough to understand that no father wants his children to be in danger,' he said. 'If there is somebody who has done something bad, a father would want to know all about it. In case such a person was a danger to his children. Do you understand me?'

'Sure,' I said. What a strange fellow, I thought.

'But you don't *think* he's done anything?' he asked. 'Aren't you certain?'

'He hasn't done anything,' I said.

'Then why did you say he had?'

'I was only making it up—for an example.'

'It seemed to come out very easily for something that was made up. Not only that, there was the tone of your voice. But I'll take your word for it. You made it up?'

'Sure, sir. What say you ask Dad or Mr Kelly? They'll tell you about Sam Phelps. If you don't believe me, sir, you could ask them.'

'I believe you,' he said.

'Mr Phelps is a nice old man,' I said.

'I said I believe you.' He was frowning again. 'Perhaps I misunderstood. Perhaps I shouldn't have asked you...'

I waited for him to make up his mind.

'Very well, you may go,' he said, turning his back to me.

A strange fellow, I thought, running out into the playground. He had better not ask Dad or Mr Kelly questions like that about Sam Phelps, they might bop him for having the cheek to suggest that such a nice old man could do wrong.

I'll have to warn the other kids about Fat Norman, I thought.

Cal and Dibs had not waited for me. But I could catch

up with them before they went to the cave, Dibs was bound to be stopping off for a piecey at his home. Anyway, I had something I wanted to think about; I must do some pretty careful thinking. I'd walk home, I wouldn't run.

Not far along the road I heard the sound of Buster Kelly's Indian starting up. Then Buster came speeding towards me. He was heading for the river crossing.

I waved to him and he stopped beside me, the Indian's engine chugging noisily.

'What you doing here, Buster?' I said. 'I didn't know you'd be here today.' This was his second unexpected visit to Calliope Bay since the carnival. He had come on Sunday too; that was when he was introduced to Caroline. He and Dad and Caroline had a good talk on Sunday afternoon.

'I had to pick up some gear from home,' he told me now. 'Brought your cousin a telegram too. It was waiting for her at the store. Came yesterday, so I reckoned I'd better hurry across with it.'

'What did it say, Buster?' I asked, worried. 'Was it bad news, do you know?'

'Don't reckon so,' Buster said. 'Caroline didn't seem to mind when she read it.'

'That's good, eh?' I said. Buster had his shirt-sleeves rolled high. His freckled arms and hands looked very strong.

'What did you say?' he said above the motor-bike noise.

'I said it's good about Caroline not caring what was in the telegram,' I said. Buster's fingers, outstretched on the handlebars, looked very tough. I moved closer to the motor-bike. I said: 'Can I ask you something, Buster?'

'What do you want to know, Harry?' He was a decent fellow, he never minded talking to me.

'I'm a bit sick of being so skinny,' I said. 'What's the best way of building muscles?'

He laughed. 'You're not too skinny, Harry. Better than being a fatso, boy.'

'I don't want to be *fat*,' I said. 'Wouldn't mind being a bit stronger, though.'

'Are you thinking of taking up boxing?' he asked. He threw a punch close to my left ear. 'Hey, you're a calm one. Why didn't you duck?'

'I knew you wouldn't make it land, Buster,' I said. 'I saw it coming. I knew which way to duck. If I'd wanted to, eh?'

'You'd make a good boxer, Harry,' he said, tapping me lightly on the chest. 'Who would you fight? My old mate Kid Savage?'

'Well, I wasn't really thinking of being a boxer,' I told him. 'I just thought I should be a bit stronger. Feel this.' I flexed my arm so that he could feel the muscle. 'Not very big, is it?'

'It's not bad,' he said, smiling. 'More like a peanut than a muscle, I suppose. But you can't expect to have enormous muscles at your age. Wouldn't be natural.'

'Anyway, how could I become a bit tougher?' I asked.

He looked at me thoughtfully for a few moments. Then he said: 'What about press-ups? Do you do press-ups?'

'No,' I said. 'Do you think they would help, Buster?'

'I reckon so,' he said. 'If you do twenty-five press-ups

a day, you'll probably toughen your arms. But I wouldn't worry too much about it, boy. You're okay for your age. I was no tougher than you when I was your age. It's hard work that's turned me into a fine figure of a bloke.' He grinned.

'Thanks, Buster,' I said. 'I'll try press-ups. I'll try twenty-five a day. See how I get on.'

'Don't overdo it,' he said, making the engine roar, ready to take off. 'I said don't overdo it, don't strain yourself, Harry.'

I stepped aside. 'I'll be all right, Buster,' I said. 'When you coming back?'

'Maybe at the week-end,' he said. 'I'll see how the work goes. So long!' He waved as he roared off towards the river crossing.

I watched till he was out of sight. I had certainly been lucky to meet Buster. What he had told me fitted in great with my plans, everything would go smoothly now. Would the press-ups be enough? I might try some extra running as well. Say I got up early every day and ran to the river and back, or along to the works then back to the river then back home for breakfast—I could do the press-ups first, then go for a run. Later I could go for longer runs. I could do more press-ups. All that would be bound to make me tougher.

I pushed out my chest, pressed back my elbows, felt stronger already. Then I got down on my mark, ready-steady, waited for it, go! Shot off for home, bare feet hardly touching the ground as I whizzed along.

Dibs called to me when I got as far as his house. He was

on the veranda with Cal. They each had a piecey, thick with plum jam.

'Where you been?' asked Dibs. 'We're going to the cave. You coming? Or you staying with Caroline?'

'I'm coming,' I said. That bread and jam looked good; I was very fond of Mrs Kelly's plum jam, but it was ages since I had tasted any of it. 'I was talking to Buster,' I told Dibs.

'Not all the time you weren't,' Dibs said, sounding suspicious. 'He only just left your place. Said he'd taken Caroline a telegram. That's what he said, wasn't it, Cal?'

'I know about the telegram,' I said before Cal could chip in. 'Buster told me about the telegram.' I could bop Dibs. Trying to make the telegram sound like a secret his brother had specially told *him* about!

'So where were you before that?' Dibs asked.

I remembered Fat Norman; it seemed a long time since I had been listening to him. 'I was with the teacher,' I said. I lowered my voice. 'I'll tell you something about Fat Norman when we get to the cave. Boy, he's a strange fellow! Wait for me, you kids. I'll tell Caroline where I'm going.'

'Why tell her?' Dibs asked.

I didn't reply, I was on my way.

I found Caroline on her bed. She was not asleep, but she looked drowsy. She was lying on her back on the counterpane, her dress rumpled above her knees. Though she seemed to be looking straight at me, her head on a pillow, she said an odd thing, she said: 'Who's that?'

I moved to the bed. 'It's Harry. What's the matter, Caroline? Are you sick?'

'Not sick, Harry,' she said, taking my hand when I sat on the edge of the bed. 'Little sleepy, that's all, Harry.' She let go of my hand; she had not moved her head or her legs.

'Are you sure you're not sick?' I asked.

'Just sleepy,' she said. 'I'll get up soon and peel the potatoes.'

'Don't do that,' I told her. 'You heard what Dad said last time. He said you mustn't do the potatoes again. It wasn't only because you cut yourself, Caroline. He thinks you needn't bother with things like potatoes.'

'I know,' she said. 'Uncle Frank's very kind.'

I looked around the room, wondering if it would be wise to leave her alone, she might really be sick. On the dressing-table and shelves were some of her presents and prizes—vases, dolls, little ornaments. In the wardrobe were her dresses. It was her room, all right; it was no longer my parents' room. And I didn't mind.

'I was talking to Buster,' I said. 'On my way home from school.'

She did not speak. I looked at her. She had closed her eyes.

'Harry!' It was Dibs shouting.

Caroline's eyes were still shut.

'Think I'll go to the cave for a while,' I said. 'Do you mind if I go to the cave, Caroline?'

'You go,' she said, not opening her eyes, not seeming to care what I did.

'Will you be all right?' I asked.

She nodded, eyes still shut.

So I left her. I went out to Dibs and Cal. I didn't want to, but I had to.

II

THE SUNDAY before Mr Wiggins died, I was at the wharf with Cal and Dibs and Bruce Norman. Bruce Norman, who had turned out to be not a bad kid, was trying to catch up with all the things in Calliope Bay we other kids had taken for granted for years. He seemed specially eager to talk to Sam Phelps about Sydney Bridge Upside Down, reckoned he had always been interested in horses and would very much like to know more about the old fellow's crock. Unfortunately, said Bruce, his father had warned him never to go near Sam Phelps, and because of his father's maniacal behaviour when angry he did not dare disobey, at least not unless there was no risk of his father finding out. In that case, I told him, the best day would be Sunday, when Sam Phelps was not as busy as he was on week-days, and the best time on Sunday would be mid-afternoon when, as Bruce had once mentioned, his father usually snoozed for two hours after an enormous dinner. Bruce said this sounded a crafty plan. So we met him near the works after he'd had his share of the dinner and we took him across the beach to the rocks, then across the rocks to the wharf. He was amazed by the funny steps, got annoyed with Dibs and me when we couldn't tell him how come the steps had been put in the wrong way up. One of the fairly interesting things about him, I thought, was that even though he was a fat kid who would not be much good in a fight he was not scared to let older kids see when he was annoyed. Another thing: although he was apparently very clever, he was not against kids having fun, he did not act superior, the way Susan Prosser had, he would never tell tales. So we didn't mind taking him to the wharf. In fact, it was good going to places we knew well—such as the beach and the rocks and the wharf—with somebody who did not know them well, it was like seeing everything for the first time, the way it had been with Caroline in the beginning.

'Mr Phelps must be having a snooze too,' I said after we'd discovered there was nobody on the sunny wharf. 'Bet he doesn't eat as much as your father, Bruce. He's skinny as a rake, old Mr Phelps.'

'So's his horse,' said Dibs. He asked Bruce: 'Have you had a good look at Sydney Bridge Upside Down?'

'I've seen him in the distance a few times,' Bruce said. 'Pulling the wagon. Seemed rather a large wagon for such an elderly steed to be pulling. I want to ask Mr Phelps about that point. Whether he thinks there is any cruelty in it.'

'Better not be cheeky to him,' I said. 'He might tell your father.'

'He'd do well to avoid Fat Norman,' said Bruce. 'Not that I'll be cheeky to him. He may have good reasons for keeping the crock working.'

'Sydney Bridge Upside Down mightn't be as ancient as he looks,' I told Bruce. 'He doesn't get very sweaty when he's pulling the wagon. And I remember the time Mr Phelps let Caroline have a ride. She sat in Sydney Bridge Upside Down's hollow, and it was all right—nothing broke.'

'What do you think of Caroline?' Dibs asked Bruce.

I stopped. We had been strolling towards the sea end of the wharf because Bruce had turned in that direction and we had kept up with him; he apparently fancied a walk in the sun before looking for Sam Phelps.

The others stopped when I stopped. Dibs glanced at me. Cal and Bruce didn't.

'I'd have to talk to her before I could answer that,' Bruce told Dibs. 'Why do you ask? Do you want to tell me something about her?'

'No, I was only wondering,' said Dibs. 'Like, you've seen more grown-up girls than us. I was wondering if you thought she was prettier than other grown-up girls you've seen.'

Bruce shrugged. 'I take little notice of girls, grown-up or otherwise.'

Dibs looked at me and grinned, as if he had just proved something. He turned to Bruce: 'Same as me, boy. I reckon it's sissy to take much notice of girls. Girls are no good, eh?'

Bruce did not reply. He had seen that Cal had gone to the wharf edge and was staring down at the water;

he went across to Cal, knelt beside him.

'Are you calling me a sissy?' I asked Dibs.

'What?' said Dibs. He was playing dumb. He was also making sure he stayed in the middle of the wharf.

'Who's a sissy?' I asked.

Bruce looked across, asked: 'Do you do much fishing here?'

Dibs took a few steps before he remembered not to move too far from the middle of the wharf. He told Bruce: 'We fish when old Phelps lets us. Plenty of fish down there, boy.'

'What sort of fish?' asked Bruce.

Dibs said loudly: 'Millions of herrings, boy. We can use the herrings for bait. We can catch snapper and gurnard and barracoutas and kingfish. Barracoutas are the ones to fight. Once I caught a huge couta and he nearly bit my leg off, he was so angry.' He glanced at me, said in the same loud voice: 'Remember that time, Harry?'

'No,' I said. 'What was that you said about being a sissy?'

'Have you got any lines, Bruce?' Dibs called.

'I'm afraid not,' Bruce said.

'You can buy them at the store,' Dibs said. 'Or you can borrow one of ours. Dad's got plenty of lines. He doesn't care when we use them. Specially if we catch a couta or a kingie. What do you reckon, Harry? Shall we come fishing here with Bruce next Saturday? Or after school one day.'

I said: 'What I want to know—'

Dibs called: 'Make sure you don't fall in, Bruce! The currents are dangerous down there. Ask Cal. Cal fell in

183

during the holidays. He was drowning. Harry saved him. Remember that time, Harry?'

Bruce turned to Cal. I could see Cal flapping his hands and bobbing his head as he told Bruce how he had nearly drowned.

I said to Dibs: 'What I want to tell you, boy, is that it's stupid to call anybody a sissy without knowing what you're talking about. Here, I want to show you something.'

He stopped moving away, watched me closely.

'Feel this,' I told him, flexing my arm. 'Go on, feel it.'

He felt it.

'Not a bad muscle, eh?' I said.

'Not bad,' he said. 'That's a pretty big muscle, Harry. Yes, that's a big one, all right.'

'Know how long it's taken me to get it that big?'

'How long?'

'Eleven days,' I said.

'Only eleven days?' he said, astonished.

'That's all,' I said. 'A few more days, boy, and I don't know *how* big it will be. Not only that, either. I feel stronger all over.'

'How come?' asked Dibs. 'You eating more meat or something?'

'No,' I said. 'Training.'

'Training for what?'

'Nothing. Just training.'

'You must be training for something!'

'Well, I might go in for boxing when I'm older,' I said. 'Buster reckons I'd make a good boxer, he reckons I could be as good as his friend Kid Savage. But I want my body to be strong before I go in for boxing. I want to be as hard as nails, I want to be able to fight anybody, anybody in the world. That's why I've been doing all these press-ups, all this running. Part of my training.'

'I didn't know you were doing that, Harry,' said Dibs. He sounded very impressed.

'If you get up early enough any morning you'll see me belting along the road,' I said.

'What do you know?' said Dibs.

'That's right,' I said. 'What do you know?'

'Anyway, Harry,' he said, 'I didn't mean you were a sissy when I said that to Bruce. That wasn't what I meant.'

'It's okay,' I said. 'Remember, though. Remember this muscle.'

'Yes, I sure will,' he said. He was studying my arms and legs. 'What's the other part of the training, Harry?'

'Some of my training is secret,' I told him. 'The other part's secret.'

'What's a secret?' asked Cal. He and Bruce were walking towards us.

'It's a secret why Sam Phelps keeps using Sydney Bridge Upside Down to pull the wagon,' I said. 'It's Sam Phelps' secret.'

'Some secret!' Cal said. 'I don't care about that secret.'

'Bruce does,' I said. 'What say we go and see Mr Phelps now?'

We headed back along the wharf. Today I was not scared by the thought of what Sam Phelps might say to me. It must be because I had grown so much stronger, I thought. It was good to be strong, I was afraid of nobody.

'Better let me handle Mr Phelps,' I told Bruce when we were nearing the woolshed. 'He doesn't like people barging in on him, especially strangers.'

'Recluse, is he?' asked Bruce.

'What?' said Cal, who was tip-toeing along one of the rails used by Sam Phelps' wagon.

'Sort of hermit, is he?' asked Bruce.

'He's a bit that way,' I told Bruce. 'He was all right in the old days, Dad says. Before his daughter ran away and his house was pulled down. He gets sulky nowadays. But I can handle him.'

'He doesn't like Harry,' said Cal, leaving the rail.

'What gave you that idea?' I said. 'We get on all right. He's a nice old bloke.'

Cal laughed. 'That's a good one!'

'I got nothing against Sam Phelps,' I told that cheeky Cal. 'I wouldn't say anything against Sam Phelps.'

'Hear that, Dibs?' said Cal. 'Hear what Harry said? What a fibber, eh?'

'I wasn't listening,' Dibs said, not looking at Cal. 'I was thinking the planks are getting wobbly down this end of the wharf. About time Mr Phelps put in new planks. This wharf has been up a good few years. Bet it was used a lot in the old days, bet a lot of heavy cargo went across it when the works were going full blast. Eh, Harry?'

Pleased that Dibs was being so friendly, I tested a plank by pressing several times with my foot. 'It's pretty wobbly,' I said. 'Mr Phelps better take care. He might have an accident.' I saw Cal staring at me and added: 'It would be terrible if he had an accident. Poor old Mr Phelps!'

I led them behind the woolshed and along the rough path towards the clearing where Sam Phelps had his shack. It was a rickety-looking place with silvery-grey boards and rusty spouting and pipes; the tin chimney was rusty too. The shack was sheltered by the cliff and the trees, and this was just as well; a good wind would blow it away. On the edge of the clearing was the shed, also rickety-looking, where Sydney Bridge Upside Down was kept.

The shack door was shut. A sack hung across the little window near the door.

'He must be having a snooze,' I said. 'Let's take a peep at Sydney Bridge Upside Down.'

'If Mr Phelps is having a snooze it would be risky to wake him,' said Dibs. 'We'll have to come back another time.' He sounded relieved.

'I don't mind waking him,' I said. Sam Phelps doesn't scare me, I thought.

But I was not quite so brave after I had looked into Sydney Bridge Upside Down's shed. Because the horse was not alone. Sam Phelps was in there too.

'Whoops whoosh groan groan!' I said, ducking. Sam Phelps had been looking straight at me.

Instead of running, the other damned kids crowded round me to find out why I'd ducked. Then Bruce Norman looked into the shed, and he didn't duck, he stayed looking.

'Good afternoon, Mr Phelps,' Bruce said. 'Do you have a few minutes to spare?'

Sam Phelps appeared in the shed doorway. He looked past Bruce at the rest of us, at me the longest. He did not seem angry. He was not happy, either. Just rough-looking, scarred, whiskery—just like always.

I decided it would be cowardly of me to leave it to Bruce to do the explaining. I could handle Sam Phelps without any help from a smaller kid.

'We called to see if Sydney Bridge Upside Down is feeling better,' I said, moving up beside Bruce. I touched Bruce's arm. 'This boy is Bruce Norman. He hasn't had a good look at Sydney Bridge Upside Down yet. What do you think, Mr Phelps? Is Sydney Bridge Upside Down well enough for Bruce to have a look?'

'I promise not to touch him, Mr Phelps,' said Bruce. 'As a matter of fact, I'm very fond of horses. I'd like to own a horse. Even a pony would do.'

'You can touch him, son,' said Sam Phelps. He was not smiling, but his voice was friendly. 'He's well enough, always has been. I don't know what Harry Baird's talking about.' He looked at me. 'There's nothing wrong with Sydney Bridge Upside Down. What do you mean? You've seen him with the wagon, haven't you?'

'Not lately, Mr Phelps,' I said as Bruce entered the shed. 'I haven't been down this way lately.'

'Don't lie, son,' said Sam Phelps. 'Who did I see tossing bricks at the works on Friday. Who did I see looking at me? Are you saying it was another lad?'

'Oh, that's right, Mr Phelps,' I said. I'd known from the start he had trapped me, but I wasn't sure if he would bother to say anything. 'I forgot about Friday,' I said. 'Yes, that's right, Mr Phelps. What I remembered was Dad saying Sydney Bridge Upside Down had been sick. I clean forgot about seeing him back on the job—on Friday, eh?'

'You Baird fellows seem to go in for lies,' Sam Phelps said. 'Unless you're making it up about your Dad, too.'

'No fear,' I said. 'He did say that, Mr Phelps. Hey, Dibs, you heard Dad saying Sydney Bridge Upside Down was sick. Remember? That day we went to the carnival. He said it just before we left, didn't he?'

'Did he?' said Dibs, looking surprised. Then he saw my stare. 'Yes, I remember now. That's what he said.' But I could tell he did not remember, and I knew Sam Phelps could too.

Blow Sam Phelps for being so talkative today, I thought; blow Dibs for not remembering. It didn't really matter, of course. It had not been an important lie, more like a small half-fib. Anyway, I didn't care what Sam Phelps thought. Sam Phelps was nobody.

Bruce Norman came from the shed. He told Sam Phelps: 'Thank you for letting me touch him. He's much stronger than I'd imagined. Seeing him from a distance was rather deceptive. His back gives the wrong impression. Why is his back such an unusual shape, Mr Phelps?'

'Too many heavyweights on him when he was a youngster,' Sam Phelps said. He talked to Bruce in a much friendlier way than he talked to me. 'Would you like to ride him, son? Give me a call when I'm along at the works end of the line some afternoon.'

'Thank you very much,' Bruce said. 'Yes, I'd love to ride your steed, Mr Phelps.'

'He certainly goes for Bruce, eh?' Dibs said to me when we were leaving the clearing. 'Fancy offering him a ride!

He's never let me ride Sydney Bridge Upside Down.'

'What about that time at the picnic?' I said.

'That time was only because Caroline was there,' Dibs said. 'He didn't give me a ride. And he didn't give Cal one.'

'I didn't want one,' Cal said. 'Who wants a ride on that old bag of bones?'

'Bruce does,' I said. I couldn't figure out why Bruce got on so well with Sam Phelps. I asked: 'Going to tell your father about meeting him, Bruce? Or do you still reckon he'd be angry?'

'Angry?' said Bruce. 'He'd be maniacal. I'm afraid I must be careful about accepting Mr Phelps' offer. Fat Norman has a knack for sniffing out anybody doing wrong. Children or grown-ups—it makes no difference. He's used to children misbehaving and he thinks grown-ups are the same. I must say that it's a nuisance of a belief. We have to be so careful.'

'What do we do now?' asked Dibs. 'Like to come and see our cave, Bruce? Shall we show him the cave, Harry?'

'If he wants to see it,' I said.

'I'd rather investigate the works,' Bruce said. 'Is it true that people have died in there?'

'A few fellows had accidents when they were pulling down the roof,' Dibs said. 'It's dangerous. That's why we're not allowed to go in.'

'Harry goes there,' Cal said.

'A girl had an accident there,' Dibs told Bruce. 'Girl called Susan Prosser.'

'I heard about that,' Bruce said. 'They were talking

about it on the first day of school. Seemed rather mysterious.'

'Nothing mysterious,' I said. 'She fell through a chute hole, that's all. It was an accident. She should have been more careful.'

'Harry's the only one who goes there now,' Cal said.

I was getting annoyed with Cal. He was looking for a good bop on the nose. I asked him: 'Why do you keep saying that, boy? Because old Phelps said he'd seen me? You shouldn't believe everything old Phelps says.'

'What were you doing with the bricks?' asked Cal, as if I hadn't just warned him by putting my fist to my nose.

I would have bopped him. But Dibs suddenly shot off across the rocks towards the beach, and Cal went racing after him.

'Fat Norman hasn't ordered me not to investigate the works,' said Bruce. 'Nobody has officially said the works are dangerous.'

I was in the lead as we went slowly across the rocks. 'It's not a very dangerous place,' I said, looking back at him. 'I can get right to the top. I've never fallen.'

'What was your brother saying about you and the bricks?'

'He was only being cheeky,' I said. I moved on a few rocks, waited for Bruce to catch up. 'What I was doing with the bricks was sorting out which ones to take to the cave, that's all.'

'I see,' he said. A little further on, he said: 'I expect there's a good view from the top of the works.'

'Not bad,' I said. 'I'll take you up if you like.'

'Yes, please,' he said.

Dibs and Cal were out of sight behind the dunes when we got to the beach.

They were out of sight somewhere else by the time we got to the works. They might be in the swamp. It was funny how Dibs liked being with Cal these days; not many weeks before Cal always gave him the pip. Although I was friendly with Dibs again, I could not really trust him, I would probably have to remind him how strong I was, he was the sort of kid who did not understand what he was told until he had been bopped a few times.

Along by the furnace-house I saw some of the bricks I had been throwing during the past week or so. I also saw that the furnace-house wall, my target, was scratched and chipped where the bricks had landed. People might wonder about those marks. Maybe it was just as well Sam Phelps had been talkative; he had warned me. I must remember to tidy up after school tomorrow night.

'Where are the others?' asked Bruce.

'Keeping out of the way,' I said. 'Scared they'll get into trouble. What about you, Bruce? Still want to go to the top?'

'Lead on,' he said.

I led him into the works and up the first lot of stairs, then up the second lot. On the way I showed him the chute opening Susan Prosser had fallen through. I also showed him how the stair-rail had been taken off so that there was a drop from the second floor to the ground floor and nothing for you to hang on to if you happened to stumble over the edge of the stair-well. But it was not actually dangerous, I said. Only a very clumsy person would stumble.

I led him up the last lot of stairs and showed him the footholds that would take us to the top. I said I wouldn't blame him if he reckoned this bit was too risky. He said he could get up there easily enough, he said he was a good climber.

He was too. Soon we were standing on the top floor, looking at the view. The bay seemed very peaceful. The sea was calm and the sun was making it sparkle. A few kids were playing on the beach, a few more were playing king of the castle on a dune. Nobody was on the wharf, nobody was on the hills. I could not see Cal or Dibs.

'Your house is easy to pick out,' Bruce said. 'The roof is so red. Redder than the others.'

'We painted it during the holidays,' I said. 'We thought my mother would be pleased if we painted the house. But we needn't have bothered.'

'Why is your mother away?' asked Bruce.

'She went to the city for a holiday, then she got sick,' I told him. 'She'll be back soon.'

'I'm glad my mother never goes away,' Bruce said. 'I'd object to being left alone with Fat Norman.'

'My father's all right,' I said. 'It's good when he looks after us. We have more fun.'

'Do you find school is fun?' asked Bruce, moving to the wall the demolition fellows hadn't bothered to bash. He sat in the shade.

'I don't have much fun at school nowadays,' I said. 'When I was a small kid I used to have fun there. I remember the first time I whistled. That was at school. I thought I was very clever because I could whistle. Susan

Prosser said I was a skite. She must have thought I was whistling at her. I wasn't. I was just whistling. I was only a small kid then. I was excited because I had discovered I could whistle. I went around whistling all the time.'

'I'm a rather good whistler,' Bruce said. 'Listen.' He whistled a soft little song, but I could not recognise the tune.

'Can you whistle with two fingers in your mouth?' I asked. 'I'll show you.'

I showed him. Maybe because I *was* a skite and wanted to amaze him, it was the loudest I had ever whistled, it was so loud Bruce closed his eyes and slammed his hands over his ears.

I grinned at him. 'What did you think of that?'

'I can't whistle like that,' he said, sounding as though he wished he could, the way Dibs had sounded earlier when I showed him how strong I was.

'It's only practice,' I said. 'You can do anything if you practise hard enough. I used to practise from the cliff behind the wharf. The first few times I fooled Mr Phelps. He'd look all round, wondering where the whistling was coming from. After a few more times, he took no notice, he didn't turn his head when I whistled.'

Bruce moved across to the edge of the floor. 'Yes, it's one of Fat Norman's sayings,' he said. 'Practice makes perfect. He means in schoolwork.'

'I don't care about schoolwork,' I said. I saw that he had his back to me, and I gave a short loud whistle to see if he jumped.

By the time he had his hands to his ears, I'd stopped

whistling. He was looking towards the swamp, and suddenly he began laughing.

I moved up beside him and had a look.

Dibs and Cal had stepped from the trees near the swamp and were staring in every direction, trying to make out where the whistler was.

'Duck!' I told Bruce. 'Don't let them see you.'

We sat down quickly.

'Cal's in a mean mood today,' I told Bruce. 'He might tell Dad if he sees me up here.' I paused, wondering if I should tell Bruce what I was thinking. Then I decided it would be safe to tell him. 'Cal would like Dad to chase me with the whip,' I said. 'Dad would do that if he knew I'd been up here.'

'A whip?' said Bruce, seeming startled.

'Sometimes he does that,' I said. 'Not all the time. Just now and then. When he's in a bad mood.'

'I think that's awful,' Bruce said. 'Fat Norman would never do *that*.'

'It doesn't happen often,' I said, a bit sorry I had told him. 'Dad's not often in a bad mood.'

'Still, it should never happen,' Bruce said, sounding like a grown-up. 'Parents should never use whips on their children. I wouldn't use a whip on a horse, let alone a child.'

'Better not tell anybody,' I said. 'I don't really mind. I can always get away from him. His crutch slows him down. I run across the swamp and escape. I don't mind. So don't tell anybody.'

'My word!' said Bruce, shaking his head.

To get his thoughts off the whip, I said: 'Think I'll see what those other kids are doing.' I moved to the crumbly edge of the wall, peeped down.

I couldn't see Dibs and Cal. Not for a few seconds. Then I saw them crossing the paddock, not far from the works. They were heading for the works.

'Heck!' I said to Bruce. Then, as I looked the other way: 'There's Caroline!'

Caroline was on the back of Buster Kelly's Indian. Good old Buster! He was giving Caroline a ride.

I watched the Indian moving slowly along the road towards the river crossing, and I did not mind at all that somebody else was getting a ride from Buster, I was very glad Caroline was the one with him.

For the past week or so, I had been worrying a fair bit about Caroline. I could tell she was not happy, and I was afraid that any day now she would say she was fed up with Calliope Bay and must leave. Thinking of her quietness, her sort of sad quietness, I was certain it had begun the day after the carnival. What had happened at the carnival had made her sad instead of gay. Even before I began early-morning training, she had changed, so that I was sure she would not want to play our old game, our running game. And although I'd had enough of that game because it made me too anxious, I would have gone on playing it if Caroline had wanted me to. Ever since the carnival she had not mentioned it, she had not even kissed me. She had certainly changed. And I knew why. I knew she was afraid of Mr Wiggins. You only had to see how she hid in her room when his van pulled up outside to know how much he scared her. I had found her hiding in there one day when Mr Wiggins was outside, and she told me she was glad Mrs Kelly had kept gossiping to him because it gave me time to get home from school and collect the meat from him. She said she could not bear the thought of Mr Wiggins looking at her today. Or any day, I knew.

Well, Caroline would not have to suffer much more, I thought. Just hang on a bit longer, I felt like telling her. But couldn't, of course.

Meanwhile, it was great that Buster should call and give her a ride. Buster would make her forget terrible Mr Wiggins.

I turned to Bruce. 'We'll go down now,' I said. 'I want to remind those other kids how strong I am.'

12

There was a hairy, cheeky lady's man who often visited the edge of the world, and his name was Mr Chick Wiggins, and he died in the place where he had once killed many animals. Sam Phelps found his body one Saturday afternoon.

I start with Mr Wiggins and the finding of his body, but now I go to our house on the afternoon of the previous day, after school, before tea. I go to Caroline's bedroom.

'You look happier today,' I told Caroline. I was sitting on the side of her bed, watching her sort out the shoes she had taken from the wardrobe.

She stayed kneeling, but turned her head to smile at me. Yes, her cheeks were pinker than usual, her eyes were brighter though still sort of dreamy.

'I was getting scared, Caroline,' I said. 'I thought you might be sick, might have some strange illness that was making you unhappy.'

'Unhappy!' she cried. 'No, I'm not unhappy, Harry.'

'Not now,' I said. 'I can see that. But when you didn't go to the wharf to watch the *Emma Cranwell* come in yesterday I thought you *must* be sick. Because I remembered how keen you were to go to the wharf last time she came in.'

'I was different then,' she said.

I waited, but she did not explain, she went on studying the shoes.

'How were you different?' I asked.

'Mmm?' she said.

'I thought you must be worrying about Mr Wiggins,' I said.

She heard me that time. '*Him*!' she said. There sure was hatred in her voice.

'I don't know why Mr Wiggins keeps bothering people like he does,' I said. 'You'd think he could see people don't want to talk to him. Except maybe Mrs Kelly. Mrs Kelly doesn't mind talking to him.'

'Are these nice, Harry?' asked Caroline, holding up a pair of brown shoes.

I didn't blame her for not wanting to talk about Mr Wiggins. I said: 'Yes, they're good shoes.'

'Flat-heeled, see?' she said, turning them over. 'Suitable for wearing on a motor-bike, I think.'

'Yes, they're just right,' I said. 'When is Buster coming for you?'

'After tea,' she said.

'Where will you go?' I asked.

'Wherever I'm taken,' she said, smiling at me. 'We might even go to Bonnie Brae.'

'Gosh, that's a dangerous road at night,' I said.

'Buster is a very careful rider,' she said. 'Especially when I'm with him. He never rides no-hands when I'm with him.'

'Seems like everybody is going to Bonnie Brae tonight,' I said, thinking she was lucky to have so many rides on the Indian, not that I cared how many she had, I was glad she had so many, Buster was good to give her so many.

'Oh, yes,' she said. 'This is the night Uncle Frank goes there with Mr Kelly, isn't it? Expect he'll leave after us. But we might see him in Bonnie Brae. I must warn—I must tell Buster about Uncle Frank being there tonight.'

'Anyway, the road won't be slippery,' I said. 'We've had no rain for a long time, eh? Remember those storms when you first came? Remember how it rained at the carnival? It sure was rainy then.'

'What will you do while we're away?' asked Caroline.

'Might play ludo with Cal,' I said. 'Or snakes and ladders. Might look at my cigarette cards.'

'No homework?' smiled Caroline.

'On Friday!' I said. 'Anyway, Fat Norman's not supposed to give us homework. We're too young for homework. It's too big a strain for kids like us.'

'Mrs Kelly says it keeps her children out of mischief,' Caroline said. 'She thinks Mr Norman is sensible to give you homework.'

'Mrs Kelly has some stupid ideas,' I said. 'Besides, what mischief would I get into? Heck, Mrs Kelly's as bad as Fat Norman. They don't like to think of kids having fun.'

Caroline laughed. 'Even so, I think you get your share of fun, Harry.'

I thought I'd be daring. 'I liked the fun *we* used to have, Caroline. You know, running up and down the passage.'

I was surprised to see her turn red. She concentrated on the shoes. 'The weather was much hotter then,' she said. 'It's rather cool these mornings.'

'Do you think so?' I said. I suddenly wished I could see her with nothing on.

'Harry,' she said, then was silent.

I waited, then said: 'Yes?'

'You didn't tell anybody, did you?'

'About what?'

'About how we used to run along the passage.'

'Cal's the only one who knows,' I said. 'Besides you and me. But Cal won't tell anybody. Because he used to do it too. He's too scared to tell.' He knew I would fix him if he did, I thought.

She slowly put the shoes into the wardrobe, all except the brown pair.

'We might play it again one day, eh?' I said, longing to see her. 'When the weather's hot maybe?'

'I don't think so, Harry,' she said.

'Why not?'

'Best not to.'

I pretended to be sulky, but in a way I was glad she had said that. I didn't know why, it just seemed to me she was right to say it. Somehow it was good for me to want to see her with nothing on, but better if I didn't.

I go now to our backyard the following morning. This, of course, was a few hours before Sam Phelps found Mr Wiggins' body.

I was bopping Cal near the wash-house when Dad came out to the porch and saw me. I didn't see him until it was too late.

'Harry!' shouted Dad. 'What are you doing to your brother?' He stamped his crutch on the middle step, seemed to sail towards me.

I thought of running, but didn't. Though Cal was making a good bit of noise, he wasn't hurt, I hadn't bopped him all that hard.

'He's telling fibs about me, Dad,' I said before Cal could change gear from squawking to taletelling. 'He said I asked Mr Wiggins—'

'I didn't, Dad!' Cal shouted. 'He didn't hear me properly!'

'Didn't you say I *asked* Mr Wiggins for a ride?' I said.

'No!' he shouted.

'I thought you did,' I said. I was sure before, now I wasn't. 'Well, I'm sorry,' I said.

'You're too quick with those fists,' Dad told me. 'Whatever he did, you shouldn't hit him like that.'

'It was a misunderstanding,' I said.

'What was that about Mr Wiggins, anyway?' he asked.

I was ready to tell him. I had intended telling him this morning as soon as I got the chance. I knew that Cal, peeping from the window, had seen me going off with Mr Wiggins last night and it would be no use pretending I hadn't gone. So the best thing would be to tell Dad. I told him: 'Mr Wiggins called last night. He wanted to see you about something, Dad. Then he said he was going to the wharf to see Sam Phelps and would I like a little ride, and I said I wouldn't mind, so I went with him to the end of the railway line, then I came straight home and went to bed. But I didn't *ask* him for a ride. He offered me one. Honestly, he did.'

'What time was this?' asked Dad.

'After eight o'clock,' I said.

'Funny time for him to be calling,' he said. 'What did he want to see me about?'

'I don't know,' I said. 'When you weren't here, he said he'd go to see Sam Phelps.'

'Odd bloke,' Dad said, frowning. He saw Cal rubbing his arm and told me: 'If I catch you hitting this boy again, I'll lam into you—you bully. I've got enough to worry about with your mother away—' He looked unhappy, not angry, and I was sorry I'd had to upset him, I thought he was right to call me a bully, and I felt annoyed at myself and miserable and frightened.

'I'm sorry, Dad,' I said. Before I knew it, I was crying, and this was as much of a surprise to me as it was to Dad.

'Hold on,' he said. 'It's not worth crying about.'

'I know,' I said. 'I'm sorry, Dad.' I could have had a good howl, but I forced myself to stop.

'How did you hurt your leg?' he asked.

That helped to stop my sniffling. 'I fell over,' I said. 'It doesn't hurt.'

'Looks like a bad bruise under that cut,' he said.

'It feels all right,' I said.

'Better go inside and bandage it,' he said.

'Yes, Dad,' I said. I saw Cal looking annoyed because

I was getting the sympathy he must think he deserved. I would make friends with him, I decided.

'You boys mustn't fight,' Dad said sadly as he hopped back to the porch.

I walked up to Cal and put my arm round his shoulders.

He tried to pull away, but I held him. 'It was a mistake, Cal,' I said. 'I'm sorry I hit you. I think I must be going deaf in one ear. Or it might be too dirty. I'll have to wash my dirty lug, eh?'

'You didn't need to hit me,' he said.

'I know,' I said. 'That's why I'm saying I'm sorry. Shake hands on it, eh?'

We shook hands, though he didn't seem to want to. He was eyeing me suspiciously.

'You can look at my cigarette cards if you like,' I said.

'I don't want to,' he said.

'Think I'll head up to the cave this morning,' I said. 'Want to inspect that pistol. I reckon I'll get a chance today or tomorrow to ask Buster about some ammo. Want to come? You and Dibs. And Bruce Norman maybe.'

'If you like,' he said.

'Dibs might have some fags,' I said. 'You can have a smoke too.'

'I don't want to smoke,' he said.

'You can if you like,' I said. 'Now I better go and bandage this leg, like Dad said.'

He said nothing. I guessed I would have to work hard to become as friendly with him as I was in the old days. When, I wondered, were the old days? They must be the days before Caroline arrived. So many things had changed since then. Most of all, I thought, I had changed. I could not exactly remember what I was like before she came. I knew what I was like today. I was scared. I kept trembling I was so scared. But I would get over it, I had got over it before.

Caroline and Dad were talking in the kitchen. I heard Dad mention Bonnie Brae as I reached the door.

'—and live in Bonnie Brae,' he said. He was not looking sad now, he was even cheerful. 'Of course, the boys are used to this school and it mightn't be a good thing to switch them. We'll see— Ah, here he is, the young devil.' He and Caroline looked at me, looked at my leg.

'Poor Harry,' said Caroline. 'How did you hurt your leg?'

'I fell over,' I said. 'But it doesn't hurt. Be okay in a couple of days. I'll bandage it.' I got a bandage from the middle drawer of the sideboard.

'Let me help you,' said Caroline. 'You sit on the chair and I'll put the bandage round your leg.' She looked up at Dad as she unwound the bandage. 'No, we didn't get as far as Bonnie Brae. Buster thought it might be too far for us to go at night.'

Dad watched her winding the bandage. 'So what did you do, Caroline? Cuddle by the river? Or go for a moon-light walk to the waterfall?'

Caroline smiled up at him, not seeming to mind his kidding.

'We went to see some people called Hobson or Dobson, some name like that,' she said. 'Buster's friends. They were nice people.'

205

'That would be Bill Dobson's place,' Dad said, nodding. 'Yes, Bill's a good fellow—'

'Hey, it's a bit tight,' I told Caroline. The touch of her fingers had been soft and warm, but she was tugging much too hard on the bandage, I'd be a cripple if she made it that tight.

'Sorry, love,' she said, loosening the bandage. 'I'm not very good at this.'

'It's all right now,' I said. It wasn't really, but I could loosen it myself later; I mustn't embarrass Caroline, she was doing her best.

'So you liked the Dobsons, Caroline?' said Dad.

'They were nice,' Caroline said. 'Buster and Mr Dobson had a few bottles of beer. Mrs Dobson and I had a little wine. We chatted. It was very nice.'

Dad laughed. 'Sandy Kelly and I had a few too. You know what it is at smoke concerts. Well, you can guess what it is, eh? I had to watch Sandy, didn't want him taking us over the bank on the way home. But Sandy can hold his liquor. It was a good night.'

A good night for them, I thought. They would never guess what a horrible night I'd had.

'Now does that feel comfortable?' asked Caroline as she snipped the safety-pin in place.

'Yes,' I said. 'Thank you, Caroline.'

'Where did you take the tumble, son?' asked Dad.

'Down the road,' I said.

'Where down the road?'

'That culvert near the school track,' I said, remembering that I had once seen a kid slip into it and twist his ankle.

'Skylarking, I suppose?' He smiled at Caroline.

'Yes, it was my own fault,' I said. 'I jumped the wrong way. Nobody pushed me.'

'All your own work, eh?' He smiled again at Caroline. 'Harry tells me we had a visitor last night. Chick Wiggins. Queer night for him to call. He knew there was a smoke concert on. He knows Sandy and I usually go. Asked for me, did he, Harry?'

'Yes,' I said seeing Caroline looking at me, maybe worriedly.

'What did he say, Harry?' asked Dad.

'I told you,' I said.

'I know,' he said. 'But Caroline didn't hear.'

'Oh, I don't mind not knowing,' Caroline said.

'What exactly did he say, Harry?' Dad asked.

I was sweating. 'He said he wanted to see you. Then he said he wanted to see Sam Phelps. He didn't say why, though.'

'And you went for a ride with him?' asked Dad.

'Just to the railway line,' I said. 'I came straight back.'

'Didn't he invite Cal?' asked Dad.

'Cal was in bed,' I said. 'He wouldn't play ludo and went to bed early and I was just sitting in the kitchen thinking I'd better go to bed too and Mr Wiggins knocked on the door—and asked for you. Don't suppose I'd have gone with him if Cal had been up. I thought it was just something to do.'

'A bit of fun, eh?' said Dad.

'Yes, Dad,' I said.

'You're a great lad for your fun,' he said. 'Well, I suppose there was no harm in it. You weren't away long, you say?'

'Only a few minutes,' I said. 'Didn't take Mr Wiggins long to reach the railway line.'

'It's a wonder he didn't call on Mrs Kelly,' Dad said. 'Soon as he found me away, he'd know Sandy was away too.' I saw the wink he gave Caroline.

'Eh?' I said.

'Nothing,' he said. 'Nothing you need to know about.'

'Can I go and play now?' I asked.

'More fun!' He grinned at Caroline, and she smiled faintly at me. 'Make sure you're back in time for lunch. Where are you going?'

'Just up the hill,' I said, moving towards the door, my right leg straight and stiff. 'Cal's coming with me. We'll be back for lunch.'

'A great lad for his fun,' I heard Dad telling Caroline as I went out.

My hands were very sweaty. I wiped them on my pants.

I go now to the time the night before when Cal was in bed and I was alone in the kitchen. Dad and Caroline had been away for more than an hour.

I was not sorry Cal had gone to bed. It gave me a chance to read Caroline's autobiography.

As soon as Cal shut our bedroom door, I sneaked into Caroline's room and grabbed two of the exercise books from her suitcase. I had been thinking of doing this for a week or so, but I'd never had the opportunity before. I had been hoping, of course, that Caroline would read me more of the autobiography, but she hadn't—and she had been so dreamy lately that I hadn't liked to ask her for more. She probably wouldn't mind if I had a peep. Anyway, it was her own fault for making me so curious about Uncle Pember.

One of the books was only a quarter full. This must be the latest. I put it aside and looked into the other book. This was filled right up, it was most likely where I would find Uncle Pember mentioned.

I turned a few pages, looking for his name. I couldn't see it. I read some lines: 'Ian, who at this stage hoped to become the credit manager, called to me from behind a grand piano one afternoon. I confess I giggled. Incidentally, he had a nickname for me, this was Blondie-baby. Blondie-baby, he said on the afternoon I refer to, would you trot out with me this evening? Not unless you dress yourself properly, I said teasingly. How do you mean, Blondie-baby, he said, then looked where I was looking. Yes, I said with a giggle, your fly is undone, Ian. At this point, I can mention that it was diverting for me, when I was going about my business in the city, to fix my gaze on men's flies as I approached them. They were usually disconcerted. I may say that I never did this in the belief that I would one day spy a penis—'

I quickly turned the pages. Still no mention of Uncle Pember. I risked reading a few lines: 'On shimmering summer nights, when the scarlet birds flew away from the black serpents and white swans glided under dark bridges etc., I wished Geoff had not been so stuffy. That is to say, I was lonely on such nights. The humidity, I may add, was very high. Sticky weather, people kept saying. As usual, I slept bare. This led to an experience (note from my wobbly writing in this passage how the memory still affects me) to an experience of some interest. First, let me say that another of the salesmen, a gentleman who often appalled Geoff with his coarseness, was reputed to be a lecher. This reputation, as my experience of him illustrated, was indeed well-founded—'

I turned some more pages. I reached the end of the book without seeing Uncle Pember's name. I turned back two pages, read: 'Although I was but seventeen, I was well aware of the pitfalls, having become familiar with them at a much earlier age, indeed as early as fourteen. Nevertheless, I was confident that a giant such as Robert, contrary to general belief, would be extremely gentle. I am not sure what grounds I had for being so confident. Whatever they were, they proved to be mistaken. No, wait a while. I may come back and change this. Robert could be tall, but not precisely a giant. Have to think about him, so often in the basement with the filing-cabinets. Did I ever speak to him? Who am I thinking of? Ronald, was it? Enough for today—'

I closed that book and took up the other one. Only three pages from the start was my own name! It was so clear it seemed to glow. I looked away from the page, telling myself I shouldn't read what Caroline had written about me, it would be better if I didn't.

After some seconds, I read: 'I dare say his attempted attentions were flattering, or would have been were he not such a loathsomely hairy little man. Small wonder that sweet young Harry did his best to protect me. I feared at times that Harry's freckles would pop, so great was the indignation he felt towards this person Wiggins. I recall a day when there was a carnival in a nearby town, and Harry took it upon himself to protect me. There were moments during the day, I confess, when I wished he were not so protective, yet I had to forgive him on reflection. I was sure that if my principal memory of the day turned on a pyramid of absolutely splendid cowboys, all of them deeply tanned and in tight-fitting trousers that threatened to burst open at any moment—if this was my principal memory, I am sure Harry's was of his duty as my protector—'

There was a knock on the back door.

I raced up the passage and put the exercise books in the suitcase. Then I tip-toed along the passage to the kitchen. I waited for another knock before I went to the door. The second knock was louder than the first.

I opened the door.

'Hello, young fellow,' said Mr Wiggins, stepping into the kitchen. 'Anybody home?'

'Only Cal and me,' I said. 'Cal's gone to bed.'

Mr Wiggins was looking round the kitchen as though he didn't believe I was the only one there, as though he might see somebody behind the sofa or under the table if he looked hard enough. He wore a navy suit and a white shirt and tie, and the suit-coat bulged with all the tough-ness it was covering.

'Dad at the smoke concert, is he?' said Mr Wiggins, walking slowly towards the passage.

'Yes,' I said. 'Only Cal and me at home.'

'So you were saying,' he said. He looked back from the passage. 'Only you and Cal?'

'Yes, Mr Wiggins,' I said.

'Then you won't mind if I have a look, will you?' he said, moving slowly along the passage.

I did not speak. And I paused before I followed him. I was thinking hard. Although I had known I would have to be strong to tackle Mr Wiggins, I had not been able to work out *how* I would tackle him. Some day, I'd thought, I would have my chance. I had no idea, of course, when that day would come. It might have taken months to come, even years. Yet I had been certain it would come, sooner or later, and I would be ready for it when it did come. Had it come already? Could tonight possibly be the time? Was I strong enough yet? How could I do it?

I was shaking when I went along the passage. I had thought of the beginning of a way.

Mr Wiggins opened our bedroom door. He felt for the light-switch. I was behind him when the light went on. Cal blinked at us from the bed.

Mr Wiggins looked behind the door, then switched off the light. 'Good night, son,' he said to Cal as he closed the door.

He crossed the passage to Caroline's room and switched on the light there. He went to the wardrobe and looked in. He looked under the bed.

I saw him frown in the moment before he switched off the light. I followed him back to the kitchen.

I stayed in the kitchen while he checked that there was nobody in Dad's room. I was pretty sure now that I had a way. And I kept reminding myself how strong I was.

'Where is your cousin?' asked Mr Wiggins.

'Out,' I said.

'So I gather,' he said. 'Where?'

I looked at him. I felt calm.

'Out with young Kelly, is she?' he asked.

'No,' I said.

'Who then?'

'Nobody.'

'Well, where is she then?'

'I don't think she'd want me to tell you,' I said.

'Nonsense,' he said. He put on a sort of smile. 'I have a present for her, son. It's out in the van. Caroline will love to get it. She loves presents.'

'Well...' I said.

'She won't mind if you tell me,' he said.

'I don't know about that,' I said.

'Come on, Harry,' he said. 'You know she loves presents.'

'Well, she's gone for a walk,' I said. I pretended to think. 'I know,' I said. 'Say you take me in the van? I'll show you where she is.'

'Just tell me,' he said.

'Best if I go too,' I said. 'To show you.'

'All right,' he said. 'Come on.'

We went out to the van. The moon was shining on it. It looked ghostly.

I got in beside Mr Wiggins. There was a parcel on the seat. I touched it.

'Is this the present?' I asked.

'That's right, son,' he said. 'Well, where do we go?'

'Only to the works,' I said.

'We could walk there,' he said.

'Best not to,' I said. 'There's a secret place.'

He glanced at me, but said nothing. He started the van and we went slowly along the road to the works, Mr Wiggins looking out carefully in case Caroline went by.

When we got to the works I told him to drive round the other side. This, I knew, would put the van out of sight.

He grumbled something about the bumps, but drove the van behind the works.

'This will do,' I said. I got out quickly.

Mr Wiggins got out with the present. 'I don't see her,' he said. 'Where would she be walking?'

'Actually, she's inside,' I said. 'We've got a secret place in the works.'

'In there at this hour of the night?' he said. He sounded suspicious.

'There's a paraffin lamp,' I said. 'Dibs Kelly's father gave it to him, so we put it in this secret place, and Caroline's allowed to go in there whenever—'

'At this hour of the night?' He was still suspicious.

'You can find her if you like,' I said. 'I'm going home. My little brother will wonder where I am.'

'Stay here,' he said. 'Show me where she is. So you have a secret place in the old works, do you, Harry? That sounds exciting.' He was being very friendly.

I went ahead of him to the works entrance. 'I'll show you,' I said as I crossed the patch of moonlight near the entrance.

I hesitated in the doorway, long enough to make sure he was behind me. When he stepped into the patch of moonlight I went fast up the stairs to the first floor.

'Follow me, Mr Wiggins,' I called, not loudly enough to cause an echo.

'Where are you?' he called, and there was a small echo.

'Just up the stairs,' I said. 'We have to go to the second floor. That's where Caroline is, Mr Wiggins.'

I went on up to the second floor and waited for him.

Now I go to our cave the next afternoon. I was there with Cal and Dibs and Bruce Norman. We were smoking cigarettes.

Although I had told Dibs I'd hurt my leg during my usual early-morning run, he kept looking at the bandage as though something about it puzzled him. I wished the damned leg wasn't bandaged; the cut and the bruise wouldn't be as noticeable as the bandage was. At any rate, I was glad I'd got up early, before Cal was awake, and had the usual run; it might have seemed odd, later if not now, if I hadn't.

'Are you feeling dizzy, Bruce?' I asked. He had not taken a puff for some minutes.

'Not at all,' he said.

'Usually need three to make you dizzy,' I said. 'Depends on the leaves.' I squinted through the murkiness, trying to see Cal. 'Cal once got dizzy on one of them. Didn't you, Cal?'

'I'm going outside,' Cal said, crawling from the darkness at the back of the cave. 'Too choky in here.'

I jerked my injured leg out of the way to let him pass.

'It *is* rather suffocating,' Bruce said. 'I'm not really fond of smoking. Half a cigarette seems to satisfy me.' He, too, crawled from the cave.

'All the more for us to smoke, eh?' I said to Dibs. I was not enjoying the cigarette, but I didn't want to leave the cave, it seemed a safe place.

'Think I'll only have one today,' Dibs said.

'Don't you want to be dizzy?' I asked.

'Not today,' he said. There he was, looking at my bandage again.

'What's the matter?' I said.

'Eh?' he said.

'Why do you keep looking at my leg?'

'Nothing, Harry. Nothing.'

'I told you how it happened, boy. I fell over. But it's not serious. It was Dad's mad idea to put this bandage on. I'll take it off tonight, you bet.'

'Good idea, Harry.'

I'd better get him thinking about something else. 'This is our chance,' I said. 'Now those kids are out of the way we can have a look at the pistol.'

'It doesn't matter,' he said. 'Think I'll get some fresh air, Harry. See you outside.'

I put up my hand to stop him, but the stiff leg slowed me, and he crawled from the cave. He seemed in a hurry, I thought. Now why should he be in such a hurry?

I crawled to the end of the cave and took the rocks from the hollow where the pistol had been hidden. There was no pistol under the rocks.

Well, I'm not surprised, I thought. I wasn't even angry. I should be angry and puzzled. I should rush out and force those kids to tell me what they had done with the pistol.

But I couldn't be bothered. I did not want to leave the cave.

I lit another cigarette and thought about the pistol. Why had Dibs and Cal taken it? Did it mean they had got some ammo and were planning to fire the pistol without letting me know? Maybe they had already got some ammo, maybe they had already fired the pistol—

No, I still did not care. They could keep it. Let them shoot off their toes. It would serve them right.

I wondered what would happen if I stayed in the cave all day. What say I refused to leave the cave when they came to get me? I could block the entrance with bricks from the fireplace. Nobody could get through. They would have to let me stay in here until I was ready to leave. I might never be ready to leave. I might stay in here until I suffocated, until I died. They would be sorry then. They would be sad. Caroline would be the saddest of all because nobody else in the world liked me as much as she did, nobody else anywhere thought I was sweet, which was another way of thinking I was all right. Maybe it wouldn't be fair to make Caroline so sad, especially when I had done so much to make her happy. Maybe it would be better if I put off staying in the cave. I could save it up for another time.

I finished the cigarette. That was the third. But I still did not feel dizzy.

'Harry?'

The stiffness spread from my leg to the rest of my body when I heard the voice. Then I saw that it was Dibs looking into the cave.

'Are you all right, Harry?' he asked.

'Sure,' I said, crawling towards him. 'I just had another cigarette. Thought I'd see if I could get dizzy. It didn't work, though. Those fags aren't as good as the last lot you made, boy.'

'We were talking about you, Harry,' Dibs said when I was out into the sunshine. 'We wondered if you'd conked it. Like, with all that smoke in there.'

They were sitting on the grass, Cal and Dibs and Bruce. They were looking at me. Was there something special about the way they were looking at me?

'One of these days we'll have to put in some air-holes,' I said, sitting on the grass not far from Dibs, looking at the opposite hill, the one above the works, as I spoke. 'By the way,' I said, still not looking at them, 'what did you kids do with the pistol?'

'Pistol?' asked Bruce.

'I don't think *you* know about it, Bruce,' I said. 'But Dibs does. And so does Cal.' I looked at Dibs. 'What happened to it?'

'You mean *you* didn't take it?' Dibs asked. He glanced at Cal. Then he told me: 'We thought you'd taken it and hidden it somewhere else, Harry. Hey, who did take it then?'

'Search me,' Cal said, staring at me as if he still thought I'd taken it.

'Why didn't you tell me?' I asked Dibs. 'How long's it been gone.'

'It was there a couple of weeks ago,' Dibs said. 'Then I checked a week ago and it had gone. And I didn't tell you because I thought you knew. Honestly, Harry, I thought you'd hidden it somewhere else.'

'I'd like to know who took it,' I said. 'That was supposed to be a secret hiding-place.' I believed Dibs and Cal, they were not pretending, I could always tell when they were pretending.

'Was it a real pistol?' asked Bruce. 'Could it shoot?'

'Sure,' I said. 'But you better not tell anybody. We might get into trouble. If you hear of anybody having a pistol, though, you can tell me. It will probably be our pistol.'

We seemed to be friendlier after that. It was as if the mysterious disappearance of the pistol had turned Dibs and Cal against me. Now they knew that I was as puzzled as they were; they believed me.

'Anyway,' I said to Dibs, 'did you ever ask Buster about the ammo?'

'Yes, I did,' said Dibs. 'He only laughed. He said he'd be a nut to give ammo to kids.'

I frowned. 'So Buster knows about the pistol. I wonder if he took it? Do you think he'd take it, Dibs?'

'No,' said Dibs. 'Buster wouldn't take it.'

'That's what I reckon,' I said. 'But I don't know who else would, either.'

We thought about it, but couldn't find an answer.

Then Bruce said he was going home, and Dibs and Cal got up to follow him, and I knew I would have to go with them, I couldn't stay out of the way any longer.

I did not hurry, though. I hobbled, as if my leg were too stiff for me to hurry.

Somehow I guessed what would happen when Bruce

reached the turn in the track and saw the works and the houses. He would stop and stare.

And that was what he did, sure enough.

But it was Dibs who called back: 'Hurry up, Harry! Something's going on at the works! Looks like everybody's there!'

I stopped. Then I took a deep breath and hobbled on.

13

AGAIN I am walking in the moonlight along the road that takes you from the railway line, from Sydney Bridge Upside Down's turnaround spot, to the river and over the river and on across the countryside, up hills and around bends and through gullies, all the way to Bonnie Brae, and further still if you are escaping, if you are trying to get as far as you can from the edge of the world. The soles of my feet are tough, they make crunchy sounds in the metal. I listen to these sounds, then I stop and try to hear other sounds. I can hear the sea. I can hear the swamp frogs. I can hear trees stirring in the little breeze on the hill above me. I look up at the hill and I see the shapes of the trees as they tremble and now I see another shape up there and this one is still and doesn't move at all while I watch, and when I look away and take two steps in the metal I hear Mrs Knowles' cat miaowing from the first house, so I look back at the shape on the hill and it is the same as before, it is Sydney Bridge Upside Down waiting there

(You can say this as well, dear Caroline. You can say that my first teacher, Miss Piggy-face, threw black-balls at me. She was in an awful temper. She said I had made muddy marks on the floor. She said I had crumbled chalk. She said I had scribbled on the desk-top. She said I had hidden Susan Prosser's rubber. She said I had picked my nose and stuck the snot on Jimmy Ling's shiny schoolbag. She said I had stolen Billy Vigars' ruler and busted it. She said I had made a rude noise with my mouth when she was writing words on the board and a rude noise and a smell with my bum when she was writing sums on the board. She said I had thumped Dibs Kelly on his ringworm scab when he wasn't looking. She said I had thrown my sandwich crusts at the girls at playtime and grabbed other boys' sandwiches at lunchtime. She said I had stolen one of the apples other children, the good children, had brought her. She said I hadn't cleaned my teeth or fingernails and hadn't combed my hair and hadn't washed my ankles or knees or elbows or neck. She said my shirt was always hanging out. She said I tugged out other boys' shirts and undid the girls' hair-bows. She said I pinched the girls and punched the boys when we were leaving the classroom. She said I had taken the cork from the red-ink bottle on her desk and used it to stamp a trail across her pretty Niagara Falls calendar. She said I wasted all the paper in the dunny at the end of the playground. She said I was always putting up my hand to leave the room when I couldn't possibly be in any discomfort. She said I chewed the ends of my pencils to shreds. She said I spat. She said I was a little monster. She said she didn't believe I really was only six, she said most kids didn't behave like monsters until they were older, like in Standard Three or Four. You are driving me to distraction, she said. That's why I threw the lollies at you, she said. She threw another one. That's the last, she said. Now listen all you other children, now you know why there won't be any black-balls for prizes at the end of the week, she said. Blame Harry Baird, she said. Blame Harry Baird) waiting up there on the hill for me, the way Sam Phelps waits on the road outside our house, staring at our front door, staring at the curtains while I stare back at him, waiting for me to go up the side-path to the front so that he can stare at me and watch me staring back at him, not speaking, not moving, just staring. I can escape by going down the yard and across the swamp to the river-bank, but I keep thinking of him waiting back there on the road, and it is no fun for me to go to the river-bank now, it is no fun to be with anybody. Now there is the horse too. Sam Phelps watches me in the day, his horse watches me in the night. Or is Sam Phelps along there now? Is that his shape by the roadside, near the spot where Mr Wiggins used to park his van? He knows I am away from the house, he is waiting for me to get back. He knows I sometimes go to the cave to be sure of not being spoken to or seen, and that is why Sydney Bridge Upside Down is waiting up there, it's to stop me from getting to the cave. If I run hard along the road I can be past him before he realises what I'm doing, I can be down the side-path and into the house before he can trap me with his stare. But when I try to run I cannot lift my feet, I am planted in the metal, it's like there are enormous weights on my feet and splints or bars keeping my legs stiff and

223

straight, as if I'm a statue and forced to stay as still as Sam Phelps and the horse. I hear Mrs Knowles' cat miaowing again. I hear the swamp frogs. I hear the waves breaking against the wharf piles and across the rocks, I hear the surf swishing and sighing along the beach. I want the moon to go so that I won't see the shapes waiting for me. I look up at the sky and I see clouds among the stars, and the clouds are moving towards the moon, and I know that when they reach the moon I can go quickly back along the road, I can get away from Sam Phelps. I wait. If I go back I can run behind the works and get across the paddocks and then cut through the swamp to home, and Sam Phelps won't know where I am, he won't know that I am lying in bed beside Cal, awake but safe. I wait. The clouds reach the moon. Now I try to lift my feet, and it is all right, I can walk away in the dark. Does he hear the metal crunching? I won't look back, I won't stop. Should I start running? It may be too soon to run. They could still catch me if they wanted to. I can run as soon as I'm past the works and in the darkness of the paddocks, too far away to be seen. Now that I am so near the works, though, I remember what happened there and my right leg seems to stiffen at the memory. The memory of how I fell as I ran down the stairs, tripping as a groan echoed in the works. Now the clouds have moved past the moon, and I am near enough to the works to see the moonlight patch by the door, near enough to hear the groans of dying animals. I drop to the grass and I look up at the hill, and I am certain the shape is moving, it is moving very slowly towards the track (Say as well, dear Caroline, that I learned to whistle after Miss Piggy-face had gone. Say that Mr Dalloway, the new teacher, found me one rainy day in the coat-room and wanted to know what I was doing, why was I being so furtive? I said I was sniffing the coats, sir. How improbable, he said. You'll have to think of a better excuse than that, Baird. I was, though. School had many smells, and the smell of damp coats and sou'westers and gumboots was one that I liked sniffing. It was the same when Mr Dalloway caught me looking into Jimmy Ling's schoolbag. Why was I interfering with another boy's property? I was only sniffing the lunch smell, I told him. I liked sniffing the smell of all sorts of sandwiches and guessing what the other kids had brought today, if they were tomato sandwiches or banana or jam or golden syrup or cheese. But Mr Dalloway did not believe me. You can't tell me you're in Ling's bag for the sake of the smell, he said. I've been warned about you, my lad. Well, I knew who had warned him, but I could see he was not nearly as angry as Miss Piggy-face would have been if she'd caught me there, I could see he almost believed me or, if he didn't, was not the sort of teacher to make a big fuss about it. So I didn't duck when he walked towards me, as I would have if he'd been Miss Piggy-face; I simply put Jimmy Ling's bag back under the desk and looked straight at Mr Dalloway as though I had done no harm. He kept me in after school to write *I must not pry in other children's bags* a hundred times, but it was not as bad as the things Miss Piggy-face used to do to me, like throwing black-balls and shouting. Another time, when I was in a higher class, Mr Dalloway said I could be milk monitor, he said responsibility might bring out a bit of whatever good there was in me; he did not make a fuss when he discovered I'd told the smaller kids the day's ration was two bottles instead of the usual one so that there was not enough milk for the older kids; he made no fuss, but I was never milk monitor again. I rather liked Mr Dalloway then. His punishments were never very tough and there came a term when they stopped altogether. This, funnily enough, was after he had met my mother to complain about something nasty I'd done—it must have been the time I set fire to the school wood-heap. He met my mother and after that I could get away with anything. Mr Dalloway didn't seem to care what I did, all he said was that he hoped I wouldn't do again whatever it was that I had done. Which was probably pretty smart of him, because eventually I got sick of bopping other kids and all that, there wasn't much fun in it if there was no risk in it. I was no longer the worst-behaved kid at school. I was not the best-behaved, either; but I did stop caring when other kids thought of interesting ways of misbehaving, like chalking rude words on the blackboard when Mr Dalloway was out of the room. Sometimes I wondered what my mother had told him about me) and I begin crawling through the grass towards the furnace-house where there are shadows, pausing every few inches to look along the road and up the hill. I cannot see Sam Phelps. I cannot see Sydney Bridge Upside Down. But I know they are there. The furnace-house is a good hiding-place. If I drop through the hole in the top, nobody can get at me. But I'll be seen on the top, because there is moonlight on the top; they'll know where I have gone, even if they won't be able to get at me. And Sam Phelps will stand guard outside the furnace-house, and Sydney Bridge Upside Down will be with him. I'll be trapped in there, worse than when I'm trapped in the bedroom at home, and it won't be any good yelling; when you're in the furnace-house you can't be heard. When I yell at home, deep in the night, Cal wakes up, then wakes me, and he tells me to stop having nightmares, he says it happens every night and he can't sleep properly because I yell so much. He tells Dad about me and Dad says it's not surprising I have nightmares, it has been an upsetting time in the bay lately, what with another accident at the works and the Bonnie Brae policeman asking questions and people giving themselves headaches trying to think why Chick Wiggins should go into the works, it will be a good thing when they pull down the rest of the ruins, which isn't far off now, as soon as they find the men for the job down will come the ruins, and though the bay won't seem the same when that happens it must be done, all these accidents are giving the district a bad name. I tell Dad my nightmares are not about the works; at least, the only one I remember, I say, was about Mr Norman the teacher, about the homework I should have done and Mr Norman's anger when he found I hadn't done it. Even so, said Dad, it had been a disturbing time and I might be affected in ways I was not myself aware of, deep-down ways that only showed themselves in nightmares. According to Mr Kelly, he said, even a grown-up like Mrs Kelly had the shivers when she thought of poor Chick Wiggins falling to his death, a man cut off in his prime, a good butcher even if his flirty ways did gave him a bad reputation. If Mrs Kelly, who was used to people dying, could be troubled by Mr Wiggins' death, it was no wonder youngsters were upset. I remember Dad's words as I hide by the furnace-house. Is Sam Phelps troubled by Mr Wiggins' death? Who else might be troubled by his death? Not Caroline, at any rate. Caroline never talks about Mr Wiggins, I am sure she has completely forgotten him. The one she talks about now, the one she looks forward to being with, is Buster Kelly. And this, I am sure, is partly because I am seldom at home; when I am not at school I am up in the cave or alone by the river, alone on the beach, alone in the trees near the swamp. Should I run for the swamp now? When I peep from behind the furnace-house I cannot see Sam Phelps or Sydney Bridge Upside Down, but this doesn't mean they are not there somewhere, waiting for me. It's safest to crawl on through the grass until I reach the trees, then I can race along the river-bank to where the swamp begins, I can cross the swamp and be home. First, though, I must get from the works yard to the paddock, quickly and without being seen. I can imagine Sam Phelps along there on the road, staring, waiting, or doing now what his horse is doing—coming to find me. They are moving towards me out there in the dark, Sam Phelps from the road, Sydney Bridge Upside Down from the hill. If I wait they'll have time to find me; if I run I can be in the paddock and crawling through the grass before they see me. I must run. I run from the furnace-house and throw myself into the paddock, and I lie still, I listen. The swamp frogs are louder, the sea is louder. Away from the shelter of the works, the breeze is stronger and I can hear the grass moving. There are many more clouds among the stars, and

I watch them rolling towards the moon and I am sure that this time the moon will be hidden longer, I'll have a good chance to get right across the paddock to the trees. So I wait for the clouds to help me. I wait. Can I hear hooves? Can I hear boots crunching on metal? If he is coming for me, who will wait back outside the house? Mrs Kelly maybe. She watches me too. Not in the same way as Sam Phelps, not with those long and knowing stares. Mrs Kelly just gives me quick and sharp looks whenever I go by. She says Hello, but she does not seem ready to chat to me, as she used to long ago. And of course she never gives me a piecey, she prefers Bruce Norman to me, he gets bread and plum jam now. I don't care. Mrs Kelly needn't think I care about her plum jam, I can get by without it, without her too. I can get by without anybody. Would anybody help me now, for instance? Nobody would help me. I lie here in the grass, listening to the hooves and the boots, and nobody will help me (Put this down as well, dear Caroline. Say that Dad was wrong when he said I didn't really remember that pongy voyage in the *Emma Cranwell*. Say it was more than hearing him tell of it in later years that made me remember it. I remembered every bit of it myself, every moment on the leaning deck in the black night on the wild seas. I remembered him throwing away my pyjamas, I remembered the pong that surrounded us as he led me back to the cabin, I remembered how he washed me and how the water splashed. I remembered, even though I was sick and weak and scared, what he said as he washed me. He said: 'Why didn't she come? Why does she do it?' He was talking to something out in the awful night, and his voice was as angry as the waves that crashed on the port-hole. I remembered his words, but I did not speak to him about them ever. When we were home again, just Dad and me, I would pretend that the night he threw away my pyjamas had been a kind of jolly adventure and that I did not mind looking back upon it and grinning with him when he said how my mother would be annoyed because I had lost my new pyjamas. It was good with him and me at home on our own; I liked following him around and helping him, he let me do some hammering and showed me how to use the big saw, and he let me scatter seeds. I did not care if she or Cal never came home, and I wished he would feel the same. I knew he didn't, because there were nights when he put his elbows on the table and put his hands round his cheeks, and stared at nothing and did not speak for several minutes. I knew he was thinking of her at these times, I knew he was worried. Then he would cheer up and we would go along to see Mr and Mrs Kelly, and he and Mr Kelly would have some beer and I'd be allowed to play with Dibs until we got too noisy and Dibs was sent off to bed, then I sat in a corner and listened to the grown-ups and pretended I was too interested in the Kelly kids' fairy-tale books and comics to hear what was being said. What they said was usually about how people were behaving to one another; it was amazing, seeing there were so few people in this part of the world, how much could be said about them. Men were always in trouble with their wives about something or other, wives always had something to be unhappy about, husbands were always good fellows in some ways, not in others, somebody was always courting somebody else, somebody was always going to have a baby, somebody was always to blame for a certain road not being graded, somebody was always to blame for the district not getting a fair deal—I preferred the gossipy bits about people and the things they did to one another, and it did not matter when Mrs Kelly began putting in things like 'you-know' and 'what-you-may-call-it' into her stories, I could guess, or thought I could, what she was trying to hide. I noticed too that the men used words like *bloody* and *damn* after they had been drinking a while, and one night I even heard Dad use the word *bitch*, and neither Mr Kelly nor Mrs Kelly seemed to mind, Mrs Kelly talked so softly to Dad after it that I couldn't hear what she said, and when I was in bed later I said *bitch bitch bitch* to myself until I fell asleep) and nobody will care what the scar-faced old man and the hollow-backed old horse do to me when they reach me. The hooves can trample on me and the boots can kick me, nobody knows, nobody cares. I must not wait in the grass. I must run for the trees. I stand, alone in the paddock, and I do not look back. I put my head down and I run for the trees. The swamp frogs are much noisier now, I hear them as I stand panting behind a tree, they drown out other noises, I can no longer hear the hooves and the boots. I might be safe here, there are trees all the way to the river-bank. If only there were a short-cut through the swamp from here—I look at the rushes, remembering. I was not far from here when I threw the present in. I could only hope it would sink or float away out of sight. I have never been back to check. What if somebody sees it floating there and fishes it out? What will he find? Flowers? A fur-coat?

A hat? An ornament? Or a joke present—like a leg of mutton? I cannot guess what Mr Wiggins thought Caroline would want from him. He would know it had better be something special, because he must know that Caroline did not like him and only something special could make her change her mind. I should have looked, only there wasn't time, I did not waste a moment after running down the stairs, falling, running on. I must stroll past the swamp during the day, glance in and make sure the present is out of sight. If Sam Phelps will let me. If he doesn't keep watching me. Where is he now? Where is his horse? The swamp frogs are quieter, maybe because the moon is still hidden. I hear a soft thud-thud, like the sound hooves might make on grass. I peep from behind the tree, look towards the works. I see nothing moving, unless that is something by the furnace-house, that could be something. Only the usual works shadows? I cannot tell. The breeze is much stronger, though. I look at the clouds and many of them are dark, and I can see hardly any stars. If I wait too long in the trees there will be a storm, I will be caught in it. I move on. I go from tree to tree, not looking back, keeping close to every tree-trunk. Now the wind is making more noise than the swamp frogs, it is making the leaves above me rustle, it is making the branches creak. I run faster, much faster than when I'd played Robin Hood games in here with the other kids, yet seeming to take much longer to reach the river-bank, the trees will never end, they go on and on ahead of me, I'll never reach the river-bank (Now you can say this, dear Caroline. You can start another page and say that one day after school my mother called Cal and me down from the passion-fruit shed and said she wanted us to go across to the store. She stood on the back porch to tell me this, and she handed me some money and told me what to get, and when I asked Cal as we went up the side-path why he had stayed behind the tank-stand while our mother was talking he said it was because Mr Dalloway was in the kitchen and was probably telling her about him not being able to do his sums today. I said she didn't seem to be upset when she was telling me what to get at the store, in fact she had the pink cheeks she usually got when she was pleased with something somebody told her or when she was excited. Cal said he hoped I was right, he said he could think of no other reason why Mr Dalloway should call. I said I couldn't either, it wouldn't be because of me since I had been doing all right at school lately, I was going through one of my good no-bopping times and was being spoken to politely by Mrs Kelly and other grown-ups. Cal and I talked about school, how it was not so bad some days and damned terrible other days, and Cal said today was one of the days when he would rather be playing at the beach than learning stupid sums, and I said we could go to the beach and have a swim as soon as we had got the things from the store— What things? I couldn't remember what she had told me to get. I asked Cal what she'd said, but he said he hadn't heard. He tried naming a few things, like butter and eggs and jam and sugar but I still could not remember. I said it was no use, I would have to go back and ask her. Luckily, we had only reached the river crossing when I realised I had forgotten, it would have been terrible if I got to the store and then found I didn't know what to ask for. Cal said he would wait for me. I said I'd run home and run back, it wouldn't take long. But it took a bit longer than I expected it to. This was because the back door was locked when I got home, which was pretty unusual; I had to wait for my mother to open it. I had to knock several times before she opened it. 'What are *you* doing back here?' she asked, and her face was angry and red. She kept the door nearly shut, but I saw she was wearing her dressing-gown, and that was pretty unusual for this time of the day. I said I had forgotten what she had asked me to get from the store. 'Oh, three pounds of flour and two packets of cigarettes, never mind the other things,' she said. Then she must have guessed that I had seen her dressing-gown and her bare feet, because she said: 'I'm having a shower while you kids are away. There's no privacy with you two running in and out. Anyway, three pounds of flour and two packets of cigarettes. Will you remember now?' I said I would, and she closed the door. No need for her to be so crabby, I thought as I ran back down the road. No need for her to have a shower so late; if we got in her way so much, she should have her shower earlier. I told Cal this and he agreed that she shouldn't have been crabby. If she was having a shower, he said, Mr Dalloway must have gone. Must have, I said. Then I thought it was funny I hadn't seen him on the road when I went back. I decided he must have popped along to see Mrs Kelly about Dibs; Dibs had been having trouble with his spelling lately. And I thought no more about my mother taking so long to open the door. I forgot all about it—until a few months later) the storm will break before I reach the river, it is as if I am running in the same spot all the time, yet I pass different trees and I am brushed by different branches. I must rest. I fall against a tree, grab the trunk to stop myself from flopping to the ground. When the noise of my panting stops at last I hear the sound of hooves back through the trees, and I do not wait to hear the other sound, I run on, the wind wilder than ever, the trees bending towards me, branches swiping me. Until suddenly I am at the river-bank. I can hear the river, I can see it rushing blackly by. Somewhere in the hills it must already be raining heavily, must have been raining a long time; I am sure there are logs speeding by in the river, maybe bodies as well. I hear thunder and look at the sky, and I know I will never see the moon again, the storm is beginning. I turn as the rain hits my face. I shout into the trees: 'Go home! Go to your shack!' They won't hear me, I can't hear my own words. I run on along the river-bank, and the wind is behind me now and I am going so fast I think I will fall at any second, or be blown into the river and swept out to sea with the logs. The thunder has stopped, the rain is heavy, mud spurts into my eyes. I stop to rub my sleeve in my eyes, and I hear sharp cracking sounds from back in the trees, and at first I think it is a pistol going off, then I realise it is the noise of twigs being snapped by heavy boots. The hooves are back there too. Soon the man and the horse will burst from the trees and chase me along the river-bank. But I will be safe if I get to the plank-bridge across the swamp. No horse can follow me there, and I can pull up a plank behind me so that the man will not be able to follow, either. It seems such a long way to the plank-bridge, though. And I can scarcely see where I'm going. I must just guess whereabouts in the rain and the dark the bridge begins. I try to stop to turn, my feet can't grip the ground, I skid, I slide in the mud. The bridge must begin around here some place, it can't be far away, it's in the rushes here somewhere, it must be somewhere near. I slide from the river-bank slope towards the swamp's edge, and I splash through the water and my feet sink into the mud as I splash on. Then I see the bridge, I see the first plank. The plank seems to be floating, soon it will be beneath the water. The water seems to be rising too swiftly. I'll never get to the plank in time (And say this, dear Caroline. Please say that I saw my mother kissing Mr Dalloway) and they can't be far behind now, I won't look, I won't listen, I must keep staring at the plank, if I stare hard enough it will stay in place, it won't float away through the angry angry wildly-waving rushes (Say I saw her, dear Caroline. Say I saw her kissing him. Say I saw them from the tank-stand. I saw them through the kitchen window. He had his hands on both sides of her head, his fingers in her hair, and he was kissing her. I saw them through the window. I was on the tank-stand. They were kissing in our kitchen. I couldn't watch. I jumped from the tank-stand and ran out to the road) and as soon as I put my foot on the plank I lose my balance and I fall, I seem to spin several times before I sink into the swamp, I am in blackness, then my head is out of the water, I am reaching for the plank, dragging myself out of the slime and the awful-tasting water. I stand on the plank. I move very slowly. I stop. I move again. My foot slides but I do not fall. I stand still. I tell myself I will not fall. I am too strong to fall again. I can get across the plank-bridge without falling. They cannot possibly catch me now (Say this as well, dear Caroline. Say that one day when I was on the back porch I heard them giggling and talking in the kitchen. They didn't know I was on the porch because I was sitting below the window-sill, taking a splinter from my heel, concentrating on getting it out and not realising for a few moments that my mother had a visitor. I crept away, but not before I heard a word that puzzled me. I asked Dad about this word a few days later when I was helping him in the garden. It seemed all right to ask him then, he was very friendly to me that morning and I was pleased to be helping him, it was one of the days, one of the great days, when I enjoyed being with my father, just him and me, like the times when she was away with Cal, leaving me with Dad, happy times. I saw him put down the hoe, then rest on his crutch while he wiped some sweat from his forehead. I smiled at him, said I would take off my shirt soon, the sun sure was hot. He said I had better take care, I burned easily and sun-blisters were no fun. I said I would not leave my shirt off too long, long enough probably to get a few more freckles. He said he had freckled easily too when he was a youngster, he said he had huge freckles on his back that he'd got when he was only four or five. This, I thought, was my chance to ask about the word. Had he, I asked, ever been called Spotty when he was a kid? He laughed. No, he said, he had been called Freckles a few times, but he'd not had enough freckles to keep that nickname for long; many of his freckles, he said, had faded. He said I could expect the same to happen to most of my freckles; as it was, he said, I did not have nearly as many as young Dibs Kelly. Good, I said. Had he, I asked slowly, ever been nicknamed Hoppy? He frowned. He wanted to know why I had asked that. I said I had read a story about an air ace in one of the Kelly kids' comics, and this ace had lost a leg in a crash-landing, and a nasty character in the story had called him Hoppy and this had made the ace feel unhappy, but his friends came to his rescue and gave the nasty character a good hiding, they said he should be ashamed of himself for calling such a brave man Hoppy. I could have gone on like this a while longer, but I saw Dad nod, obviously agreeing with what the ace's friends had done, so I guessed I could leave it to him to answer. He said he had been called various things in his time, but he could not remember being called Hoppy. Of course, he said, some nicknames were friendly and some weren't, much depended on the way they were used, on how the person using a nickname felt about the person he was talking to. Hoppy, as I had probably guessed from reading the air-ace story, was not a friendly nickname, he said. None of his own friends had ever called him Hoppy, he said. They knew that he, like the air ace, would be unhappy if they did. On the other hand, he said, a man could not help making a few enemies during his life, and it was quite possible, though he had not heard of it, that one of his own enemies had referred to him as Hoppy, it was an obvious enough thing to call a one-legged man. He bent down for the hoe. I said I would never call a one-legged man Hoppy, it would be cruel. Good lad, he said. He went on hoeing. So now I knew what it meant when my mother used that word, when she said: 'I promised to make Hoppy and the kids some scones for tonight. Better let me go now, Pet.' It meant she was my father's enemy) unless I slip and fall into the swamp, Sam Phelps could catch me then, he could find me lying in the swamp and pick me up and take me to the river-bank and throw me into the river and let me be washed out to sea. Has he reached the beginning of the bridge yet? He might already be at the first plank, Sydney Bridge Upside Down watching while he comes after me. The wind cuts, the rain stings, the water streams down my body, my dingdong frozen. I steady myself, push the hair from my eyes, move on. I must be half-way across the swamp. The water is still rising, but if I can keep my balance I'll be safe. Anyway, the frogs are silent and I can no longer hear the hooves and the boots. I'll soon be across. I know this because I have reached the open part where Kingsley, our wonderful Muscovy, used to do his tricks. I don't want to see Kingsley. I don't want to remember him. Kingsley is dead. I didn't mean to kill him. I meant to scare him, but I did not mean to kill him. I miscalculated. I landed on him instead of beside him. Whatever Susan Prosser said, I did not mean to do it. Poor dead Kingsley, poor dead Susan Prosser—I scream at the swamp, I scream, I scream. Sam Phelps screams back. He screams that he is on his way, he is coming for me, he is right behind me, he will lift me on to his horse and carry me off to the sea. You will never escape, he screams. You will never catch me, I scream back. I am too strong for you, I scream. I begin to run, guessing where the plank is, where the next plank is, certain I will keep running even if I miss the planks, I am too strong to fall (And if there's room, dear Caroline, you can say this

239

too. You can say that when she comes home I'll tell her what I know, what I've seen, what I've done. Ha ha! See how she likes that) too strong to care when I leave the last plank and go up to my knees in the swamp, too strong to be stopped now. I reach the bank. Now it is only a short climb to the passion-fruit shed and our backyard. Just grab the vine by the track and clamber up. The vine breaks. I fall. I crawl back to the slope, begin clambering, slide to the bottom. I look across the swamp. Only the rising water, the bending rushes, only the rain, the wind. All I have to do is get to the top, I have done it many times every day, it is not even a hill, it is only a slope. I run at it and grab the higher part of the vine as I slip. The vine holds. It is as if the slope has become a steep cliff, but I hold on. I move inch by inch. The vine breaks, but I do not fall. My fingers dig deep into the mud, I force them to drag me higher. I am at the top. I stand by the passion-fruit shed and look across the swamp. The wind is lighter, the rushes are straighter. The rain stops. Nobody is out in the swamp. Now I can hear the frogs again. I look at the sky and see the clouds moving from the moon. There is moonlight on our garden when I walk by it to the wash-house. I take off my clothes in the wash-house and turn on the tap in the tub. I climb into the tub and wash off the mud. I wipe myself with grubby clothes from the heap in the corner. I run naked into the house. I get into bed beside Cal. He does not move. I lie there. I think I am asleep. Then I hear Cal whimpering. He is crying in his sleep, his body is trembling, he is whispering something in a little-boy voice. He is whispering, 'Mummy, Mummy.'

14

ONE SUNNY Saturday, two weeks after Mr Wiggins' accident, I was hiding in my room when I heard voices out the front. Although the window was up, the blind was down, so I could listen without being noticed. I crawled from under the bed and stood by the blind, listening. The voices were angry. They belonged to Mrs Kelly and Fat Norman.

'You haven't been here long enough to know us,' Mrs Kelly said. 'If you knew us you wouldn't dare suggest such a thing. You're an educated man, surely you can control your emotions.'

'This is a matter of reason,' Fat Norman said. 'I've reasoned this out, I'm not rushing into it. My wife and I have given it a great deal of thought. I assure you it's no instant reaction, Mrs Kelly.'

'But it only happened yesterday!' Mrs Kelly cried. 'You haven't had enough time to think about it.'

'Yesterday?' he said. 'This began long before yesterday.'

'I thought you said it was yesterday he let your son, let your Bruce, have a ride,' said Mrs Kelly. 'Isn't that what you said?'

'Yes,' he said. 'But I don't—'

'Well, how *can* you have given it much thought?' she asked. 'Even if you and your wife sat up all night talking about it, it still wouldn't be long enough.'

'Yesterday was the climax,' he said. 'I can assure you I gave it a great deal of thought before yesterday. In fact, I began thinking about it only a day or so after I arrived.'

'How *could* you?' asked Mrs Kelly. 'Do you expect me to take you seriously, Mr Norman? Do you know what you're saying?'

'Perfectly well,' he said. 'I'm saying I find his behaviour distasteful in the extreme. I'm saying I should tell him so.'

'You're saying a lot more than that,' Mrs Kelly said. 'You're accusing him of something wicked.'

'I'm saying he is capable of such behaviour,' said Fat Norman. 'Nothing more than that—at the moment.'

'I'm surprised by one thing, Mr Norman,' said Mrs Kelly, her voice turning very serious. 'For an educated man, you seem surprisingly unaware of the implications of what you say. Don't you realise it's slander?'

'Nonsense,' he said. 'I'm a parent. I'm expressing a natural concern for the welfare of my children.'

'But you don't have to be slanderous about it,' said Mrs Kelly.

'Leave me to be the judge of that, Mrs Kelly,' Fat Norman said in his classroom voice.

'I certainly won't!' she cried. 'Not when it concerns

somebody who has done *you* no harm. I'll tell you this: I'm beginning to wonder if you're the right sort of person to have charge of *our* children. There!'

This was shouted so loudly it seemed to have shut Fat Norman up. It was so loud it must have reached Dad, who was in our kitchen. I heard him hopping along the passage and opening the front door. I stood stiffly by the blind, wondering if I should risk peeping. I wondered if Caroline, across in her room, was listening too. She had been out late with Buster last night, and Dad had told Cal and me at breakfast that she was having a lie-in today, but I didn't reckon that anybody, even Caroline, could sleep through the noise Mrs Kelly and Fat Norman were making.

'What's going on out here?' I heard Dad ask. 'Where's the fight?'

'We were on our way to see you, Frank,' said Mrs Kelly. 'Mr Norman has something on his mind. Tell Frank what you have on your mind, Mr Norman.' I could imagine what sort of look she was giving Mr Norman, I had stopped that sort of look many a time myself.

'It's quite straightforward,' Fat Norman said. 'Nothing to be hysterical—'

'Tell Frank what you told me,' said Mrs Kelly.

Fat Norman said: 'I'm saying, Mr Baird, that I'm entitled to tell that chap at the wharf not to pester my children. Now that's all I'm saying.'

Mrs Kelly said: 'That's not all you were saying to me. You were saying Sam Phelps was an evil fellow.'

'Sam Phelps?' said Dad, sounding amazed.

'I said he *might* be up to no good,' said Fat Norman. 'His

243

interest in my children could be perfectly innocent for all I know. But I prefer not to encourage him.'

'Slander, isn't it, Frank?' asked Mrs Kelly.

'Sounds like a misunderstanding,' Dad said. 'There's no harm in Sam Phelps, Mr Norman.'

'That's what I told him,' Mrs Kelly said. 'But you can't reason with him. He decided as soon as he got to Calliope Bay that poor Mr Phelps was evil, and nothing will shift him. I'm surprised an educated man can be so old-fashioned—pointing the finger at somebody because he lives alone and minds his own business.'

'It wasn't his business to give my son a ride on his horse,' said Fat Norman. 'And why does he stand on the road and look at the houses? He's looking for the children!'

'Oh, I wouldn't say that, Mr Norman,' said Dad. 'I get what you mean. But you're barking up the wrong tree. We all know Sam Phelps. There's no harm in Sam Phelps.'

'Exactly what I told him,' Mrs Kelly said. 'I'm blowed if I can see the danger in young Bruce riding the horse. You should be ashamed of yourself, Mr Norman. You'll want us to go down and lynch Mr Phelps next. Would that satisfy you?'

'All I'm saying—' Fat Norman began.

'Ask anybody in the bay about Mr Phelps,' said Mrs Kelly. 'Ask my husband—here he comes now.'

I peeped out. Mrs Kelly, Dad and Fat Norman were looking along the road. I heard the Reo, then I saw it. It stopped outside the Kelly place.

'Yoo-hoo!' Mrs Kelly called. She beckoned to Mr Kelly, looked at Dad and nodded twice, as if to say that Mr Kelly would soon deal with Fat Norman.

I hoped he would. I was scared Fat Norman would say when he first got the idea Sam Phelps might have done something bad. I didn't want to be brought into their argument, I didn't want them to think of me, I didn't want to be noticed. Even while I was hoping I'd be left out of it, though, I was thinking that Fat Norman certainly was dopey. No wonder Bruce didn't seem to like him. Making all that fuss because Bruce had ridden Sydney Bridge Upside Down! What would he say if he knew Bruce was on the wharf now, fishing there with Dibs and Cal? Probably turn maniacal.

I saw Mr Kelly reach the others. 'I was coming along, anyway,' he said. 'Picked this up at the store, Frank.' He handed Dad a letter.

'The meat was there too, was it?' asked Mrs Kelly. When Mr Kelly nodded, she told Fat Norman: 'We can never be sure about the deliveries now. It was different when we had Mr Wiggins. He was always so regular.'

I saw Dad frowning at the envelope before he put it in the back pocket of his pants; he hadn't read the letter.

Mr Kelly turned. 'I'll take the meat in,' he said.

'Come here!' Mrs Kelly said. 'Do you know what Mr Norman's saying about Sam Phelps? Go on, Mr Norman, tell my husband what you think of Sam Phelps.'

'All I said—' Fat Norman said.

'He wants us to lynch Mr Phelps,' said Mrs Kelly.

'Nonsense,' said Fat Norman. 'All I said was I don't want him hanging round my children. I don't trust old men like him.'

'Sam wouldn't look so old if he shaved more often, spruced himself up,' said Mr Kelly. 'He doesn't think it matters. I can see his point of view.'

'Fancy suggesting he's an evil man!' said Mrs Kelly, looking scornfully at Fat Norman.

'No harm in Sam,' Mr Kelly said. 'Minds his own business.'

'Well, I can see you're all on his side,' Fat Norman said. 'But you don't blame me, do you? You don't blame me for being concerned about my children?'

'We understand that,' said Mrs Kelly. 'You shouldn't slanderise him, though. You must be careful what you say.'

'Very well,' said Fat Norman. 'I'll accept that he's a nice, normal old fellow—or not-so-old fellow. But I reserve the right to tell him to stay away from my children. Is that reasonable enough?'

'I still don't know what you have against Sam,' said Mr Kelly, who had taken out his tobacco tin and was rolling himself a smoke. He licked the cigarette paper. 'What's he done, eh?'

'Oh, he reckons—' Mrs Kelly began.

'No, let him tell me,' said Mr Kelly. He lit his cigarette, looked calmly at Fat Norman.

'Specifically, he gave my son a ride on his horse yesterday,' Fat Norman told Mr Kelly. 'Wait!' he said as Mr Kelly took the cigarette from his mouth to speak. 'I admit that ordinarily I wouldn't mind if Bruce rode somebody else's horse. I know he is very fond of horses. But I believe that recluses like your Mr Phelps are often—well, a little peculiar. We can't be sure what form this peculiarity will take. No, no, I'm not saying Phelps *is* peculiar! I'm talking of men like him. You look sceptical, Mr Kelly. But don't you think it's a *little* peculiar how he stands on the road looking at the houses? Why does he do that? And what about the accidents at the works? I gather he found the Prosser girl's body. He also found Wiggins' body. Now isn't that a *little* peculiar? Two people die in mysterious circumstances, and Phelps is involved on both occasions—'

'Now hold on!' Mr Kelly shouted. 'Just a minute!' He looked at Dad. 'This is getting serious, Frank. What do you reckon? How do we handle this fellow?'

I saw Dad look from Mr Kelly to Fat Norman, then to Mrs Kelly. Mrs Kelly was deep purple and speechless.

'I don't know what he's driving at,' Dad told Mr Kelly. 'What have those accidents to do with Sam? Sam only found the bodies.' He frowned at Fat Norman. 'What are you driving at, Mr Norman?'

Now Fat Norman looked rather scared. 'Please don't misunderstand me,' he said. 'I'm simply suggesting—'

'What have the works got to do with Sam Phelps?' Mr Kelly asked him. 'Are you worried about the works, Mr Norman? Is that why you're having these queer thoughts? Don't worry about the works. They'll be pulled down next week. Bill Dobson and his lads start first thing on Monday. Does that make you feel better, Mr Norman?'

Mrs Kelly found her voice. 'What a cheek saying Mr Phelps is peculiar! I know who's peculiar around here!' She glared at Fat Norman, then walked away. I heard her shout: 'I know who's peculiar!'

'Well, what do you say, Mr Norman?' asked Mr Kelly.

I did not wait to hear what Fat Norman said. I got back under the bed. I curled up under there, my hands over my ears to make sure I heard nothing the men said. They had said enough to make me shake and sweat. Especially Fat Norman and his talk of mysterious circumstances. Heck, the policeman from Bonnie Brae hadn't thought there were mysterious circumstances, so why should Fat Norman try to cause trouble? I knew that whatever Dad and Mr Kelly said to him, however much they went on about Mr Phelps being a good fellow, Fat Norman would still think he knew better. And sooner or later he would call on Mr Phelps and go over all the dopey things he had already gone over with Dad and Mr Kelly. I didn't think Sam Phelps would say why he waited on the road, but I couldn't be sure; there was no telling what he would say if Fat Norman made him angry enough. He might even say *I* was the one Fat Norman should be worrying about, *I* might be dragged into their damned argument. I wished Mr Dalloway had never left Calliope Bay; he was certainly better than a trouble-maker like Fat Norman.

I tried to forget Fat Norman by thinking of what else Mr Kelly had said. He had said the works would be pulled down next week. Of course, I'd already heard Dad say they would be pulled down, but I hadn't realised it would be so soon. Calliope Bay would seem strange without the works. Ever since I was a small kid I had played there, I had looked down from the top floor, I had hidden there. I could not believe that one day soon there would be no works to go to. They couldn't pull down the works, surely there was somebody who could stop them—

I heard a motor-bike. Even with my hands over my ears, I could hear the Indian.

I crawled out again and went to the blind. I peeped. Buster was parking the Indian. Now he was walking to our house. He was smiling and pointing to our front door.

Caroline must be looking from her window, there was nobody else Buster could be smiling at; Dad and the other two men had gone.

Yes, I heard Caroline's footsteps, I heard the front door being opened, I heard their voices. I did not want to listen; I put my hands over my ears.

Back under the bed, I wondered if Dad and Mr Kelly had got Fat Norman to stop being dopey. Maybe they were all at Mr Kelly's place, drinking beer. Or maybe Fat Norman had apologised for being so dopey and had invited Dad and Mr Kelly to his place. Maybe everything was okay again.

It was dusty under the bed. Dad usually gave the house a sweep-out on Sundays, and sometimes I went round with the broom before school, but neither of us was much good at reaching under the beds, some of the dust under this bed had probably been here for as long as my mother had been away. I should be out in the sun, I only got gloomy under the bed, I kept waiting for somebody to call for me, I expected the Bonnie Brae policeman to arrive at any moment and say he had discovered my secret. If I were at the wharf, fishing with Cal and Dibs and Bruce, I would not think about the policeman. These days, though, I could not be bothered with Cal and Dibs and Bruce; they seemed too young, too ignorant. I no longer got excited about the same things as they did. Like the pistol. Dibs reckoned he had worked out who was the only person who could possibly have stolen the pistol. There had been no strangers at the bay, no tramps, no visitors from places like Bonnie Brae, he said. So the thief must be somebody who lived in the bay, and the only person likely to know about the cave was Sam Phelps. What did I think of that for an idea? I said I didn't care. Would I care, he asked, if he sneaked into Mr Phelps' shack and looked for the pistol? No, I said, I wouldn't care, the pistol could stay stolen for all I cared. It was the same with the other things he talked about. I was not interested. Until, in the end, he gave up talking to me. He concentrated on Cal and Bruce. And I got under the bed.

Maybe it was not so much the other kids as the bay itself. I was tired of Calliope Bay. So was Dad. I agreed with Dad when he said after tea one night that it would be easier for everybody in the family if we lived in Bonnie Brae. He said Cal and I would get better schooling at Bonnie Brae, he didn't think Mr Norman was all that hot as a teacher, seemed too jumpy to be a good teacher. He said he could easily get a good job in Bonnie Brae and would not have to ride miles to work. He also said, lowering his voice and looking at Caroline, that my mother would prefer Bonnie Brae to Calliope Bay. He said she had often complained about the loneliness of Calliope Bay, had often said it would be nice to be able to pop down to the shops when she felt like it. When she got back from the city, said Dad, he would talk it over with her; in fact, he would not wait for her to get back, he would write to her about it. That was a good plan, I said; we would have more fun in Bonnie Brae. He laughed and said he would write the letter straight away.

He had not talked about Bonnie Brae since that night. I hoped he hadn't given up the plan to move there. It would be good to get away from Sam Phelps and Fat Norman. And what fun would there be here when they pulled down the works?

I heard voices. Buster and Caroline. I heard the front door being opened. Buster and Caroline were going for a ride. Caroline was lucky. I wished I could be on the Indian, zooming round bends, speeding through gullies, whizzing over hills.

But when I peeped from behind the blind, I was surprised to see them walk past the Indian and stroll along the road. Caroline was happy. I saw her turn to laugh at Buster, and she looked very beautiful. She wore a white dress, her blue sandals were the ones she usually wore when she went to the beach. How brown her arms and legs were! They had been very pale when she came to us, so many weeks before. She seemed small beside Buster. Buster, with his sort of golden-coloured arms and legs and his ginger hair and his bright yellow-and-blue shirt and his white shorts, looked the right person to be walking with Caroline; it seemed right for them to be together, to hold hands as they walked. Tucked under Buster's right arm was the green travelling-rug from Caroline's room. They were going to the beach to sit in the sun.

I left the window, but I did not get back under the bed. I sat on the bed, wondering. I wondered if I should go along the road too. I wondered if I had been silly to stay inside so often lately. Seeing Buster looking so strong made me realise how skinny and weak I had become. I no longer did exercises, so I was no longer strong. I no longer ran around much in the sun, so my skin had gone pale, the freckles were more noticeable. No wonder I thought Buster looked right as he walked with Caroline; it was because I knew I would look wrong if I walked with her. Once I was seldom far from her; now I was seldom near her. The times when I played with her, when she read to me from her auto-biography, when we explored, seemed long long ago; it was hard now to believe that I had been the one with her, the one who had saved her from Mr Wiggins—

I'd go to the works. I would have a last look at the ruins. No ghosts were there in the daytime, the sun would be shining, it would be warm and secret on the top floor, I could sit there for the last time. One day in years to come I might wonder what it was like in Calliope Bay, and I would remember how I had gone for the last time to the works, and I would not need to wonder any more. I must go there now.

I was soon there. Nobody, I was sure, had seen me leave the house. Nobody had watched me walking slowly along the road. Nobody had spied on me as I crept past the furnace-house and into the works. And all alone, making no sound, I went to the top of the works and I sat there, high above everybody. And it was the last time I would ever be there.

No more bricks for the cave. In fact, no more cave. If we went to Bonnie Brae, we would have to find different ways of playing. Anyhow, feeling like I did about Dibs and the other kids here, I would want different ways wherever I was. There would be many more kids to choose from at Bonnie Brae, many more places to explore. Yes, it would be good to live in Bonnie Brae. There was no fun left in Calliope Bay. I could look down from here and see it all, and nothing about it would surprise me—

I got up and went to the crumbly wall and looked across the paddocks and the beach. I looked at the sea, green and shiny in the sun, then at the wharf. Right at the end of the wharf were Cal and Dibs and Bruce. I could see them sitting on the edge, waiting for the barracoutas to bite. Back along the wharf, not far from the woolshed, were Sam Phelps and Sydney Bridge Upside Down. I could see Sam Phelps carrying a sack from the woolshed to the wagon. Sydney Bridge Upside Down just stood there.

I looked at the beach. Three of the small Kelly kids were playing near the rocks. I could see no grown-ups. Then I saw Caroline on a dune. She had run up from the other side and now she was looking back, and I knew she was laughing. She began running again, and Buster came in sight and ran after her along the dune, then she jumped out of sight and so did Buster. I watched, hoping they would appear again, but the minutes went by and they stayed out of sight. If I went on looking long enough, I thought, I would probably see them going for a swim. They were lucky to feel like playing in the sand and swimming. A few weeks ago I would have felt the same way; now I did not care. I would rather stay here at the top of the works.

I looked in other directions. I looked at the river crossing. I looked at the swamp, then back at the river crossing. I looked at the trees near the swamp, I looked harder at the swamp, as if I might see something from here that I had not been able to see when I was nearer, jewels sparkling in the sunlight maybe. I looked at the houses, our roof the brightest of all, our garden the tidiest. I looked at the passion-fruit shed up from the swamp, then I looked again at the swamp. Then at the river and the road that went on across the countryside, up hills and around bends and through gullies, all the way to Bonnie Brae, and further still if you were escaping.

I saw Fat Norman. He must have been walking close to the houses, because he suddenly popped into sight from behind the Knowles house. Now he was turning to the road. He was walking along the road towards the works. He was walking quickly, as if he had something urgent to do.

I looked at the wharf. Cal and Dibs and Bruce were still waiting for the barracoutas to bite.

Fat Norman did not turn from the road when he was near the works, down there below me. He walked on, he was heading for the railway line.

Cal and Dibs and Bruce were still waiting.

Fat Norman was on the railway line.

Cal and Dibs and Bruce were—

I saw Caroline and Buster. They were crossing the paddocks from the dunes. Fat Norman would see them if he looked their way; he didn't. They didn't look across at him, either. They were strolling, holding hands. Buster had the rug under his arm. They must be coming for their bathing-suits.

Fat Norman was striding along the railway line.

Cal and Dibs and Bruce were standing. Dibs was pulling in his line, the others were staring at the water.

Caroline and Buster were nearing the works. They would be out of sight while they short-cutted to the road.

Fat Norman was striding on.

I saw Sam Phelps leave the wagon and go behind the woolshed. Sydney Bridge Upside Down just stood there.

Cal and Dibs and Bruce were dancing around. Dibs was holding up his catch. I couldn't see what it was.

Caroline and Buster were out of sight.

Caroline and Buster were still out of sight.

I still couldn't see Caroline and Buster.

Caroline and Buster must have stopped to look at something.

No sign of Caroline and Buster.

Caroline and Buster were still out of sight down there.

I heard voices. They were talking down there.

I left the edge of the top floor and sat in the shady part. I wanted to give them time to get to where they were going. I didn't want to watch them any more. I wanted Fat Norman to reach Sam Phelps, I wanted Dibs and Cal and Bruce to run along the wharf to the funny steps and escape across the rocks, I wanted Caroline and Buster to reach home and get their bathing-suits—and I did not want to see them doing all this. Next time I looked, in five minutes maybe, I would want them to be gone, everything done that they were now about to do.

I heard voices. I thought I heard footsteps.

Caroline and Buster were walking around down there.

They have five minutes, I thought, putting my hands over my ears and counting the seconds.

They have four minutes.

They have three minutes.

Two minutes.

One minute.

I took my hands from my ears, went to the edge and looked, I could see nobody anywhere. I could hear nobody.

For the last time, from the top of the silent ruins, I looked at the bay.

And now I saw Dibs and Cal and Bruce. They had come from beneath the wharf. They were running across the rocks. I would beat them home, I thought.

I ran to where the stairs had been. I skimmed across the footholds to the floor below. And, as I ran towards the stairs, I heard the sort of cry I used to hear on windy days when I was on the top floor. There was no wind today.

I stopped, not sure where the cry had come from. It could have come from the floor below.

It came again. Ooo-ooo-ooo!

Now I knew. It had come from the killers' special room.

This was my last chance, I told myself as I walked slowly across the killing-floor to the special room. If I don't look now, I thought as I took the first brick from the peep-hole, I'll always wonder, I'll always be sorry I didn't. Now

I'll know, I thought as I reached for the second brick.

I looked into the special room.

They were on the rug.

He was on top of her. They were moving together. Her arms were around him. Her legs were slowly waving, as if to me. His head hid her face, but I could see her hair spread on the rug, yellow against green.

Her legs were waving quickly now, as if to keep me looking, like don't go don't go. He paused, bent one foot on the rug and pushed forward, and her legs stopped waving while he did this, her feet hooked behind his knees as he pushed, her fingers scraped his back. Then they moved together again, and slowly her legs began waving again, and I saw the sweat glistening on the gold and brown and red and white of their bodies. While they still moved together, like one animal wriggling and sweating on the rug, he moved his head from her face and seemed to whisper into her ear, and while his head was turned I saw her face. Her eyes were closed, her tongue was out and going from one side of her mouth to the other. Her legs kicked, her fingers scratched, she groaned, she cried: 'Aaahhh!' He stopped the cry by pressing his mouth against hers, but the kicking and scratching went on, and his elbows churned up the rug as he pushed faster and faster. His head kept turning from side to side, following hers. Then her legs were kicking not so quickly, they were waving slowly, they came down slowly on the backs of his legs, her fingers were still, and he was no longer pushing. Now their bodies moved with the quickness of their breathing, but there was no kicking or scratching or pushing. Their breathing slowed, their bodies were still, he staying on top of her, her fingers now smoothing his back, stopping suddenly as they reached the blood of the scratches. She turned her head from his and murmured something, and he murmured back. Presently he slid on to his side, facing her. His eyes were very close to hers, he must be looking through them, as I had once tried to do. She kept gazing at him, her eyes very dreamy, as she drew up her legs; then she turned and leaned across him to look at the scratches. She circled the scratches with one finger, murmuring to him as she did so. He put his arm around her and pulled her down beside him again. When their faces were close, his hand moved in circles across her back and sometimes further down, then to the front of her, to her breasts and further down. She seemed to tremble from her toes all the way up to her head, and he took his mouth from hers and laughed. He laughed into her face, then sat up. She laughed too. Then, when she looked at his body, seeming to study every inch of it, she saw something that made her put her hand to her mouth and open wide her eyes, pretending to be scared. He kissed her breasts, she pulled his hair. He pinched her, she squealed. She stood up, her back to me, and looked down at him. Then he stood up, and I could see all of him, I could see why she had pretended to be scared. I must go. I had seen too much. I had imagined all this, but not exactly this; I had always imagined her lying still and soft, not kicking, not scratching, not yelling. I did not want— Now she was kneeling and straightening the rug, now she was on her knees, now her elbows were on the rug too, she was crouching, waiting. Now he was on his knees behind her, moving towards her, closing in behind her, his arms reaching out and going around her. She gave a little cry as, in this different way, they were together again. She gave a louder cry as I turned from the peep-hole. I seemed to hear the echo of it as I put back the bricks, it seemed to go on and on, filling every corner of the works as I ran to the stairs and down the stairs and out into the sunshine.

I ran. They're no different, I thought. The squeals and groans are the same. Like the cries of dying animals. Hit by hammers, stabbed. How could she let such a huge thing go into her? No wonder she laughed at mine, no wonder she gave it a baby name. I was a baby. He was a man. I could do press-ups all day long, all week long, and never be like him.

I ran.

I ran down the side-path and on to the porch and into the kitchen, and past the table, towards the passage—

'Harry!' shouted Dad.

I ran into the passage.

'Harry!' he shouted again.

I stopped, did not turn. 'Yes?' I said.

'Come here,' he said.

I looked at him from the passage.

He was sitting at the table. His crutch was on the floor beside him. Both his hands were on the table; he had a piece of paper in one hand.

'What's wrong with you?' he asked.

'Nothing,' I said.

'Come here,' he said. 'Why are you looking so miserable? What have *you* got to be miserable about?'

I went to the table. I said: 'I'm all right, Dad.'

'Look as if you've seen a ghost,' he said, frowning.

'No. I didn't see anything,' I said. 'Honestly I didn't, Dad. I didn't see them—'

'See who?' he asked.

'Anybody,' I said. Quick, who else had I seen? 'Only Mr Norman,' I said. 'I saw Mr Norman going to the wharf—'

'To hell with that fool,' said Dad. 'Serve him right if he's shoved into the sea.' He looked at me, then at the paper in his hand, then at the table. He seemed to forget me.

He's the one who is miserable, I thought. Heck, I don't care about Caroline, I care about Dad. Caroline is a is a is a bitch. Dad is good. I'd rather help Dad. I shouldn't have wasted my time helping Caroline. I should have been helping Dad.

'Dad?' I said.

He went on staring at the table.

'I'm glad we're going to live in Bonnie Brae,' I said. 'I'll be glad not to have Mr Norman for a teacher. There'll be better teachers in Bonnie Brae. Dad?'

He looked at me, but he did not speak.

I sat on a chair opposite him. I looked at the paper in his hand. It was a letter. It must be the one Mr Kelly had given him.

'Anything you want me to do, Dad?' I asked. 'Shall I get some driftwood for the copper?'

'What?' he said. He shook his head a few times, as if to wake himself up. 'What were you saying about teachers?'

'I just said there'll be better teachers in Bonnie Brae,'

I said. 'Then I was wondering if there's—'

'Don't mention teachers to me,' he said, sounding very bitter. 'Not after this!' He waved the letter.

'All right, Dad,' I said.

'And you can forget about living in Bonnie Brae,' he said. He waved the letter again. 'She's told me what I can do with Bonnie Brae. *And* with Calliope Bay!' He looked closely at me, could see I was puzzled. When he spoke again his voice was quiet: 'She's not coming back, Harry. She prefers the city—and Dalloway. I'm afraid she's left us.'

'She can't!' I said. 'She's not allowed to!'

'It's her choice,' he said.

'What about me?' I said. 'What about Cal?'

'She apparently prefers Dalloway to her children,' he said.

'She can't!' I said.

'She's made her choice,' he said. 'She won't come back.'

'She has to!' I shouted. 'What about Cal?'

'She's made her choice,' he said bitterly.

'I hate that Mr Dalloway!' I shouted.

He reached across and patted my shoulder. 'Don't cry,' he said. 'She's not worth crying about.'

'I'm not crying!' I shouted, slapping the damned tears.

15

I WAS walking along the dusty road that took you from the river and across the countryside, up hills and around bends and through gullies, all the way to Bonnie Brae and further still if you were escaping, if you were trying to get as far as you could from the edge of the world.

It was a sunny day, mid-morning. I had left Caroline in bed. Cal was at school, Dad was at work. I might see them again some day.

I was walking pretty slowly because I knew that sooner or later before I reached the store, one of Bill Dobson's lorries would catch up with me and give me a lift. Bill Dobson's lorries made several trips from Calliope Bay every morning with the rubble that had once been the works. I was not sure how far they took the rubble, but I reckoned it would be some way past the store. After that, I could get another lift. I was hoping to reach Bonnie Brae by early afternoon. I must be as far from Calliope Bay as possible by the time Dad was home from work. I knew the other two would not notice I had gone. Caroline, who was out every night with Buster, spent most of every day either asleep or half-asleep. Cal, who had scarcely spoken to anyone since Dad gave him the news about our mother, was too unhappy to care what I did or where I went. Only Dad would care. But he wouldn't know where I had gone. Even if Cal told him I hadn't been at school today, it might be hours before he guessed I was running away. He would have to search all the hiding-places in Calliope Bay before he guessed.

Should I have left him a note? No, this would put him on my trail sooner. Best to send him a letter tomorrow or the next day. I would try to explain why I had left, why I had taken his money, why it might be a long time before I saw him again.

I felt very sad at the thought of how he would look when my letter arrived. He would look miserable, the way he had looked for days after getting my mother's last letter. Every day after that letter he had written to her, but she had never written again. Eventually he seemed to realise she really had finished with us, and he stopped looking miserable and looked angry instead, then he went around with his face stiff and frowning all the time, and he was still like that. I wished I did not have to make him miserable again. I wished he were a cruel father and I hated him, so that it would be easier for me to run away, so that I would not have to think of the unhappiness I caused him. But there was no other way. I could not stay in Calliope Bay now that the summer was ending, now that everything had changed, now that she and Dalloway were having fun in the city. No matter how much it hurt Dad, I must go. And maybe he would understand later that what I had done was the only thing I could have done.

I whistled. Everything would be all right. It was good to be walking along the road. My boots, crunching in the metal, were already covered with dust. But the schoolbag over my shoulder was not yet heavy even though it was crammed with a macintosh, a pair of sand-shoes, a shirt, a towel, some sandwiches, two apples, my father's whip and my collection of cigarette cards. I'd whistle all the way to Bonnie Brae, and further still.

I stopped whistling when I heard the lorry. I turned to greet it.

It pulled up beside me. Bill Dobson himself was in the cab. He was a big tanned man who always, it seemed, wore a black singlet and khaki shorts. From what Dad and other men said, he was a decent fellow.

'Hop aboard!' he called to me, leaning across the cab to open the door.

I had a look at his load while I climbed up. He was carrying bricks mostly, but there were bits of iron as well, and I recognised the furnace-house doors.

'Going to the store?' he asked when I was in the cab and the lorry was on its way again.

'No, I'm going to Bonnie Brae,' I told him. 'How far you going, Mr Dobson?'

'You're in luck,' he said. 'Bonnie Brae is where I'm going.'

'Hey, that's good,' I said. 'I didn't think you'd go that far.'

'Special trip,' he said. 'Got a buyer for those bricks on the back. Lot of good stuff at the works. They built that place solid.'

'I used to play there,' I said.

He laughed. 'So your Dad was telling me. No school today, Harry?'

'I have to go to Bonnie Brae—for Dad,' I said.

'With your lunch, I see,' he said, patting my schoolbag; I was nursing it.

'Yes,' I said.

'What to do, Harry?'

'Just a message,' I said. 'I got to pay a bill. Dad says it's important.'

'Must be,' he said. 'Wouldn't send you on a school day if it wasn't, eh?'

'I don't mind missing school,' I said. I had to keep his mind off the message. 'I'm not very fond of our teacher, Mr Dobson. He doesn't seem to know much. We call him Fat Norman.'

'Yes, I hear he's making himself unpopular,' Mr Dobson said. 'Tried to give Sam Phelps a rough time, I hear. Got more than he bargained for, one of my lads was saying. Sam dropped him, eh?' He laughed. 'Sam's not as fragile as he looks. This fellow Norman didn't know what hit him.'

'Fat Norman said he'd get the policeman to Mr Phelps,' I said. 'He's silly. Mr Phelps hasn't done anything.'

'You find these crazy fellows,' Mr Dobson said, swerving into the parking space outside the store. 'Won't be a moment, Harry. Have to get some baccy.'

I kept my head down while he was in the store.

265

Somebody in there might recognise me.

I sure was lucky to get a lift all the way to Bonnie Brae, I thought. This meant I would be there not long after lunch. I would soon be pushing on down the coast, zooming on my way to—I wasn't sure how the towns fitted in further down the coast, but I could look at the destination signs at the start of the highway south from Bonnie Brae. Did Laxton come before Port Crummer? And how many miles was it to Wakefield, the furthest-away town down the coast? I knew the city was about two hundred miles from Wakefield. It would be good if I could reach Wakefield in time to catch a bus to the city in the morning. Or I could hitch-hike all the way to the city. It depended how lucky I was. So far I seemed lucky.

Bill Dobson climbed back into the cab. We pulled away from the store.

'I was talking to your Dad last night, Harry,' he said. 'We were talking about you and your brother. He didn't say anything about sending you to Bonnie Brae.'

'Think he only decided at breakfast,' I said. Heck, I had forgotten that Bill Dobson sometimes dropped in to see Dad after work. If he dropped in tonight, Dad would soon be on my trail.

'How do you reckon on getting back?' he asked.

'Back?' I said.

'You'll be coming back later today, won't you?'

'Oh, yes. Well, I can get the bus back as far as the store. Then I don't mind walking home. The bus leaves Bonnie Brae at four o'clock. That will do me.'

'I'll be leaving there myself about half past two,' he said.

'Be glad to give you a lift back.'

'Thanks very much, Mr Dobson,' I said. 'But I wouldn't mind looking around Bonnie Brae for a while. I think I'll catch the bus at four.'

'Fair enough,' he said. 'Might as well make the most of your visit, eh? Not often you Calliope Bay people get to Bonnie Brae.'

'My last time was for the carnival,' I said. 'We had a lot of fun. Until it rained.'

'My word, it certainly rained,' he said. He changed gears as we began climbing a hill, climbing very slowly. 'Yes, a patchy summer,' he said. 'More storms than usual. Not one of our best summers.'

'No,' I said. The lorry was hardly moving, we'd be lucky if we ever got to Bonnie Brae. I sighed. 'What were you and Dad saying?' I asked. 'About Cal and me.'

He glanced at me, grinned. 'Got you worried, eh? Afraid he was putting your pot on?'

I grinned. I did not mind his kidding. As long as the lorry moved, however slowly, I could put up with his kidding. I said: 'I'm not worried. I'm glad not to be at school.'

'My lads are the same,' he said. 'Best thing about school is when you don't have to go, eh?' He laughed, I joined in with a few loud ha-has. 'No,' he said presently, 'we didn't get round to discussing lessons, Harry.' His voice became solemn. 'We were talking about how you boys will manage when your cousin goes, I mean, now that your mother— well, now that she isn't coming back as soon as your Dad hoped.'

'It's okay, Mr Dobson,' I said. 'I know she never wants to come back. I know she's made her choice.'

'Tough on your Dad.' He shook his head. 'On you boys too.'

'We'll be okay,' I said. 'Besides, Caroline doesn't help much. She doesn't like housework.'

'Even so, a woman's influence is always good to have in a house,' he said. 'If you know what I mean, Harry.'

'I know,' I said, glad the lorry was nearly at the top of the hill; we should be speeding soon.

Mr Dobson waited until we were on the straight, going pretty fast. Then he laughed. 'Better not let Buster hear what you think of Caroline's attitude to housework,' he said. 'Might put him off marrying her!'

'No, it won't, Mr Dobson,' I said, not smiling. 'He knows already. But he doesn't care.'

'Don't blame him,' Mr Dobson laughed. Then, seeing I wasn't smiling, he became serious. 'I was only joking, Harry. Time enough later for a pretty girl like Caroline to learn about housework.'

'Oh, she's all right,' I said. I tried to think of something in her favour. 'She used to help with the washing. Sometimes she used to wipe the dishes.'

'Good for her,' Mr Dobson said.

I looked down at the cliffs and the breakers.

'Anyway, your Dad says he'll bring you and Cal to the party,' Mr Dobson said. 'You can team up with my lads, Harry. Plenty of fun and games, eh?'

'What party?' I said.

'You know, the engagement party,' he said. 'Didn't

you hear about it?'

'You mean for Caroline and Buster?'

'That's the one, Harry.'

'I knew they were getting married,' I said. 'But I didn't know they were having a party. Dad didn't tell me that.'

'Probably keeping it as a surprise for you,' he said. 'Yes, we're turning on a big party at my place, Harry. A lot of fun for young and old. How does that strike you?'

'Very good, Mr Dobson,' I said.

I watched the road. I didn't care about missing the party.

'Your Dad says you'll be coming with the Kellys in the Reo,' said Mr Dobson. 'Looks like the whole district will be there. We might even kid Sam Phelps into coming.'

'A good idea,' I said. Another reason why I wouldn't mind missing the party, I thought.

We sped into a gully, the lorry swaying so much I was sure we'd lose the furnace-house doors. We crawled up another hill, then we were speeding along another straight, nearer and nearer to Bonnie Brae.

'Mr Dobson,' I asked when there was only about a mile to go, 'which comes first—Laxton or Port Crummer?'

'On the way down from Bonnie Brae? Port Crummer's first. Why, Harry? Thinking of going there?'

'No,' I said. 'Gosh no. I was thinking of the other places on the coast, that's all. No, I don't want to go there. Not until the holidays maybe.'

'Not a bad spot for a holiday,' he said. 'Well, there we are, Harry. There's Bonnie Brae ahead. Journey's end, eh?'

Not just yet, I thought.

16

WOULD YOU believe me, I ask, if I mumble mumble mumble? No, says my friend in the brown velvet jacket, white polo-neck shirt, tight sky-blue pants and black cowboy boots. I'll bop you, I tell him. You can't stay at my place any more if you do, he says. I'll find another place, I tell him. Let's buy those peanuts, he says. We walk to the peanut stall, but a fellow in a long grey coat beats us there, takes his time deciding what size bag he wants, buys a very large bag, grabs a handful and shoves them into his mouth. Noisily munching, he watches us while we buy our two small bags, then he jerks forward and spits everything out. When he straightens up, he tells us he has broken a tooth. You were gobbling, my friend tells him, popping one peanut into his own mouth. The fellow, fingers to his teeth, tries to kick my friend, misses, nearly falls. Don't blame me for your busted tooth, my friend says. I'll bust *you*, the fellow says. Come on, I tell my friend, let's go before there's trouble. We leave the peanut stall quickly and turn the corner into the main street. Now I can start looking again. I am always looking, sometimes alone, sometimes with my friend. He thinks I am looking at the lights and the flashing signs. I don't tell him why I am really looking because I know he won't believe me. He thinks, when I tell him other things, that I make them all up. I do this, he thinks, because I lived so long in a place where nothing happened, now I must pretend a lot of things happened. I make up things, he thinks, so I won't feel bad about missing all the things that went on in the city while I was a kid. Do you know, I say, that there was a castle near where I lived? There are no castles in this country, he says. Do you know, I say, that I once saved a beautiful short-sighted girl from being captured by a hairy monster? You must have read too many fairy-tales, he says. Do you know, I say, that I slew the hairy monster *and* a skinny witch? No doubt, he says. Do you know, I say, that I was once the strongest hero, inch for inch and pound for pound, in the world? Of course, he says. Do you know, I say, that I used to run along halls and up and down stair-cases with this beautiful girl and that neither of us wore clothes and she used to lie on a big satin-covered bed and let me look at her breasts and pussy and say what a nice big cock I had and let me lie with her and let me cry on her breasts and if I'd been a few years older would have let me marry her and would probably have waited for me to grow a bit if an older hero hadn't turned up in a Daimler one day and taken her to the castle and fucked her right left and centre while I looked on? Let's go for a walk, I feel like some peanuts, says my friend. Do you know, I say as we leave his basement, that I had a secret cave— Look, he says, when did all this happen? Not so many years ago, I say. Like shit it was, he says. Well, a fair number of years ago, I say. Like when you were a skinny scabby kid having your first randy nightmares, that's what you mean, he says. Doesn't seem long ago, I say. It's time you grew out of it, let's get those peanuts, he says. He does not believe me. He doesn't know that when we walk up the glittering main street nibbling our peanuts, I am not looking for girls in short skirts and white boots, I do not care about the brilliant windows full of record sleeves, I do not want the snappy trousers jackets shirts shoes in other windows, I am not looking for new kicks. Mine is a much older curiosity. Just as when I first came to this city, I am looking for her. I no longer knock on doors, it is true, but this is because I knocked on so many when I first came, I knocked on all the doors it was possible for a grubby country kid in dirty boots to knock on. Does Mrs Janet Baird live here? What makes you think she might live here? I had her address on a piece of paper, but I lost it in Wakefield. Can't you remember it? I can't remember the street-name exactly, but it was something like Pecker or Peckham or Peckworth or Cocker or Cookham or Peck or Packer or Docker or Dockworth or Hackett or Bickworth or Decker or Peckham or Packer or Peckworth, some name like that. You'll have to do better than that, son. No, she doesn't live here. Why don't you try Duckett Street? What number is it, anyway? You don't know the number! You *have* got a job on your hands! Why don't you find a street directory and see if any of the names ring a bell? Mrs Janet Baird, you say? What is she like? Oh, she's a little taller than you, she has brown hair, she walks quickly, she talks quickly, she turns pink when she's excited, she smokes a lot of cigarettes, she has a pair of red ear-rings and a pair of black ones, she doesn't like sitting down for long, she likes to keep moving about, she taps her chin with her fingers when she's crabby, she likes to be tidy and puts on a clean dress and lipstick even before she goes to breakfast, she is angry if other people go to breakfast in their pyjamas, her favourite colours are red and blue and black, she doesn't like washing clothes and she isn't fond of gardening, she makes pretty good ginger beer, she doesn't make very good jam, she doesn't like people who get sick or stay away from school or work, she gets angry if anybody farts, she reads travel books, she thinks sums and spelling are good for kids, she sometimes cries when she is in bed and thinks everybody else is asleep, she calls my father Hoppy when he's not at home to hear her, she sleeps with other men when my father is at work, she has a special friend called Mr Dalloway. Sorry, son, don't know any lady who answers that description. If she calls, will you tell her Harry is looking for her? Yes, but I'm not expecting her to call, never heard of her before, don't expect to again. But if you do you'll tell her, won't you? Yes, yes. Why aren't you at school, son? I'm looking for my mother. Well, tell her to give you a bath when you find her. You can't sleep here, son, I'll have to take you along to the station if you try to sleep here. Please sir, I'm only resting, I'll go home now, my mother's got a big feed waiting for me. Off you go then, and tell her to give you a wash, you could grow spuds in those ears. Yes sir, I'll hurry home, sir.

Mrs Janet Baird? Nobody of that name lives here, son. Have you ever heard of anybody called that? Not as I remember, son. Relation of yours, is she? She's my mother. How come you lost your mother, son? She ran away. Where from? From Calliope Bay. Where in God's name is Calliope Bay? It's at the edge of the world. Maybe she fell over the edge, ever thought of that? Yes, but I'm sure she's in the city somewhere. Does she know you're looking for her? No, but she won't be angry when I find her, she'll come back with me to Calliope Bay to see Dad and Cal, as soon as I explain how miserable Dad and Cal are she'll want to hurry back, she won't want to stay with Mr Dalloway. Who is Mr Dalloway? He used to be my teacher, then he captured my mother and brought her to the city, he's probably got her locked up somewhere, in a little room maybe with no furniture except a rug on the floor, and he makes her lie on the rug and he does things to her and makes her groan and scream, he's got two legs. Heard no groans or screams from the lodgers lately, son. What if she won't go back with you, what will you do then? I won't hurt her, I won't try to make her miserable the way she made my father miserable, I won't chase her with the whip I've got in my schoolbag. Why do you carry a whip, son? In case the bullies grab me again. Again? Yes, they roared up beside me in big old rusty cars one night when I was walking along a street and they grabbed me and took me to a castle and put me in a dungeon and whipped me with my whip, and I never cried out, I never said a thing, I just stared at them when they said they had kidnapped me and would keep me in the dungeon until my family paid them a lot of money. So your family paid up? Eh? Well, how did you get away if they didn't pay up? Oh, I did press-ups until I was very strong, then I knocked out a bully when he came to the dungeon one day, and I ran up the stairs and escaped. And now you're looking for your mother? Yes, I walk along street after street, I knock on door after door, I peep in window after window, I stare at face after face, I follow woman after woman, and all the time I am looking for my mother. Best of luck in your search, son. Thank you, sir. Yes, they all wish me luck, they hope that one day I will find my mother. But I do not tell my friend about her. Having him for a friend is handy, he will not stay my friend if I tell him about my mother, he will order me from the basement, he will say that at last I have gone too far, he is sick of my fibbing. So I pretend, as I walk up the main street with him, that I am as excited by the girls with plump legs and white boots as he is, I grin when he makes remarks from the side of his mouth about the ones leaning through the windows of the old cars parked by the pavement, cars full of hunters, ready to roar off with their catches as soon as they have gone through all the kidding that the girls with plump legs and white boots seem to want before they'll climb in. I also pretend, when two hunters take off from a doorway after three girls, that I share my friend's doubt about whether the hunters will be in luck, I know that inside a block they will be certain of their catches. My friend, of course, is a hunter. I will leave him when we reach the coffee bar, I will go on alone and stay away from the basement until he has thrown out his catch, I have my own kind of hunting to do. Would you believe me, I ask as a car tries to back into us, if I mumble mumble mumble? Certainly not, he says. Would you believe me, I ask as the car roars off, if I say I was the loudest whistler in Calliope Bay? Show me, he says. I show him. Girls along the street go on tip-toe and turn when they hear the whistle. A country kid's trick, he says. Would you believe me, I ask as we stare up at a floodlit fifteen-storey tower, if I say I was in love with the most beautiful girl ever to sail in the *Emma Cranwell*? You don't know what love is, he says. But do you believe I was in love with her? I ask. No, he says. Why not? I ask. Because, he says, you live in nightmares, you don't know where the nightmares end and real-life begins. Why do you say that? I ask. Because you have them at my place, he says. I don't, I say. You do, he says. All right, he says, who is Fat Norman? How do you know about Fat Norman? I ask. Ho ho, he says. I haven't told you about Fat Norman, I say. Of course you haven't, he says. So how do you know? I ask. Because, he says, you talk about him in your nightmares, the way you talk about your dear Caroline and your killing-floor and your furnace-house and your swamp. No, I say. Yes, he says. I'll have to leave your place, I say. Why? he asks. Oh, I don't want to upset you with my nightmares, I say. I don't mind them, he says. Of course, if you bopped me you'd have to leave, I can't stand being bopped. Nightmares I can stand, but never bopping. By the way, he says, who is Uncle Pember? I wait, I consider. Then I ask: Would you believe me if I say I saw Uncle Pember the other night in this street? Continue, he says. I continue: He was riding a horse called Sydney Bridge Upside Down and at first I did not recognise him, I thought he was a butcher named

Mr Wiggins. This was because of his whiskers. Then I remembered that Mr Wiggins did not usually have whiskers. So I went up to this man and I said: Are you Uncle Pember? He said: Yes. And you're Harry Baird, are you not? I said I was. He said he was mumble mumble mumble and would I like to hop up behind him and go out to see his chandelier. I said: No thanks, I've heard about your damned chandelier. Please yourself, he said, and galloped away on Sydney Bridge Upside Down. And that, I tell my friend is how I at last met Uncle Pember. I ask: Do you believe me? Sure, he says. Thank goodness, I say. Well, he says, I'm off to the coffee bar. Thanks for believing me, I call as he crosses the road. He gives a hunter's brisk wave. I go on alone.

17

LATER IN the story of my life I will tell what happened when I met Mr Dalloway on the fifteenth floor of a city tower. For the time being, I end with these memories of a summer on the edge of the world.

Text Classics

Dancing on Coral
Glenda Adams
Introduced by Susan Wyndham

The True Story of Spit MacPhee
James Aldridge
Introduced by Phillip Gwynne

The Commandant
Jessica Anderson
Introduced by Carmen Callil

A Kindness Cup
Thea Astley
Introduced by Kate Grenville

Reaching Tin River
Thea Astley
Introduced by Jennifer Down

The Multiple Effects of Rainshadow
Thea Astley
Introduced by Chloe Hooper

Drylands
Thea Astley
Introduced by Emily Maguire

Homesickness
Murray Bail
Introduced by Peter Conrad

Sydney Bridge Upside Down
David Ballantyne
Introduced by Kate De Goldi

Bush Studies
Barbara Baynton
Introduced by Helen Garner

Between Sky & Sea
Herz Bergner
Introduced by Arnold Zable

The Cardboard Crown
Martin Boyd
Introduced by Brenda Niall

A Difficult Young Man
Martin Boyd
Introduced by Sonya Hartnett

Outbreak of Love
Martin Boyd
Introduced by Chris Womersley

textclassics.com.au